This book is a work of fiction. All characters, names, locations, and events portrayed in this book are fictional or used in an imaginary manner to entertain, and any resemblance to any real people, situations, or incidents is purely coincidental.

SOUNDS AND FURIES
Seven Faces of Darkness

Tanith Lee

Copyright © 2010 by Tanith Lee

All Rights Reserved.

Cover Art:
"Sounds and Furies," Copyright © 2010 by John Kaiine
Back design also features images and composition by John Kaiine.

Cover Design Copyright © 2010 by John Kaiine and Vera Nazarian

ISBN-13: 978-1-60762-060-0
ISBN-10: 1-60762-060-X

Trade Paperback Edition

March 1, 2010

A Publication of
Norilana Books
P. O. Box 2188
Winnetka, CA 91396
www.norilana.com

Printed in the United States of America

Sounds and Furies
SEVEN FACES OF DARKNESS

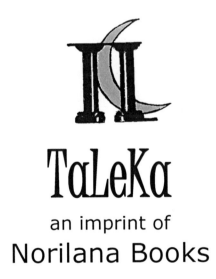

TaLeKa
an imprint of
Norilana Books

www.norilana.com

Sounds and Furies

SEVEN FACES OF DARKNESS

TANITH LEE

CONTENTS

WHERE ALL THINGS PERISH	9
MIDDAY PEOPLE	52
COLD FIRE	79
CRYING IN THE RAIN	92
WE ALL FALL DOWN	111
THE BEAUTIFUL AND DAMNED BY F. SCOTT FITZGERALD	115
THE ISLE IS FULL OF NOISES	142

WHERE ALL THINGS PERISH
From a Tailored Concept by John Kaiine

I

It was glimpsing Polleto again, between trains, at that hotel in Vymart, which made me remember. Which in its way, is quite curious, for how ever could I have forgotten such a thing? So impossible and *terrible* a thing. And yet, the human mind is a strange mechanism, and the human heart far stranger. Sometimes the most trivial events haunt our waking hours, even our dreams, for years after they have happened. While episodes of incredible moment, perhaps only because they have been marked indelibly upon us, stand back in the shadows, mute and motionless, until some chance ray of mental light discovers them. And then they are there, burning bright, towering and undismissable once more. At such times one knows they are more than memories, more than the mere furniture of the brain. Rather, they have become part of it, a part of oneself.

"What is it, Frederick, that you are staring at?"

"That little man at the table over there."

"What, that little clerkish chap in the dusty overcoat? He hardly looks worthy of your curiosity. Of anyone's, come to that."

"No, he probably isn't. A very ordinary fellow, the sort you wouldn't recall, I suppose, in the normal way of things."

"I should think not. But you do?"

"Well, as it happens, he was resident in a place where something very odd once happened to me. And not to myself alone."

"He was involved in this odd thing? He looks blameless to the point of criminality."

"I imagine that he is. No, he was simply living there at the time, had been there two or three years, if I remember correctly. I met him once, in the street, and my aunt introduced him as a Mr Polleto. We exchanged civilities, that was all. He had the faintest trace of a foreign accent, but otherwise seemed a nonentity. My aunt confessed they had all been very disappointed in him because, learning his name before his arrival, they'd hoped for some sort of flamboyant Italian theatrical gentleman, or something of the sort."

"He looks more like a grocer."

"My aunt's words exactly. Those were the probable facts, too, I believe. He'd been a shop-keeper, but come into some funds through a legacy. He bought a house in Steepleford, which was where I was visiting my aunt."

"This is a remarkably dull story, Frederick."

"Yes." I hesitated then. I added, "The *other* story isn't, I can assure you."

"The story which you recollect only since you caught sight of your Mr Polleto? Well, are you going to blab? We have four long hours before the Wassenhaur train. Let's refresh our glasses, and then you can tell me your tale."

"Perhaps not."

"Oh, come, this is too flirtatious. What have you been doing all this while but trying to engage my attention in it?"

"I protest."

But the brandy bottle intervened. And presently, sitting on that sunny terrace of the Hotel Alpius, I recounted to my friend, Jeffers, my friend and traveling companion, the story which I will now relate. That was the first time I ever told it to anyone. And this, now, I trust, will be the last.

2

The modest town of Steepleford had some slight notoriety in the eighteenth century, when it was one of the centres of a cult known as the Lilyites. These people believed so absolutely in the teachings of Christ, and acted upon them so unswervingly, that they soon turned the entire Christian church against them. There were a few hangings and some riots, as is often the way in these cases, until at last the cult lost both dedication and adherents, and ebbed away. Even so, through the succeeding years, (from about 1750 to 1783), now and then some murmur might be heard of the Lilyites. Being however still generally feared and loathed for their extreme habits, they were soon rooted out and disposed of, one way or another. The last hint of the cult seemed to surface, nevertheless, in sleepy Steepleford. During the July of 1783, one, Josebaar Hawkins, was harangued in Market Square, for holding a secret meeting of seventeen persons, at which they had, allegedly, sworn to slough their worldly goods and to love all men as themselves, in the celebrated Lilyite manner.

At his impromptu trial, Hawkins either denied all this, or ably recanted. He was said to have laughed heartily at the notion of giving up his fine house, which was the product of successful dealings in the textile industry, and stood to the side of Salter's Lane, in its own grounds. He asked, it seems, if the worthies now questioning him thought he would also abandon his new and beautiful young wife, who went by the unusual name of

Amber Maria, or drag her with him in the Lilyite fashion, shoeless and penniless, about the countryside.

Hawkins was presently acquitted of belonging to the sect. No others were even interviewed upon the matter. Thereafter no more is heard, in the annals of Steepleford, of the Lilyites, but there is one more mention of Hawkins and his wife. This record states that in 1788, Amber Maria, being then twenty years of age, (which must have made her fifteen or less at her wedding), was taken ill and died within a month. Hawkins, not wishing to part from her even dead, obtained sanction for her burial in the grounds of his house.

All this, though possibly of local interest in Steepleford, where as a rule a horse casting its shoe in the street might cause great excitement, is of small apparent value on the slate of the world. Yet I must myself now add that even in my own short and irregular visits to the town, I had been, perhaps inattentively, aware of a strangeness that somehow attached itself to the Hawkins house, which still stood to the side of Salter's Lane.

The Lane ran up from Market Gate Street. It was a long and winding track, with fields at first on both sides, leading in turn to thick woodland, that in places was ancient, great green oaks and mighty chestnuts and beeches, some over two hundred years of age. I can confirm from walks I have taken, that there exist, or existed, areas in these woods which seemed old nearly as civilisation, and when an elderly country fellow once pointed out to me a group of trees which had, he said, stood as saplings in the reign of King John, I more than half believed him. But this, of course, may be attributable merely to an imaginative man's fancy.

Some two miles up its length, Salter's Lane takes a sharp turn towards the London Road. At this juncture stood the house of Josebaar Hawkins.

It was built in the flat-faced style of those times, with tall, comfit-box-framed windows and a couple of impressive chimneys like towers, behind a high brick wall. Although lavish enough for a cloth merchant and his wife, the 'grounds' were not vast, more gardens, and by the time I first happened on the place, these had become overgrown to a wilderness. Even so, one might make out sections of brickwork, and the chimney tops, above the trees.

I asked my aunt about the house, having found it, idly enough I am sure. She replied, also idly, that it was some architectural monstrosity a century out of date, standing always shut up and empty, since no one would either buy it or pull it down. Perhaps I asked her even then why no one lived there. I know I did ask at some adjacent point, for I retain her answer. She replied, "Oh, there's some story, dear boy, that a man bricked up his wife alive in a room there. She belonged to some wild sect or other, with which he lost patience. But she had, I think, an interesting name . . . now what can that have been?" My aunt then seemed to mislay the topic. However, a few hours, or it may have been days, later, she presented me, after dinner one night, with a musty thick volume from her library. "I have marked the place." "The place of what, pray?" I inquired. "The section which concerns the house of Josebaar Hawkins." I was baffled enough, not then knowing the name, to sit down at once in the smoking-room, and read the passage indicated. So it was I learned of the Lilyites, of whom neither had I ever heard anything until then, and of Hawkins and his house off Salter's Lane. Included in the piece was the account from which I have excerpted my own note above on Hawkins' impromptu 'trial'. It also contained a portion quoted from Steepleford's parish register, with record of both the marriage and the death of Amber Maria Hawkins. This was followed by the notice of her burial in the grounds of the house, which had been overseen both by the priest, and certain officers of the town. Then my aunt's book, having set history fair and straight, proceeded, in the way of such tomes, to undermine it.

According to this treatise, Hawkins, first an enraptured husband, had come suddenly and utterly to think his wife an evil witch, and growing afraid of her, he tricked her to an attic room of the house, and here succeeded in locking her in. Thereafter he had both the door and the window bricked up, by men who, being sworn in on the scheme with him, turned blind and deaf eyes and ears to her screams and cries for pity. My aunt's book was in small doubt that both the priest, and the officers who later pretended to Amber Maria's death and burial, were accomplices in this hideous and extraordinary act. (I have to say that, perusing this, some memory did vaguely stir in me, but it was of so incoherent, slight and indeed uncheerful a nature, having to do, I thought, with a childrens rhyme of the locale, that I did not search after it at all diligently.)

As I have already remarked, I seldom then visited Steepleford. On that visit I may have offered some comment on my reading, or my aunt may have done. I fail to recollect. Certainly the rest of my visit was soon over, nor, having gone away, did I return there for more than a year, and during my next dutiful brief holiday, I remember nothing seen or said of the house in Salter's Lane.

But now I come to my next *relevant* visit, which occurred almost three years after those I have just described.

I had been in Greece for ten months, and come back full of the spirit of that place, thinking to find England dull and drab. But it was May, and a nice May, too, and by the time the train stopped at the Halt, I had decided to walk the rest of the way to the town through the woods and fields. So, inevitably, I found myself, just past midday, on the winding path of Salter's Lane. It was the most perfect of afternoons. The sky was that clear milky blue which certain poets compare, (quite wrongly, to my mind), with the eyes of children. Among the oaks which clasped the track, green piled on green, wild flowers had set fire to the hedges and the grass, and sunlight festooned everything with shining jewels. Birds sang in a storm, and my heart lifted high. What is Greece to this? thought I, staring off between breaks in the trees at luminous glades, steeped in the most elder shadows. Why, this might *be* Greece, in her morning.

And then, between one step and another, there fell the strangest thing, which I could and can only describe as a sudden quietness; less silence than absence. I stopped, and looked about, still smiling, thinking the world of nature had fallen prone, as is its wont, to some threat or fascination too small or obscure for human eye or mind to note. I waited patiently too, for the lovely rain of birdsong to scatter down on me once more. It did not come.

Then, and how curious it sounded to me, as if I had never before heard such a thing, I picked up the song of a blackbird—but it seemed miles off up the Lane, the way I had come. And precisely at that moment, turning again, I saw something of a dull, dry red, that thrust between the leaves. At once I knew it for a chimney of the Hawkins house.

I was taken aback. Imaginative, as I freely admit I am, I would not say I was especially superstitious. But something now disturbed me, and that very much, and not being able to divine what it was, beyond the presence of that wry old house, discomposed me further.

Accordingly, I stared at the house, right at it, and crossing over, gazed up the outer wall, over which the vines and ivies hung so thickly. What an ugly house it was, I thought, and no mistake. Even its windows of filthy glass, largely overgrown by creeper, were ugly. While that window there, above, was the ugliest of all, an absolute eyesore, stuck on at quite the wrong architectural moment.

While I was thinking this, and standing there, staring so feverishly and insolently, with no warning the childish rhyme came back into my head, from out of some store-cupboard of the brain. And with it a host of tiny bits and pieces that, over the years of my visits here, and all unconsidered, I had apparently garnered. I heard my aunt say again how a woman had been bricked up in 'that house', and a friend of my aunt's, a titled lady

I barely knew, I heard saying once again, as she must have done years before: "Oh, the peasantry won't go by the place after dark. No, it's a fact. They go all out of their way by Joiner's Crossing. And this, mark you, because of a tale more than a hundred years old."

And the rhyme? I had doubtless heard children singing it in play, in the streets and yards of Steepleford, and maybe they still do so, although, I wonder if they do. I will set it down, for having remembered it, I have never since forgotten.

She looks through water,
She looks through air,
She leaps at the moon
And she looks in.

Give her silver,
Give her gold,
And bind her eyes
With a brick and a pin.

"Aunt Alice," I said to her that evening, when we were pursuing some sherry before the meal, "I want to tell you about something I saw on my walk today, coming here to the town."

Pleased to see me, she turned to me a willing, expectant face, but no sooner did I mention the house in Salter's Lane, than she laughed.

"Dear boy, I shall have to think you obsessed by the place. Are you intending to buy it? I should certainly be delighted to have you live in the town, but not in such a miserable property."

I replied, rather irritably, that nothing was further from my desires, and looking rather crushed, she amended, "I'm sorry, Frederick. I am sure that London is more suited to your temperament than such a dreary backwater as Steepleford." After which much of the evening was spent in my praising

Steepleford and herself, for I felt ashamed of my bad temper. When I was a boy, this aunt had been very kind to me, and deserved far better of me than three-yearly visits laced with petty ill-humour.

By ten o'clock we were friends again and playing cards, and so I reintroduced my topic. Although, I admit I stuck strictly to facts as I saw them, omitting all the other sensations I have outlined.

"The oddest thing, Aunt, is that I could swear the window which I saw had not been there previously. It was very high up, almost into the roof, rather small, yet somehow extremely noticeable. Although I have only once—to my recollection—looked at the house before, yet I thought I remembered it quite well, and I truly believe there never was a window in that position—however fantastic this may sound."

As women will, my aunt then said something damningly practical. "So many of the house windows there are closed up with ivy and creeper. Could some of this overgrowth simply have fallen away, and so revealed the casement you speak of?"

Such a banal solution had not occurred to me. I agreed that she was probably correct. To myself I said that I must put up with the necessary boredom of my visit, and not try preposterously to dress it up with invented supernatural flights.

The following morning, I penitently accompanied my aunt on her round of social calls. By midday, my face had set like cement in a polite smile, and thus, as we crossed Market Gate Street, I found myself beaming at a small, nondescript man in unostentatious dress, who had touched his hat to us.

"Ah, Mr Polleto," said my aunt, magnanimous to a fault. "What fine weather we are having."

Mr Polleto conceded that we were. He had a flat dusty voice, old even beyond his bent and well-aged appearance. In it my ears caught just the trace of some foreignness. Then I found myself introduced, and not standing on ceremony, as my aunt had not, I shook hands with him. What a hand he had! It was neither cold nor hot, not damp, but rather dry—it did not have much strength in it, certainly, yet nor was it a weak hand. But an uncomfortable hand it was. It did not seem to *fit* in mine, and I sensed it would not fit in anyone's.

"Mr Polleto has resided in the town for quite three years now, I believe," said my aunt, when we had parted from him. She then told me of the general disappointment that he had not lived up to his name. "He has the cottage by the old tiltyard."

But I was not interested in Mr Polleto and his indescribable handshake; his face I had already mislaid, for he was one of those men who are eternally unmemorable, or seem so—for if ever seen again, somehow they are known at once, as I have already demonstrated, and later must demonstrate further.

However, now I wanted my lunch, and was dismayed to find my aunt was leading me to yet another doorstep. I rallied rather feebly. "And which lady is this, Aunt Alice?"

"No lady, Frederick. This is the house of our local scholar. I have some purchases to make and will leave you here, with Mr Farbody, who has written and published pamphlets."

"Indeed," said I, but just then the maid let me in, and presently I was taking a glass of very drinkable Madeira, in a sunlit library, with Mr Farbody, who had at once addressed me with: "My good sir, I understand you are interested in the history of the Hawkins house."

"Well, it is a curious tale," Farbody continued, requiring little prompting from me. "Did you know that the farm-hands hereabouts, and workers and their families in the town, have kept up a tradition that the spot is cursed?"

"I remember someone saying that people refuse to go along Salter's Lane by night."

"Well that, of course, isn't always to be avoided, but they make a to-do about it. The thing is, it seems, not to *look* at the building. I've heard of girls, if due to be married, still binding their eyes with a scarf and having to be led, if they should need to pass the house even in daylight."

"And all this because Amber Maria Hawkins was thought a witch?"

"Ah, she *was* a witch, if the tales may be believed," and here he winked at me. "She could see treasure in the ground, for one thing. No one knows her origins. Josebaar said he came across her one day in the woods. She was probably a gypsy girl, but all alone, bright-haired and straying with her arms full of wild flowers. He took a fancy for her, and perhaps she for him, it seems so—or else she liked the idea of his status in the town. He had already made some money and his family was an old one. And if she was a gypsy or itinerant, homeless and without kin, all that may have appealed to her, do you see. So there and then she is supposed to have said to him, 'You may sport with me, and I will let you. Or you may marry me and I will make you rich.' And he said, 'How might that be, seeing you are in rags?' To which Amber Maria replied simply, 'You I will bring silver and gold.'

At this, the rhyme came into my head again and I interrupted. "I thought it was she was to have the gold and silver?"

Farbody smiled, and lit his pipe. "It does seem she might have been rich on her own account for sure, if she'd cared to be, for the next thing she did was point at the ground under a tree and say to Hawkins, 'Dig there, and you will find a large store of coins.' Even money likes money, so he dug in the ground, and *hey presto!* found a box of gold pieces, deep down and undisturbed for a century. When he asked her how she knew where to dig, she shrugged and said, 'I saw them.' Nor did Amber do this only once, but several times, apparently. And in the same way she could find items that had been lost. And once she is supposed to have seen a sheep that had fallen down a deep well, which animal was then got out alive. She could see, you understand, *through* things. Through the earth, through stone, and through certain other natural materials, though not, I think, through metal, which may account for the metals in the rhyme."

"What does the rhyme mean?" I asked him.

"It's essentially to do with binding her, shutting her up where she couldn't do harm. You see, Hawkins was besotted with her some while, but then he began to be afraid of her. He's said to have told the priest, 'She will sit quiet all day and only look at me,' and when the priest said that many a man would be thankful for such a placid, adoring wife, Hawkins replied she did not look *on* him, but *into* him. And he said that once he had told her hotly to leave off, for he was a sinner like all men, and if she would keep on staring in such a way, she would see his foul and mortal corruption. To which she gave this strange response: 'Men say always they are wretched and tainted by flesh and sin, but in all men there is such goodness and beauty, as in the earth and all living things, that it is to me like my food and drink, and I can never be tired of having it.'"

When Farbody told me this, there in that warm and pleasant room, the sunlight on the books and the domestic pipe-smoke mild in the air, the hair rose on my neck.

"In heaven's name," I said.

The scholar smiled again, pleased with himself, and with the peculiar tale he had memorized so well. "Yes, something in that gives you a turn, doesn't it. She seems to be speaking so charmingly, innocently, and it makes the skin creep. I can tell you, sir, I read this story first when I was a boy of eleven, and I was awake nights after, until my mother scolded some reason into me and hid the volume I'd been reading. Which may explain," he amiably added, "my life-long quest for such hidden trifles of knowledge."

Farbody then went on with the narrative.

Josebaar turned quickly from love to shrinking horror at his young wife. At first he tried to arrange a separation between them, but she would have none of this; then he had thoughts of escaping her by going overseas. But she guessed his course, and is said to have assured him she loved him too well to let him go. If he must leave, she would find and follow him, and he did not doubt that she had the powers to do so.

In the end, Hawkins, pale and harried, went to his friends, among whom was the priest, and confessed he was in such fear he should not 'soon remain alive, since the woman eats me up from the inside out.' By what grim stages the others came round to Hawkins' state of mind, Farbody said, one might only conjecture, and similarly if any money was involved in it. "But those were ignorant and superstitious times," he reflected. "Alas, they are still." Whatever went on, or the span of its duration, a plan was presently constructed to rid Josebaar Hawkins of the woman.

"He pretended to her that he had only been testing her with his talk of going off, to see how much she loved him. And finding her so faithful, he meant to reward her. He told her he had put by an especial gift for her, an heirloom of his family, kept in a wooden chest in the attics of the house. But it would amuse him if she would go up and look first *through the wood* of lid, and so say what she saw, before he unlocked the chest and gave her the trophy. Well, it seems she could easily see through wood but not through her husband, and up she went. No sooner was she in the room with the empty chest, than he slammed closed the door and secured it. And then at once came a gang of men and bricked the door up, and others came along the roof to seal and brick up the window."

The bizarre quality of Farbody's recitation was added to, for me, by a sense of historical fact which seemed to underlie the whole. I found I asked abruptly, "Could she not have opened the window—or broken the pane, before the roof-gang reached her?"

"No, dear sir. Remember, the glass in those days was of much thicker and sturdier stuff than the flimsy crystal of our day. Besides, he had previously *pinned* the window shut. I mean, he had driven iron pins through the frame to the brickwork, and hammered in long pins lengthwise all across."

"Hence the horrible rhyme, a brick and a pin."

"Just so. Besides too, she was very high up, and the men anyway would have thrust her back, she was physically no match for them. They must have been a harsh crew. All the while they were doing it, blocking her in to die the slow death of starvation and thirst, Amber Maria was shrieking and imploring them. And after they had finished, she screamed and howled in her prison uncountable days and nights, before she fell silent for ever. There are many reports of this."

I shuddered. "In God's name, you speak as if it happened.

He looked at me. "My dear sir, it did. I can make no claims for her sorcery, but the facts of her death are undoubtedly true. Some years after, Josebaar Hawkins was hanged for her murder. For he confessed to it, having had not a quiet hour since."

"And then. Did they unlock the room?"

"That they did not. The story concludes with that asseveration. No one would go near the house, let alone pull bricks away from any part of it. That they left, and leave, to the mercy of God."

I sat some while in silence. Perhaps, very likely, I looked grim or rattled, for the scholar came and refilled my glass and moved the biscuit plate nearer my elbow.

"The children's rhyme," said Farbody, "as you're aware, has its own oddities. The brick and the pin relate to the window and door, the sealing of the room. I've come across one text which states that Amber Maria could see *only* through natural substances, and that therefore a brick, which is man-mixed, would defeat her gaze, just as would refined metal; obviously the very reason why she could detect coins in the ground, rather than see through these also. But do you recall that other line, *She leaps at the moon?*"

I said that I did.

"Salter's Lane," said the scholar, "has nothing to do with the salting trade. Indeed, one wouldn't expect it, so far as we are here from the sea. No, the word *salter* relates to the Latin, *Saltare, to leap.* In Mediaeval times, that area of the woods was known to be a place where witches held their revels, and danced the Wild Dance for their lord, Satan, 'leaping high as the moon'. Which moon, of course, is a calendar feature of the sabbat, whether full or horned for the Devil."

Just then the door-bell jangled. My aunt had returned for me. I was astonished to see, glancing at Farbody's clock, that only half an hour had elapsed. But then I suppose, I was struggling back to my own time, across the centuries.

I thanked him, and going out with my aunt into the summer street, I resolved to shake myself free of the unnaturally strong emotion that had dropped upon me. And so we went to our luncheon.

Three or four days later I, reluctantly, but evincing cheerfulness, accompanied my aunt to a church tea-party, in honour of the new bell which had recently been installed, and for which everyone had, the year before, been engaged in fund-raising. Here the social classes mingled with uneasy and ill-founded camaraderie, and I was revealed to a succession of people of all types, to whom it seemed my aunt wished to show off her nephew. Touched by her pride in me, I did my best to be jolly.

"And look," said Aunt Alice, "there is Daffodil Sempson. Or rather, Mrs King, as she is married to a hotelkeeper at St Leonards now, and has come for the first time to visit her sister. They are somewhat an estranged family. None of them is in service now, but in her youth, Daffodil was lady's maid to the Misses Condimer, and travelled all over Europe with them, before she was even seventeen. A great advantage for any girl."

Struck I admit by the name Daffodil, I turned, and saw a very pleasing young woman, dressed most stylishly, a trick no doubt learnt during her travels with the minor aristocracy.

"By all means introduce me to her," I told my aunt, with a more genuine enthusiasm.

But neither of us was able to catch the lady's eye. She seemed to be fixedly interested in something that went on at the far end of the room, where several people were walking about, and the tables groaned beneath their cakes and lemonade.

"I wonder what has engaged her attention so," speculated my aunt.

Mrs King, née Sempson, was staring now almost unnaturally. Then I saw her turn her pretty head, seem to check, and then once more compulsively gaze back towards the tables.

Suddenly she quite changed colour. I have been witness to several instances of abrupt illness, slight or extreme. Mrs King seemed in the grip of the latter. Her face took on not a white, but a thickly-shining, greenish pallor. Without thinking I moved towards her. But in that moment she dropped to the ground.

At once she was surrounded by women, one of whom must have been her sister. Presently she was carried away.

On all sides were sympathetic murmurs concerning the heat.

To my sorrow, Mrs King did not return to enjoy the overbountiful Tea. My aunt made enquiries of her sister, who said that Daffodil had been obliged to be sent home in the pony-cart. "It is a great nuisance, as she intended returning to St Leonards tomorrow, and now she won't be well enough."

"Is her indisposition more serious than we had hoped?" asked my aunt.

"Oh," said the sister, blinking at me with eyes not half so fine as her sibling's, "she makes a fuss about it. She has these delicate ways from her younger years. I may say, she'd never have dared go on so *then*. They would have dismissed her."

"I thought," said I sternly, "that she seemed most unwell."

"No, it isn't that she's ill," declared the vulgar sister, whose hat might have been a lesson to us all in the virtues of regret. "She says it's something that she saw in Austria, once." My aunt and I evidenced incomprehension. The sister said, "*I can say nothing of it. She refuses to explain. She says it's too dreadful, and it's taken her these six years to put it from her, and now she's been reminded and will need to stay in bed, with me expected to be flapping round her all day long, and neglecting my duties and Pa.*"

We extricated ourselves from the uninspiring Miss Sempson and soon after left the Tea-Party. As we were going out I remember that Aunt Alice said to me, "There is disappointing Mr Polleto. I understand he contributed generously to the bell-fund, which I find curious, since he's far from affluent, and never attends the church. Nor is he sociable. Did you happen to notice him this afternoon?"

I said he might easily go unnoticed, but that I had not, I thought, seen him. Nor had I.

The day before my departure from Steepleford, I had planned a walk through the woods. Whether or not I would approach the stretch of Lane that ran by Josebaar Hawkins' house I was myself unsure. In any event a sudden thunderstorm erupted. Its violence and tenacity were such that I gave over any idea of walking, and spent all that last day with my aunt. The following morning we parted most affectionately, and I returned to London. A month later I went abroad, and spent the rest of the year in Rome, in which ancient, imperial and legend-haunted city it may be supposed Steepleford, and all its tales, sank in my memory to a depth of fathoms.

Just after the New Year, I employed a day or so again at Steepleford. This time, there was snow down, but a flawless snow, thick and solid to tread upon, the weather chill and fine. Had I truly forgotten the house in Salter's Lane? I think that I had in everything but my heart. I took my way across the white fields, admiring the shapes of everything, each changed by its cover of pale fleece, then strayed off into the ancient woods, which were like a cathedral of purest ice.

And then somehow, in the way these things turn out, I took at random another of the silent avenues, and found myself ten minutes later at one of the several openings of the Lane. I had been walking by then more than two hours, and it seemed foolish not to follow this path back to the town.

Soon I reckoned I had been wise to do so. The low afternoon sun was clouding over and a mauve cast had the sky. So I strode briskly, and thinking of a warm fire ahead, and other cheer, I came level with the high wall of Josebaar Hawkins' ill-starred house.

At first I think I did not recognize it, for like everything else it was plastered with white. But then I got a great shock, and stopped dead in my tracks.

"What has happened here?" I asked, perhaps aloud. Until that time, the trees of the old estate had made a second wall behind the first, and the pile of the building been visible only in portions, as I have previously described. Now, beyond the range of one huge holly tree, I gained abruptly a view of the entire front aspect, all of it, its timber, stone and brickwork, the roof and chimneys, and every cold window, glaring as if it were eye to eye with me, like some person who has suddenly whipped from their face a mask.

Astonished, I attempted to reason how this should be. It was not that the trees were bare. No, it was that every tree, saving the holly, which in any case stood this side of the wall, had been brought down.

I confess that meeting the house like this, head-on, unnerved me. I made to myself no secret of that. But in a moment or so, I had a rational thought. Some vandal had been at work in the 'grounds'. They had chopped down the trees and carted them away, no doubt to provide firewood for needy winter hearths.

On the wing of this rationale, an unusual, perhaps a boy's desire took me, having seen so much, to scale the wall and peer over into the precincts of the house, now open to be studied. I have to say too that my peculiar eagerness to do this was prompted, I now think, more by an *aversion* to doing it, rather than a longing after secrets. It was like a dare one must not evade, for fear of being thought, and worst of all by oneself, a coward.

I am quite strong and fit. The wall had inconsistencies and irregular stones in plenty. Despite the snow, I got up it in less than three minutes, and, perched there on the top, stared down into the gardens.

They were the most desolate sight. The snow lay all about, but it had turned dark, and in places black, partly melting away as on some of the higher trees it did. There was a good reason for this. Any sun which fell here must fall directly over all, since nothing now stood between, only the house and its ground. While every tree and shrub which had grown, rampantly and untended, within the walls, had been levelled and presumably taken away. And I wondered who could have made so bold after all these hundred and more years.

Then, something else caught my eye. There was, towards the side of the house, a sort of ornamental little building, perhaps a folly. It was ruinous and falling down, and its demise seemed hastened by a young oak tree, which had toppled aslant upon its roof, and leaned there yet. And why then, I wondered, had the wood-stealing vandal not carted off also this ready-felled tree? There it lay, as useful as any other timber, bare and lean, its dislocated branches creaking in some unfelt wind, clear as complaining voices in the stillness.

There were no birds, of course. There was, as before, no sound. But this effect had been common through much of the woods, as the day advanced and the winter sun prepared to leave the earth. This time, I had not noted it particularly only here.

Now I did. For here the absence of all sound, save that sinister creaking whine of broken branches, seemed heavy with presage. The air smelled sour, and faintly dirty, like what one might expect in the centre of an industrial town, where smoke and cinders fall and make each breath lifeless, and potent with disease.

And then, even as I sat there gazing at it, the unlikeliest thing occurred. The leaning dead oak tree swayed, and out of it there burst a shower of dry pieces, splinters of wood ejected, and then one whole limb snapped off and dropped, disintegrating even as it went, so that by the instant it touched the ground, there was no more of it than dust. What had occasioned such a thing? The action of some animal—no animal was in the vicinity, so much was plain. The simple process of a slow decay then, electing to finish its work coincidentally with my scrutiny. I had the strangest notion that, by *staring* at the tree, I had hastened the breaking off and dissolution.

And then, and then, I knew it was not I. *I* had not caused it. Across my scalp my hair crawled as if filled by icy tricklings. Against my will, it seemed to me, yet no more resistible than as if at the pull of a chain of steel, my head turned and tilted back, and I looked up the unmasked face of that house, towards its highest casements.

There was not a creeper left upon any of them. Even the snow had been leached away. But oh, something white there was, which stood at the window, looking out, and out.

I can put down here only what I saw. I saw a woman's shape. Her gown I cannot detail, nor how her hair was dressed, though it seemed to me that both were disordered. Her features I could not see, and that had nothing to do with distance, and I believe nothing to do with light or shade. She had no features, none. That is, she had only one feature. She had two eyes. But her eyes were set in that featureless whiteness of a shape like two burned holes. They were not eyes at all—but, they were eyes, more eyes than are possible to any thing which lives.

I remember little of my descent of the wall. Perhaps I fell from it. Certainly I think some of it crumbled and broke away too, as I slipped down. And then I fled along the Lane, and this I do recall. I fled and I whimpered like a man pursued by the dogs of hell, that are really fiends, and they will tear him, even his soul, if they catch him. But they did not catch me, and I reached the town. And then came maybe the most sinister and curious thing of all.

For running out into Market Gate Street, in the wintry dusk a carriage passed me, and in the carriage a friend of my aunt's, who greeted me as she went by most graciously. And I raised my hat, and nodded, and then walked on to my aunt's door, like some man who has not just met the devil on the road.

"Aunt," I said to her that evening, "why not come up to London for a spell?"

"Oh, no, dear boy," she said. "I'm too comfortable here. Why should I wish to be in London?"

"Well, I am there. And half a dozen theatres and shops and museums that are the envy of the country."

But she would not be moved, saying it would put me against her, if she encroached upon my 'London World'.

And so, after another day I went again away from Steepleford. And naturally, I had spoken to no one of what I had seen, and no one had asked me what I had seen. Nor did I hear a single mention about the town of Hawkins' house, or its current state, let alone of anything else.

However, as I sat in the train, I took myself sternly to one side, and told myself that perhaps ghosts did exist, for there are nowadays even photographs of some of them, but of all things, the dead could not harm the living; their power was done.

3

Less than a month later, I was at a supper given by my then acquaintance, Lord D——. The food was of the best and the wines Olympian, which made up, somewhat, for the conversation. At midnight I well remember we had some music, amongst the rest an attractive rendition, given by a female singer of superb voice, of the words of Alexander Pope's *Pastorals,* the melody being, I think, Handel's. As it finished, one of the servants came discretely in, and presently handed me a telegram.

To my dismay I read that my aunt had fallen seriously ill, and begged my attendance on her. My own man had taken alarm and brought the message directly on to me.

I hurried to my rooms and flung some things together, and was next on the train for Steepleford Halt.

I have said, I had great affection for my aunt, and with good reason. My agitation was increased because she had never, until then, that I knew, been afflicted with any ailment more than trifling and swiftly over. Other thoughts I believe I dismissed from my mind.

The morning was young when we arrived at the Halt, where her carriage had been sent in readiness. It was a dismal day in February, sleety and cold, with leaden skies. Everything looked horrible to me in the deadly light of it, and the light of my anxiety, and all the station buildings, the gaunt trees, covered by an air of desuetude and darkness. This impression only increased as we bumped among the wintry woods, and I cannot describe my abrupt unease, as I thought we must turn into Salter's Lane. Then the carriage veered away, and went instead by the other route, to the Crossing. On asking the coachman, he told me that some trees had come down in the Lane, which made it impassable, and I dare say I was ridiculously relieved.

I barely noted the town. No sooner had we reached my aunt's than I sprang from the carriage and hastened indoors.

In the hall, I met her doctor, a solid man, who reassured me somewhat. "It is a kind of low fever we've been seeing in the town recently. Unfortunately, given your aunt's age, it has stayed with her longer than one might have hoped." Then he frowned, and I asked him why he did so. He said, "Ah, well, there have been rather a lot of such cases in the past month. But there. The old and the very young are always vulnerable. Your aunt, of course, is not yet sixty."

I said, "Have there been fatalities?"

"No, no, nothing like that."

None of this prepared me for the sight of my aunt, who, lying propped on her pillows, looked white, and, to me, near death. I took her hand, and she murmured at once, "I called you here, my dear, because I was afraid I might not be able to remain much longer. But today I feel rather better."

I told her she was a fraud, and that I was happy to find her so.

Despite my nervousness, my aunt rallied. She improved. But she did not entirely get well. Two weeks later, when pressing concerns of my own urged me to go back to London, she too implored me to leave. "I was being very foolish," she said. "What nonsense. I shall see the New Century, I am determined on it." And I realized I made her more uncertain by remaining so faithfully, as if hourly fearful of her collapse.

The doctor too grew confident. "She is completely out of danger, or I'd never concur with your departure. And she has the best of care. I'd like to see more progress, but then her age has been against her a little. When the spring weather comes, then we should see a change for the better. Although," he added, rather insensitively and ominously, "I find that all those who have succumbed to this pernicious malady take a great while over mending. There's a young woman I have heard of, of only three and twenty, of the working families, you understand, but well-nourished and fit, and the mother of healthy children, who has been sick with this same fever off and on for eight weeks.

She was one of the first to contract it, and again and again she seems to throw it off, only to sink down once more."

Receiving this news, I was now in two minds whether or not to go. However, in the end a telegram arriving the other way, from the metropolis, forced my hand, and I caught the train.

Truth to tell, it was a relief to escape the atmosphere of a convalescent house, not to mention all Steepleford, which had seemed unbearably dreary and run down in the rain and mud of a new-born and unfriendly March. Indeed, I had never seen the place look so forlorn; it had depressed me. And when, having been returned to the city only a few days, a firmly-written letter came from my aunt, assuring me she had now taken the upward path, and even given a tea-party for some friends, I resolved to stay where I was. Soon after this, and in the light of a further optimistic bright epistle from Steepleford, I allowed myself to be lured to France with Nash and his brother, and then was persuaded on to Italy again.

In retrospect I gain a terrible impression of my short time there in the awakening summer, and of that previous more leisurely summer I had spent in Rome, happily gravitating among the bronzes and the marbles, both inanimate and human, while concurrently there ran on and on, behind the veils of distance and inattention, that dreadful horror of which I could know nothing, and yet which I do believe I sensed, for had it not shown itself to me behind its own shadow, brushed me with its noiseless wing?

I shall not try to excuse myself. Perhaps I was afraid. I might have seen there was good reason to be.

Certainly I did not ponder that chance vision I had had of a 'ghost' in the window of Josebaar Hawkins house. I did not even offer the experience as a suitable gothic tale, one hot Tuscan night among the soft blue hills, when others were telling ghost stories. Did I even call it to mind? Perhaps, I cannot remember. But of course, too, what I had seen was not a ghost. Not that at all.

Needless to say, when I got back to England late in July, I was at once assailed by feelings of unquiet and guilt, and instantly wrote to Aunt Alice—there had been no letters from her waiting for me, but as a general rule she did not constantly put pen to paper. I asked how she did, and if I might come down and see her.

After a little delay, I received her reply, which was brief and penned in a careful, rigid style. She said she was in her usual health, and would be glad if I would 'take time to call on her'. I thought the whole tone of her letter sulky, and was peeved she had not mentioned some presents I had sent her on my travels, for which may I be forgiven.

For some reason, as I saw to the packing of my bag, I had upon my brain that fragment of Pope's *Pastorals,* which I had heard the very evening the telegram reached me of my aunt's illness. The gracious verse was in every way unlike the rhyme which had accrued about Amber Hawkins and her murdering spouse, yet now it too lodged fast in my head, and repeated itself over and over. Never came warning in a stranger guise.

The words are well-known, of course, but I shall put them down even so, such is their unconscionable significance to me now:

> *Where'er you walk, cool gales shall fan the glade,*
> *Trees where you sit shall crowd into a shade;*
> *Where'er you tread, the blushing flowers shall rise,*
> *And all things flourish where you turn your eyes.*

The train reached Steepleford Halt soon after three o'clock of a peerless summer afternoon. London had been somewhat stuffy and overheated, but as we entered the countryside beyond, a wonderful honeyed peace descended, balmy, lazy, and a-flicker with butterflies. Flowers blazed from every hedge and bank, the trees were laden with heavy green, the sky as blue as the mysotis.

Descending from my carriage I was struck initially only by the sense of the huge sun, which was hammering the earth, but looking about me, I perceived at once a quality in the light, both dry and harsh. Where it fell, not only did the sight seem wounded, but the place beneath. Everything looked to me, in this glare, drained of colour, faded like a woman's lovely gown worn too often.

The veteran who oversaw the station was standing to one side, consulting his watch as the train pulled out again. It was my habit to exchange a few pleasantries with him when I met him, and I prepared to do so now, but he forestalled me. Looking up, his face was not as it had been, less older than used up. He nodded with no smile.

"Good day. I regret the train was late."

"No matter. It was a delightful journey today."

"But a poor arrival, I dare to think," he said. He sounded surly, which surprised me very much; he was not of this sort. Then he pointed straight by me. "D'you see that tree?"

I turned, to humour him, and gazed towards an old copper beech which had guarded the ground above the railway for as long as I had been coming there, and no doubt some regiments of years before that.

"The tree. Indeed I do."

"See how it leans?"

"Why yes—what can have happened?"

"The good Lord knows," said he. "The roots are out to one side. Dying it is."

"What a great pity. Can nothing be done?"

He made a noise. He was angry, not merely at my paltry concern, but at all things, which had somehow conspired to ruin the beauty of the tree.

"It's got to be felled," he said, "tomorrow. A danger to the trains if it falls, d'you see."

I said again I was very sorry, as I was, and gave him something for his trouble, at which he looked as if it were the Thirty Pieces of Silver themselves.

I was glad to get out of the station after this.

My intention had not been to walk, it was too sultry, and here for sure there was a dull storminess to the air that already made my head ache. The station further up the line lay five miles beyond the town, but in an outpost where a cab might be accosted. Here, however, I had been promised my aunt's carriage, which now, going out on to the path, I did not find. This I could have understood more readily if the train had been early, or on time.

I half turned back to ask the station-master if a carriage might be procured from the local inn, but then thought better of it. The walk to the town would not take so long, providing I struck off at once for Salter's Lane, and followed that to Steepleford.

There I idled then, on the gravel, under the impoverished shade of some spindly, desiccated sycamores, as if a decision must still be made. I was reluctant to go on. But go on I must, and would.

Until this moment I had, I think, almost entirely suppressed or driven away my utter unease at the prospect of the Lane where witches once had leaped in their revels, and where lay the house of a murderer, and his wife who, as I had seen and still credited, haunted its window. Now my fears rushed in like the sea tearing through one small crack in a dam, and carrying all before it.

I broke out into a sweat which even the leaden heat had not occasioned, for it was cold, and my heart thudded in my breast.

Come, I thought, in heaven's name, you are not a baby. What is there to be afraid of? If the wretched nook affects you so, do what the others do, and look away from it.

What finally galvanized me was a dawning grasp of what the absence of the carriage might mean. In the past, when it was promised, it had been reliable. If my aunt had forgotten to order it forth, or her coachman not brought it, then something must have occurred to interrupt the mission. And all at once I was vastly unsettled as to what.

Then I did set off, striding the path between the fields, towards the woodland which lay, like a smoky cloud, upon the nearest horizon.

I must have noticed as I went, the state of those fields. They were bleached and barren-looking, the grain in parts fallen, and where upright, then not usual in its colour, and in areas seeming burnt. At the time I suspected a fire had taken place, or infestation of some sort. My mind was not truly on the fields, or did not want to be.

But then I reached the edges of the woods. And with the best will in the world, I could no longer delude myself very much.

Only after the most serious of gales would so many great trees have fallen. Looking in, at what had been the greenest of green shades, I now beheld bald, wide avenues, all railwayed with these broken pillars, which had tumbled in every direction, taking in every case more than one or two fellows with them. Besides these fallen giants, the standing wood was sickly. There could be no mistaking it. A yellowish tinge was on each leaf, or worse, a blackened scorching, as if some acid had been thrown over and among them all. The canopy besides showed great holes.

I advanced like some soldier into enemy territory, where any lethal hazard or trap may be encountered. No sooner was I in, however, than again I paused. Upon the raddled ground, bare of anything but for the most hardy weeds and brackens, (and these burnt and brown), I had begun to see strange heaps and drifts of a dark dust. I knew at once what these were, but going over to one of the fallen trees, I tapped it, nor very hard, with a strong-looking stick I had found on the outer path, and picked up thoughtlessly, as one sometimes does on a walk. No sooner did the stick make contact, than the bole of the prone trunk, for about five feet either side the light blow, gave way in a shower of what appeared to be the finest black sugar. The sturdy-looking stick also snapped in half, brittle as charcoal. And the sugar-like substance sprayed out also from this. I dropped the stick then. As it hit the ground, it shattered into some twenty further fragments. The dust—the dust was all that persisted of trees which, last summer, had seemed to touch the sky.

But I must go on through this wreckage of a poisoned wood. I followed the carriage-ride doggedly, which normally at this time of year would have been rather overgrown. Surely I had seen it so myself—with sprinklings of woodland flowers everywhere the sun could penetrate, thick moss and large lacy ferns where it did not. There was no hint of that now. Not even the toadstools and other funguses, that colonize any woodland, good or bad, had ventured in. Nor was anything else to be come on. No beasts or birds ran or fluttered or fluted through the trees, or played about the tracks. Silence ruled the woods. Absence ruled them. And here was I, forging on perforce, like the last man quick upon a dying earth. And my feelings of horror and dejection increased with every step I took.

By the time I got out into Salter's Lane, I may say I was prepared for anything. Had I not been, the quantity of felled trees which marked the exit point, would have alerted me, and the expanses of the deadly dust, which resembled here nothing so much as the encroachment of a desert.

Even prepared, yet I halted where I stood. I looked down the Lane, and knew it for an avenue accursed. It was—and I do not exaggerate—like some landscape of the damned.

Nothing stood in it, its length was paved by horizontal trees, and between, the dust had formed mounds which had partly solidified, in a friable, hopeless manner, perhaps from the direct action of weather. Where hedges had been, there were sometimes left some bare black twigs and poles. I did not want to enter the Lane, I did not want to travel it over.

I had no choice, unless I turned back and retrod my path, then going on to Joiner's Crossing, which would now add almost an hour to my hurrying journey.

So, I went on. I walked into the Lane and advanced, having, every yard or so, to get over the fallen trees, most of which gave way under my feet, meaning I must scramble and jump to save myself also from a fall. The mounds of dust were much the same; I sank in them as in the dunes of some hellish beach, or else the humps of powdery 'soil' they had formed crumbled, and I unsafely slithered.

This was very exhausting, and addedly foul from the dust which was constantly clouding up, as if purposely to stifle me.

Above, the sky was no longer blue. It had a tarnished sheen to it, like unpolished metal. True clouds were hung out on it, grimy-looking and peculiar in shape, like torn banners, each a mile across.

Of course, I knew I must come to the house. I knew I must pass it. I had vowed I would not give it one glance. The perils and obstacles of the Lane would assist me, surely, in that, since I needed all my attention for the road.

However, I reached the house of Josebaar Hawkins, and did not keep to my vow.

The holly tree was gone. There was no trace of it, it had become one with the dusts. The wall too had come down. It lay scattered all over the Lane, the bricks and bits of stonework disintegrating, like everything else. Behind the wall stretched a vast piece of ground that was like a bare, swept floor. It had nothing at all growing upon it, and even the dust had blown or died away. It was a nothingness, in colour greyish. And upon this table of death there rose—the house. With by it the little ornamental building I had spied on my last excursion here. This I now saw, with an unnerving pang, had been a small mausoleum, no doubt the supposed resting-place of Hawkins' wife. Now it comprised a part of a roof upon a couple of columns, and within, too, was nothing. Of the toppled oak which had leant there, naturally, there was no sign.

Of everything which had been there, of nature or contrivance, that house alone remained, but not intact. Its roof had come away in broad segments, one saw the gaping joists and beams, which were in turn disbanding. Both chimneys were down, crashed inwards. On the lower floors was not a window that held its antique glass, or its boxed decorations. The creepers had slipped from it, and after them the bricks had tried, and still tried to come out. Yet the building, what there was of it, jutted upright. And in that spot, this made it a thing of unbelievable terror. Ruined and dislodged and every moment giving more, nevertheless *it* had so far *stayed,* where nothing else had been enabled.

All this while I had not raised my eyes beyond the lower floors, or where I had raised them, I had selected their progress with much care. But in the end, I knew I would have to do it, would have to look full on at the upper window under the roof.

I had been in Rome, I had been in Siena and Venice. Among the hills and waters, among the bronzes, had I not somehow understood that *she* stood here, on and on, stood here looking out, eating with her eyes first the bricks and mortar, then the pins, that sealed her up, patient as only a hopeless thing can be, taking a century over it; next eating out the glass, and next, what lay beyond the glass, the trees, the air, the Lane, the countryside.

They must have known, the people of Steepleford town, in 1788, when they passed by on the Lane, hearing her weeping and shrieking in agony and fear, all those endless days and nights. They must have known what he had done to her. What then did *they* do, but cross themselves perhaps, or use some older, less acceptable mark. But they knew, they knew.

She had loved too well, that was her sole crime. She had seen too much in mankind that was beautiful and good, and for sure too much in him, in Josebaar Hawkins, and for this they had condemned her and killed her. How she must then have hated them. How she must have *looked,* fixing despairingly her mad eyes upon the impenetrable dark. And if she had not survived her death, *something* that came of her, and of her hatred, and of those eyes—and which learned too new skills whereby to use those eyes—that did survive, and lived still, and saw and looked—and fed. And it was there, there in that window, drawing up the whole world in its slow and bottomless net.

"Oh, God, Amber Maria, poor lost piteable hideous residue—"

My eyes were on her window, her death's window. My eyes were stuck there and now could not pull away. I felt my heart turn to water inside me and the occluded atmosphere blackened over.

I did not quite lose my senses. Instead I found I leaned on my hands, kneeling in the desert of dust among the slaughter of the trees.

To myself I said, *But what did I see this time?*

For I had not seen a single thing. The window—*her* window—was empty of everything. Of creeper and of bricks, pins and glass. Of light and shadow, and of any shape. As with the rest, nothing was there. And yet . . . the nothing which was in that window was not empty. No. She was there in it, there in the core of it, as things hide in darkness. Or, her eyes were there, those pits of seeing, her *looking* was there, her *looking* looked out. It had looked even into me, and through me, and away, to have all else.

Presently I got up, and as before I ran.

The town—I wondered after why the station-master had not warned me. I wondered too why the newspapers and journals in London had not carried some mention of it, why no sensational word seemed to have escaped from it. Perhaps there had been some news which was disbelieved—or believed too well and suppressed. Besides, events had raced to their final act as swiftly as a wave.

I have read of times of siege and plague in Mediaeval Germany, Italy, France, and in certain of those occult little towns, crouched at the foot of deep valleys, hung like baskets from the sides of cliffs, the dim and winding alleys make such images still but too conjurable. But Steepleford was a slow, flat, gentle settlement, prosperous and mild, where the horse, casting its shoe, caused a stir, and they had longed for a foreign theatrical gentleman to liven them up.

Getting near the outskirts, I saw a cloud hung over the fields and town. It was a wreathe of smoke. The dead gardens along the approach I had scarcely noticed, nor the untended houses, which seemed to have been afflicted too by a kind of partial hurricane, ripping the tiles from roofs and setting askew anything that had been in the slightest vulnerable. There was a dearth of people brisk at their trade or gossip. Instead, there hung there a *presence* of incredible raw heat and turgid staleness. I have never smelled such air, even in the sinks of greater Europe.

I came into Market Gate Street before I properly knew it, and there, as in some canvas by Hieronymus Bosch, I saw what I took at once for plague fires burning in arches and at the corners of houses, reeking of sulphur and other purgatives.

The fumes by now were thick nearly as a London fog, and in them, as I moved on, persons came and went unknown, their heads down and swathed in scarves, none looking at another. They were creatures from the self-same painting, at large between torments.

Then came the River Styx, for the street was awash with a black, stinking body of fluid. I had splashed into it before I could prevent myself, but in any case, there was no other way across.

Up towards my aunt's part of the town, a pony and trap leapt rattling by, the unhappy animal tossing its head, and red-eyed as the horses of Pluto from the smoke. A man hailed me and pulled the horse in. Amazed to be recognized in the Inferno, I stopped. There was my aunt's doctor, peering down.

"Thank God you've arrived, young man. We sent off a wire this very morning."

My heart clutched at me. "It must have missed me by an inch. Is she so bad, then?"

"I fear she is, now. It's the same all over the town. The deuce knows what the illness is. We have three specialists down from London, and one from the Low Countries, and they have drawn a blank on it. My own sister, who has never taken sick in her life—well. But besides all this business of burst pipes and subsiding walls across the entire town—But I won't trouble you with that, either." The pony shook its head violently. The doctor raised his voice to curse. "Be damned to these confounded fires! What do the fools think they're doing? Have they heard nothing of modern hygiene, our only reliable ally against disease—to fill up the air with such muck? Superstition, ignorance—Make haste to get on!" And with this baleful cry, either to me or the pony, I was unsure, the doctor whipped the beast on, and like King Death himself flung off into the smother.

But I ran again, and so reached my aunt's house. And ten minutes later I was in her bedroom, by the side of her bed, but she, although living yet, did not see or hear me.

When I was a small boy, and my youthful mother died suddenly and without warning, this aunt of mine, then an elegant and pretty fashion-plate of an Alice, herself not much above thirty-five, sheathed in softest clothes and scented by vanilla, took me in her arms and let me sob out my soul. And now again I leaned by her, and I wept. But she never knew it, now. And oh, any pity I had felt for that other, for that thing once known as Amber Maria Hawkins, you can be sure I had given it up.

So now I must come to the strangest part of my abnormal tale. To a conclusion, indeed, which any writer of fiction would be ashamed to set before his audience, having brought them thus far, and by such a fearful road. Therefore, prior to the last scenes of the drama, I will say this: One piece evidently missing from my narrative has since been supplied, and only the discovery of that unique absentee has brought me, at this time, and so many years after these occurrences took place, to write them down at all.

My aunt, where she lay on the bed, did not stir. Only the faintest movement demonstrated that she breathed at all. I looked ardently for this proof, and once or twice it seemed to me it faltered, and then I too held my breath. But always the slight rise and fall of her breast resumed. At least she was not in pain or distress. That was all, at this time, I might be thankful for.

Near midnight the doctor called again. He was worn out, as I could see, by his conscientious tours up and down the stricken town, through the acrid fumes of the fires, the stenchful spilled waters, and the furnace heat, which even nightfall had not abated. When he was done with his examination, a frighteningly swift one, I had them bring him some brandy, and he thanked me, then solemnly announced that he 'did not think it would be long.'

"Is there nothing can be done?" I asked like a child.

He shook his head. He was doubtless exhausted too by this question, which must have been asked of him everywhere that night, by tearful wives and white-faced husbands, by daughters, by fathers, by one third of the folk of Steepleford, who in that hour had been made the people of Egypt, when the Angel of Death did not pass over them, but took from them, across all the boundaries of age and condition, their first-born.

After the doctor had gone, I sat down again, and drank some of the wine which had been brought me on an untouched dinner tray. Then I think I must have slipped into a doze.

I was woken, as were some countless others, by the most fearsome noise I have ever heard.

Starting up I gave a cry, and as I did so, heard below and above me in the house, and everywhere about, many other throats exercised in similar startled exclamation.

The sound I can only describe as being like an exact representation of that phrase: the Crack of Doom. It was as if a thunderbolt had been hurled from heaven and struck the town, cracking it open with one awful brazen clang.

Finding myself unharmed, and the house still entire about me, I turned in fear to the bed. But a glance at my aunt showed her still insensible. Going to the window then I stared out, but the street was thick in smoke and darkness, its few lamps half blind. Worse for being unseen, vague noises of fright and panic had risen all around, and I made out windows lighting up here and there like red eyes. Then a man came running by. I opened the casement and called down to him. "What was that sound? Do you know?"

But he only raised to me a face peeled by terror, and flew on.

I truly believed some apocalyptic conclusion was about to rush upon us all. The most primal urge came on me, and going to her, I meant to lift up my poor aunt in my arms, so we might at least perish together. But as I reached the bedside, I stopped dead once more. For I saw her eyes were open and looking at me lucidly. And where the lamp shone on her face, her colour had come back, not feverish but soft, even attractive.

"How nice to see you, Frederick," said my aunt. "I have had the most refreshing sleep and feel so much better now." Her voice was not weak, nor did she seem to be lying to console me. She added, nearly winsomely, "I hate to trouble cook, I know the hour is late, but perhaps Sally might boil me an egg? An egg with a little toast. And oh, a cup of tea. I'm so thirsty."

And then, before my astounded gaze, she was sitting herself up in the bed, and as I sprang to forestall and help her, she laughed. "You're gallant, dear boy."

When accordingly I went out into the passage, I found the maid, Sally, standing there and looking at me with great eyes. Before I could speak of the wonder concerning my aunt, Sally announced, "They say the new church bell has fallen right down the spire and landed in the chancel. The roof there is all damaged and come down, too. Did you hear the horrible noise, sir? We thought the End had come."

Distractedly I asked, "Was anyone hurt?"

"They say not." (I learned later 'they' was the carter's boy, who had bustled in with the news.) "But the whole town has been woke up."

This was, it turned out, true in more than one way, if the process of waking may be associated with revival. For my aunt was not alone in her abrupt and miraculous feat of recovery. It transpired, as over succeeding days I learned in more detail, that of all the six hundred odd persons lying sick that night, or even at the point it was thought of death, not one but did not rouse up an instant or so after the appalling clangour of the bell. And not one thereafter but did not take quickly a swift and easy path to full recovery. (Even, or so I was assured, a cat that been failing grew suddenly well, and a canary, that had sunk to the floor of its cage, flew up on its perch and began to sing.)

Shamelessly it was spoken of as a miracle, this reversal of extreme illness to good health. And there were those who spoke religiously of the falling bell, some claiming that it had cast itself down in some curious form of sacrifice, which it achieved, having cracked and buckled itself beyond use. Others averred that it had been itself unlucky or impure in some sensational but mysterious way, and therefore fell like an evil angel, at God's will, after which the town was freed from its curse.

These notions, of course, were ludicrous, but everywhere for a while one heard them, and small surprise. For the saving of so many of the town's lives, both young and old, affluent and poor, and in so abrupt and unheralded a form, did smack of divine intervention. While I did not for a moment credit this, yet I thanked God with every other there. And as the days went on, and Steepleford hoisted itself, slowly but surely from its own ashes, the streets cleared of water and debris, the baleful fires vanished, and the summer sun took pity and shone with greater brightness and less heat. The smell of furnaces and dungeons melted away.

Ten days later, accompanying my aunt on her first walk up and down the thoroughfares, I saw fresh roses flaming in twenty gardens, and now and then, where a tree had come down or been axed, new growth rioting, shining green, from the stumps.

They had found by then that the bell-rope had been eaten away. By rats, some said, as Steepleford moved, a rescued ship, back upon its even keel.

"Such a nuisance." added my aunt, flighty as a girl. "Now the rector will want another one."

I said that this would mean more fund-raising bacchanals, and Aunt Alice remarked that the strange Mr Polleto at least would spare them all his disappointing presence. "Lady Constance, when she called, told me he had left the town only last Monday. Generally such a thing would never have caught her attention, but it seems the cottage is now for sale, and she wishes to buy it for a young painter she has found."

But I had then no interest at all in Mr Polleto.

My aunt, meanwhile, had more than become herself again. She seemed to me younger and more active than she had been for years. The doctor too assured me he now thought her good for 'three decades'. And when she said to me one evening, "Do you know, dear boy, I think being ill has done me good," I could only agree. And so it must be confessed, at liberty to do so, I began to hanker after my own life.

Of course, I was bemused too. I wanted time to myself to think over events. One instant I felt I had been the involuntary party to a delusion. At another, the unreal seemed actual. But we seldom trust ourselves upon such matters, I mean upon matters that may contain the supernatural. There is always some other explanation that surely must be the proper one.

I am not unduly superstitious, but now, in the glow of returning normality, I began to prefer to think myself to have been in the grasp of a wild obsession, where I had imagined some things and brooded upon others, until I could make them fit my vivid scenario.

When finally I commenced my preparations to leave Steepleford, I was told, in passing, by a neighbour, that no carriage could be got now along Salter's Lane.

"Are the fallen trees still uncleared?"

"No, no. It's the new growth shooting out there. It's become one great coppice, with trees bursting, they say, from the stumps. Those that have seen say they've never had a sight like it. But there's a deal going on with trees and other plants, after that drought we had." Here he gave me a long list of things, which I will not reproduce, then, as I was tiring, said this: "Perhaps you may have noticed the old beech at the station? A fine old tree, but it was twisting and due for the axe, but now spared, and they say the roots have dug down again, if such a thing is to be believed, and the trunk is straight again too. And the leaves coming out on it as if it were May not August. A strange business and no mistake. Did you ever get a peep at that house in the Lane? The Witch House some call it."

Sombrely I replied that I had.

"Well, that's all come down, like a house of cards. Not a wall of it standing, nor one stone on another. A great heap of rubble."

I had a dream, not while I remained in the town, but a month later, when Nash had persuaded me back to France, in the south, in a little village among the chestnut woods. I dreamed I was on the roofs of Steepleford church, and pale, glassy arrows flew by through the air, that were the looks of a woman who stood at a window in Salter's Lane. These arrows severed the rope of the bell in the church spire. And when it fell there was no sound, only a great nothingness. But in the nothingness, I knew that woman was no more.

"What's up?" said Nash, finding me out in the village street, smoking, at four in the morning, the dawn just lifting its silver lids beyond the trees.

"Do you suppose," I said, "that something thought fully virtuous, if attacked, might rebound on the attacker, might destroy them?"

"History and experience relate otherwise," said Nash. And so they do.

4

That then, was my story of Steepleford, all I had of it at the time, but which I gave to my companion, Jeffers, on the terrace of the Hotel Alpius, as we waited for the Wassenhaur train.

I was nevertheless moved to regret to him the unsatisfactory lack of explanation concerning the final outcome of events.

"I haven't been back now to the place for years," I finished, "and so can add nothing. My aunt, you see, grew sprightly—she still is—and moved to London, where she has a fine town house."

"Hmm," said my companion. He drew upon his cigar, and looked covertly again at the instigator of my tale, that same quaint little shop-keeper Polleto, who still sat at his adjacent table.

Precisely then the untoward took place. Or perhaps I should say the apt, as it had happened before, and neither of us could now miss its significance.

A party of three gentlemen and two ladies had just now been coming across the terrace, and taken their seats to my right. So it was I heard, from behind my right ear, a stifled little cry, and next the splintering crash of a water glass dropped on the paving.

Jeffers and I both turned sharply, and in time to see that the second young lady of the party, ashen in colour, was being supported by her friends. As they fussed and produced a smelling-bottle, and called loudly for spirits, Polleto darted to his feet and went gliding quickly from the terrace.

"Now I fancy," said Jeffers, "you've witnessed something of this sort before. And I too, in a way, since you told me of it."

"You mean Daffodil King, who fainted at the church Tea."

"Just so."

"You imagine that she, and the lady over there, gave way for a similar cause—that they had seen Mr Polleto?"

"Don't you imagine it?" asked Jeffers laconically.

I thought, and answered honestly, "Yes. But why?"

"I wonder," said Jeffers, infuriatingly. Then he added, "No, I'm not being fair to you. You see, I've read of the case, and viewed a rather poor photograph once, in a police museum, in circumstances I shan't bore you with. When you first pointed him out, I had a half suspicion. But in the light of both ladies swooning at the sight of the man . . . Recollect, Austria is only over the border here. I believe you told me the charming Daffodil had been in Austria once, and said she had seen something there so awful, it had taken her six years to recover from it?"

"Yes, or so her sister informed me."

"What she saw then was that same man, Polleto, in the street probably, on the day that the people of a well-known Austrian spa almost lynched him. I have no doubts the other lady to our right, saw him in a similar style. Unless she had the singular misfortune to have met him."

"Then he's notorious?"

"No. Of course, his real name *isn't* Polleto. I was never told what his real name was. The documents referred to him only as The Criminal. And the crime too was hushed up in the end, and rich acquaintances got him away to avoid a most resounding scandal, which would, I believe, have brought down the Austrian government of the hour."

"In God's name—what had he done?"

Jeffers shrugged. "That's the thing, Frederick, what *had* he done? No one would say. Not even the file on him, which I was shown, would say anything as to the *nature* of his crime. Not even the policemen I spoke with. It was something so vile, so disgusting, so inhuman, that no scrap of it has ever been revealed by anyone who knows. They won't—can't—speak of it. They try to push it from their minds. And if they see him, like that lady across the terrace, some part of them withers. There now, she's looking a little better. All the better, no doubt, since what made her ill has left the vicinity."

I sat staring at him.

Presently I said, "Are you then saying to me what I suppose you must be?"

Jeffers stretched himself in his chair, and smiled at me. "Even you," said he, "asked yourself whether or not something of great perceived virtue, like a church bell, could have halted Amber Maria, should she set her sights on it. But it wasn't virtue she avoided, was it? She loved the earth and all the people in it. I, too, Frederick, have heard of the Lilyite sect, and of course she must have been a member of that sect. No doubt Josebaar Hawkins let her have her meetings in his house, and protected her after by lying. But maybe in the later years he feared that in her too, that she was one of the Lilyites and put the teachings of Jesus before all other things. What did she do but love others and want to help them with her precious gift of seeing, from which she herself had never tried to profit? She saw good and beauty in all men and all things, and loved them like—loved them *better—*

than herself. And where have you heard such philosophy before, save from the lips of Christ?"

I was shocked a little, to have missed this clue. Humbly I waited for him to go on. He did so.

"Amber Maria looked with her eating eyes through her window, and after the blocked-up bricks and pins, she had the glass, and then, as you said, the trees, the air and the Lane. And next Steepleford she ate up with her eyes. And it would have gone on like this, like rings spreading from a pebble thrown into a pool, and God knows where it could have ended. But ended it must have done, at last. For in this world, along with all those who, despite their colossal failings, carry in them the seeds of goodness and beauty, there are a few, only a few, I trust, who have nothing like that inside them. Who are composed only of the grossest and most foul of atoms, who are, though human, like things of the Pit. In them there is not, I daresay, one hint of light. Perhaps there is no soul. And meeting one of these persons, Amber Maria, who fed on goodness and beauty and drained it to dust, fed instead upon the worst poison, that which would scald away the psychic core of any such vampire. It was Polleto, you see, Polleto, that little ghastly human demon, whose crime is so unspeakable that never is it spoken, Polleto who had come to live in the town, placating it by helping it buy a bell, Polleto that at last her devouring eyes reached. Like everything else then, she tried to eat him up. And then she must have tried to spew him out.

But it was too late. She had touched and tasted in a manner only vampires know. She who had once loved God and once loved others as herself, until they let her die in that atrocious manner. And after that she who hated, and would have eaten the world, save in due course she came to Polleto and ate at Polleto. *Polleto!* And it killed her, Frederick, in all and every way. It killed her to a death more deep than any grave, more cold than any stone."

MIDDAY PEOPLE

1

The Ancient Romans had called noon the Ghost Hour. She had been told this, or read it, but could not remember why. The Italian light perhaps, she thought, staring out across the square. It took away the shadows, it bleached and turned the buildings to flat gold, and any people walking there, they were golden too, and without physical depth.

Unlike Chrissie, sitting under the dark pink umbrella of the café table. She could never tan; she even found it quite hard to *burn*.

"It's fucking hot," observed Craig.

Chrissie turned to him attentively. "Yes, it is."

"And that food. Too heavy. Oily. I'm going in for a lie-down. Or a throw-up. Whatever comes first."

She thought probably it was the *amount* of food he had consumed, rather than its type, (surely even Craig had known that Italy meant pastas and cheeses and olive oil?) Also the two bottles of red wine they had drunk between them. Although he did not like wine.

"Oh, I'm sorry," she brightly said. "Yes, of course. Let's go in. It's almost siesta time, isn't it."

"God, get your facts straight. Not yet."

"Oh, I see." He could be right or wrong, but was right of course. And she, stupid.

As they rose, she imagined the few people around them might think the English couple were going in so soon because they were eager for fervent holiday sex. This was not at all the case. Craig would indeed go straight to sleep, lumpen on his bed, his thick short sweaty hair plastered to the pillow. She would lie on the bed next to his, and look up at the curious patterns of pale stains in the white ceiling. She was, after three days at the little hotel, getting to know these stains. She tried to make them into something interesting, (childishly attempting to enjoy even this). Then, adult, she would try to go to sleep instead. But she was always awake, wide, wide awake.

At about five, Craig would himself wake, lumber into the bathroom and piss, grumbling, angry at his leaden head. At the room. At the hotel for something—some noise that had irritated him, a fly that might have got in, Italy, Italians. Her.

As they crossed the square, Chrissie looked longingly over at the church, with its biscuity façade and carved doorway. She wanted to go to the church, look inside, maybe attend a service even, decorous, with a scarf respectfully tied over her hair. She was not religious, yet she would like to do that, here. And she would like to walk round the town, go out into the countryside, admire the olive trees and the vineyards in the dust-haze, the round hills with villas tucked up on them under old red roofs—

So far, they had not done much. They had seen more of the hotel than anything else.

Why had he wanted to come, she wondered? Oh, that was easy really, he had been showing off to a colleague when he produced the idea of the trip. More to the point, why had Craig wanted Chrissie to come with him?

They were only in their thirties. They had only been together, that is lived together, for two years. It had never been much good. They both worked, but he considered what she did with her group of decorators to be *'fey'* and useless. "Tarting up the houses of rich cunts," was Craig's term for it. Meanwhile his high-powered job kept him out a lot, drinking and eating with his clients. Coming back, he had no time for her, yet expected, as a man much older might have done, the flat cleaned and, if he had not had a meal, one ready. If this meal was then not to his taste, he told her so. Usually it was not.

She had tried, blaming herself, making excuses for him.

But by now she wondered why they stayed together. Fear she supposed, on her side. She was in looks thin and ordinary, and before Craig, had had very little interest taken in her by men. As for him, probably she was convenient. One day some other woman would appear on the scene and sweep him off. And Chrissie dreaded the inevitable shame. But then, it might not happen, because Craig was no catch himself. Not very tall, heavy and thickset and now, from all the wining and dining, getting extra chins and quite a belly, his small-eyed, discontented face had no compensatory attractions, his voice grated, and his personality was—well, what?

Void, she thought.

And, humiliated as he pushed rudely in front of her into the side street, almost shoving her out of the way, she pretended instead to have stopped on purpose to look at something. And she cursed herself. All this should end. He loathed her. Surely there might be one man in the world, someone with low enough standards, who might care for her, actually like her, find her talented and appealing despite her 32 B bra-size and her limp dull hair? And even if there was no one—could she truly not manage on her own? Probably, if she suggested they part, he would shout for joy. Only it was all so complicated now—the flat in both their names, the joint account and—coward, coward, she thought.

And—

saw that, pretending to look at something, she *was* actually looking. *Staring.* Back across the square. At two people, there by the fountain. Two golden people, glittering in the middle-of-the-day light bright as the scattering water.

Oh, typical Italian young, gorgeously clad in their shining youth. *Am I jealous or simply having a religious experience?*

She could not take her eyes off them. And they, in their perfect new-minted world, would never notice, so it was quite all right.

They wore jet-black shades. His hair was as black, and the girl's was corn-blonde, like the bars of sunlight. Their clothes, smart, white, or simply whitened by the glare—the bare arms strong and graceful, the long throats and mouths that had not lost, like fruits, their juice—

She was in love with both of them. And really, they were not so young. No. They did not wear the fashions one saw the young put on everywhere—yet wealthy they must be. They glowed with health and money, as with light.

Something made Chrissie glance along the side street, after Craig. Walking away, he had either not noticed he had lost her, or else he was entirely indifferent. Either way, it meant much the same. In the shadow that did not fall from anything, but simply amassed in the channel of the narrow street because the sun had not got into it, Craig looked extremely thick. Physically, that was. Too solid, as if he were trying to prove his existence, his importance; opaque as a block of stone.

Chrissie looked back towards her beautiful ones. They were still there, not speaking, leaning at the fountain's rim, oblivious of the water spotting their flawless garments and skin. Lizards, she thought, golden lizards from another planet.

And then both their heads turned, and *they* looked, each of them, right at her, through their inky shades.

Chrissie felt herself colour. *"'Scusi,"* she muttered. Her Italian was hopeless and virtually non-existent—and anyway, they could not hear her from this distance.

She turned herself, quickly, and walked after Craig into the thunder-shade of the street.

By the time she reached the hotel, Craig was nowhere to be seen.

"Has my husband gone up?" she asked the man hovering at reception. She said it happily, as if this loving 'husband' and she had been separated by unavoidable circumstance, and arranged to meet again, lover-like, in the erotic seclusion above.

The man agreed the *signore* had taken the key and gone upstairs.

Chrissie began to walk towards the stairs. They would take longer, and also provide a little exercise. She had nearly reached them when she hesitated. She fumbled in her bag, pretending to search for something without which she could not go up. She could not face it. Not again, lying so close to Craig and a hundred miles from him, divided by wine, sleep and his utter antipathy.

She would not cry. *God, don't let me cry.*

Oh the hell with it, cry if you want, she thought, this is Italy not bloody Cheltenham.

Oddly, the urge to cry at once receded.

Across from her she noticed the bar, open and airy, the now-one-thirty light streaming in over small marble tables and rococo chairs. Above the counter, every bottle had become a lamp, with a flame of sun blazing inside, green lamps and scarlet ones, indigo and apricot.

Should she, after the wine?

Apparently she should. She was *in* the bar, and now another, smiling man approached, with coal-black curls, and she ordered her drink from him, a large vodka, not especially Italian at all, but when it came, dressed in its glass, it was an Italian vodka, with Italian ice.

The room was empty, save for herself and the barman. She sat drinking slowly, looking out into the street to which the sun had now miraculously soaked through. She wondered how that was? In the light, everything sprang alive out there, the burnt sienna of walls, the terra-cotta roofs, the red and rose geraniums—

Chrissie put down her glass and shrank back into the little chair. Caught in a window, there on the street, *They*. They idled by the bar, past the hotel, framed in sun and geraniums. Her Beings from the fountain.

She named them abruptly, she did not know why, Arrigo and Gina. Arrigo and Gina moved over the windows, one window after another, making each window wonderful a moment. Then they were beyond the last window. Where were they going?

It was the vodka of course which made Chrissie get up. She walked hurriedly from the bar now, back across the hotel lobby, out into the street—as if to an appointment. Not with an unmarried husband in a loveless bedroom, but to something—strange, inexplicable, crazy, *terrible.*

What was she doing? This was stupid. She stood in the street, looking along it, the way they must have gone. The sun scorched now directly down on her—and yet, shadows were beginning to come back, yes, creeping like spilled darkness from the edges of things.

Chrissie started to walk rather fast along the street. A merry dog ran by. Some children were laughing in a doorway. In a yard a fair young man perched on a stationary Lambretta, and a fair girl, hand on hip, hair streaming. But these were not They.

When she reached the street's end, a huddle of buildings stood around a space with a tall tree, perhaps a plane, and the shadows were coming—but nothing else. She had lost them, lost Arrigo and Gina. And that was just as well. What would they have said to her, *done* to her, with those slimly muscled bronze arms, those cruel serpentine fruited tongues—some torrent of abuse and a calling of *polizia?* What was she, some stalker?

She braced herself to retreat. Precisely then she became aware of them once more.

It was almost as if they had not been there until she made the (mental) move to give up, which was absurd.

And they waited—were they *waiting?*—at the mouth of an alleyway, where a bunting of gaudy washing hung, doubtless deceptive to the eyes. But they—once more they were staring back at her. Chrissie felt a wave of fright and dismay, and next second—they were sliding away from her, as if they stood on a platform with wheels—how could that be? And the washing and the alley were all she could see.

Astonished, she found she bolted forward, she also on wheels attached to *their* wheels... And running across the space, under the deep metallic flags of the plane tree, right up to the alley mouth, and there, only there, she stopped, as if—ended. For they were not to be seen any more. Finally they had eluded her and slipped away.

Lovers, she thought. Let them alone.

I must be mad, she thought.

She felt sick, but it went off. Then she only felt ludicrous and shaken, as if she had fallen over on the cobbled street and made a fool of herself. By that time it was just after two o'clock, and in the square the church bell was ringing.

II

By the evening Craig was very hungry and needed, he said, a stiff drink. So they went out, but only back to the small restaurant in the street the other side of the square, which they had visited every night so far. Craig ate voluminously, but without enjoyment. It was Chrissie who complimented the waiter on the very good food. They—Craig—drank a lot of alcohol. Chrissie watched the bottles and the brandies mount up. She was unable herself to eat or drink much.

When they came out, the evening had arrived, and filled the street and square with soft blue ashes, lit by the gentle globes of old-fashioned, wrought-iron lamp-standards. People were there who strolled arm in arm, gladly together—plump matrons with young dark eyes, benevolent men in shirtsleeves, and many Romeos with their Juliets.

"Isn't it a lovely evening—shall we—"

"You do what you want. I have to see to some work."

"Work." Her voice sounded flat and childishly silly.

"You don't think I can just laze about like you, do you? Where do you think the money came from for this jaunt? Not your pathetic little rich-cunt-pleasing rubbish. No way." Craig explained/told her that now he would go up to their room and make some international calls on the firm's mobile. He would also, she knew, order a bottle of brandy or whisky to go with this, and smoke a pack of Marlborough. If she stayed with him then, in the cramped bedroom, that was it. A desert storm of smoke and fumes and his important voice talking loud across continents. She knew, because this was how it went at home.

"Okay," she said. Neutral. "I'll just—"

"Get on with it then. Do something on your own for a change." And he left her, standing there.

She poised in the square, pretending they had planned all this beforehand. She watched the couples going round and round her, talking to other couples or groups seated at outside tables, all under the great wild-eyed stars that were swarming in the sky, and the coloured lightbulbs that were coming on. Music sounded, a horn, a mandolin, then an accordion, perhaps from a radio, or from some unseen orchestra. And the carousel of loving couples were dancing, some of them, though not the younger ones, who strutted to and fro like warriors who will always win their war. Or some swayed into the shadows, and two became one.

Chrissie thought abruptly of Arrigo and Gina. But that was not true. She had been thinking of them all the time.

She walked to the lunch café and found a little table going spare, just inside. She ordered an espresso to bring her round.

Of course, she had been looking out for them, even if she had not admitted as much. At the restaurant, out of the restaurant windows, in the square and streets both going and coming back.

Other men and girls were by the fountain now, splashing each other with its spray, amused and drinking cola.

Had she ever done that? Ever, ever? On frigid English nights?

There had been summers, so perhaps. But always it was done in disappointment, sadness, alone, then as now.

Stop it. Have some coffee. Forget all that.

Chrissie drank her coffee.

Outside, the darkness grew darker. There was absolutely no sign of Arrigo or Gina. Obviously they had only been passing through, and were now gone, in a slim white car, back to some extraordinary other place, some sparkling city, some villa on the navy blue hills, strung with lights, a vivacious party, or a deep bed.

Not until it was ten o'clock did Chrissie return to the hotel. She idled even then, and in the street, not at all dark now with its ornamental street lamps, wondered if she might be mugged, an unattractive woman loitering by herself in the night. But the night was not dangerous, not here.

When she got back to their room, Craig had annexed the bath. She took the opportunity to open windows. Moths would fly in and he would shout at her, but that was better than the stench he had created.

She thought about throwing his mobile phone from the window and down on the cobbled courtyard below, between the pots of roses and lavender. But she did not.

All she did was undress and get into the twin bed which he had told her, on the first night, was hers.

She thought she would take a long while to get to sleep, especially after the espresso, but her encoffeed heart drummed her excitedly fast from wakefulness.

She regained consciousness, surprised, in the centre of the night, and saw Craig's bulk, like some mountain she could never get over.

The windows were once more shut. Yet when she went to clean her teeth, some silvery thing sang. Was it a nightingale?

She had been dreaming—of what? She wanted to recall. Then she remembered a man in the dream, an old man, who had emerged from the carousel of dance in the square, and said to her, "Why do you think we take luncheon, and make siesta, at those hours? To keep us safe off the streets and the squares."

How puzzling. What a peculiar dream—but dreams were *dreams*.

Craig rumbled in his slumber like a train, or an approaching earthquake, and then was silent again. As if even to snore would be to offer her too much companionship.

The next day she asked if they might go to the city. She had always wanted to see the cathedral. Also, could they not browse in the shops, visit the museum—the Roman ruins of a circus? "Well, go," he said. "Why do I have to hold your hand?"

"But I thought you wanted—"

"This jaunt was your idea. I'm just the one paying for it."

I am paying for it too, she thought.

And then, *Is* it my fault? Have I dragged him here against everything he wanted? He can after all drink brandy and whisky and make calls at home. I'm inadequate. Should I have come on my own? But then he would have complained because the flat was dirty and no one did the shopping . . . And he's told me I can't cope, not on my own. Yes, I'm a fool. I do see that. I make a mess of things.

She recollected how Craig had criticized her choice in music. He only liked classical music—"What else is there? That? That's not music." But then too, only certain classics were all right. Bach, and Mozart. Rachmaninov, apparently, was a load of 'soapy crap', and Bartok and Prokofiev 'certifiably insane'. Sometimes Craig played Wagner at top volume, and the flat shook, and twice a neighbour had come to remonstrate, and Chrissie, trembling, had had to deal with this, before the neighbour gave up on reason, and began instead to retaliate with the most appallingly bad loud pop music at all hours of the day and night.

After recalling all that, Chrissie shook herself and went out into the street and meandered towards the square. She had tried to talk herself into hiring a cab to take her to the city, but her Italian was so poor—*he* spoke it quite fluently, though his accent was not good, so sometimes people would seem bemused: "Fucking cretins," deduced Craig. Even so, he could usually make them understand, could understand *them*. He had told her, on her own she would be a laughing-stock, monetarily cheated, perhaps physically attacked, in the city. Told her all that before he told her to go alone.

Chrissie sat at the table under the dark pink umbrella. She had drunk two glasses of rough white wine, and was thinking, if the city cathedral was out of bounds, she might try to see the church across the square.

But she kept glancing at her watch. As if she were waiting for someone. Who?

She knew who exactly.

And now the watch said 12:00 p.m.

No one much was in the square. Like yesterday, and the days before.

A stooped man scurried over it, darting from one side to the other, as if evading enemy surveillance. A woman went by with baskets, walking fast, disappearing into a doorway.

Those that were here seemed to cling to the square's edges, the outdoor tables closest to the three cafés, the steps of the church. It was completely relaxed, reasonable. Sensible to avoid the midday sun, the blare of trumpets in heaven that continued from noon until two—

Chrissie finished the last of her wine. As she put down her glass, she saw, through the base, the stem, the globe of it—

They were there. Her Beings. Arrigo, Gina.

By the fountain, as before.

She had not seen them enter the square, missed it, as she had the going away of the boys who had been sitting smoking on the church steps, and the people from nearby tables.

How very odd. It had not been this way yesterday, had it? She—and They—were alone in the square.

Alone in the light, the glistening, glistering gold.

Golden Arrigo, with his crow-wing of hair, golden Gina, with her lemon, Botticelli Venus hair, and herself, Chrissie, a small nothingness taking up, (and wasting) a tiny bit of space.

Don't stare. For God's sake.

She lowered her eyes.

In the side of the wine glass, however, she saw them still. They were moving now, out of the square. She felt a pang of loss. Where were they going? The same destination as yesterday? *Stay put. Don't get up.*

Chrissie found she had got to her feet, and tried to discover an excuse for this. While she was doing that, again she glimpsed them, how they paused. And then—it was irresistible—she looked at them again.

Made of spun crystal, coloured like Murano glass.

Perfect.

They—were gazing back at her through their sunglasses. *At Chrissie.*

And then, infinitesimal, perhaps imagined, the slight motion of their two heads, the flicker of light on hair. *Come on then,* the movement seemed to say. *Come with us.*

Chrissie, rooted in earth. Heart in mouth, palms wet—
While they stood. Waiting.

A kind of sound that had no sound—

She too moved, quickly. She ran, forgetting she had not paid for her drinks, towards them. And now they ebbed away, so she must *really* run—

She did not think what this must look like, as normally she would have done. Her thoughts seemed absent now, as under great pleasure, horror or agony, sometimes they are.

Which was *this,* anyway? What were they doing, calling her, summoning her, yet never letting her catch up. Ah, she was thinking again now.

She saw she had reached that open area between buildings, the spot with the curious, metal-leafed tree, and she had not seen the street she ran through before that, or anything.

They were under the tree.

Under the tree, and in front of her. And

she had reached them.

Chrissie stopped running. She was panting. It did not matter, not really.

They were only three or four feet away.

Oh God how splendid they were. Not like anything as human as a film star or a statue—they were like fabulous insects made of ivory, gold leaf and gems. And somehow, through the black shades, she could make out—the blue of his eyes, aquamarine, and her's, like platinum over pearl—but it was guesswork, maybe. She could not truly see.

"I'm sorry, I thought—"

Chrissie heard herself blurt that, but this was all.

And then he, Arrigo, beckoned with his hand.

Although like jewels, they wore no jewelry. Not even the expensive watches she would have expected. And their clothes, so seamless, elegant and simple, were of a material that reminded her of Egyptian linen. Not only their flesh then, translucent and shining.

Now they were walking on. The three of them. Not too far. Just to this corner, where this rose-brown masonry craned into a half-shade, and there, between the plaster and the cobbles underfoot, Gina bending, brushing with her fingers, a sort of green frond which grew from the stone.

Is it a weed? Chrissie did not ask. Not necessary. She was meant to pick it, that was all. Why? Oh, but she knew. She knew everything.

She knew who they were.

All in that moment.

And an internal singing, like the nightingale's, rushed through her, music gold not silver, sharp not sweet.

She bent also, to the frond, and watched her thin hand with no nail varnish or rings, and the hand snapped off the frond.

Chrissie raised the weed to her face and sniffed at it. It smelled pungent, like a herb. Neither appetizing nor un.

It would be a little bitter, she thought, like paracetamol. And tingle on the tongue, like aspirin.

At that instant too, suddenly, essentially, she could smell *them*. They had a scent like honey, and the clean fur of cats. But also they smelled of dry heat, like sand.

She twirled the frond of weed-herb between her fingers, admiring the green suppleness of it, which had forced its way, spinelessly, through the hard plaster and adamant cobbles. She was happy. Then, all she could smell was the afternoon.

She flung round—there was no one else there. That is, they were not.

Children were playing under the plane tree. Women called across from upper windows in a mellifluous Italian Chrissie could not fathom. Gusts of a rich spaghetti sauce hovered through the air. The town was awake. It was noisy, and five past two.

III

She did nothing. Nothing at all. Days passed—how many?—two, three—probably only one—and she did nothing.

The frond-weed-herb, whatever it was, wilted in the glass of water in the bathroom.

He never mentioned it. Never *noticed?*

Was that bizarre?

Yes, it was bizarre.

Chrissie however, looked at the frond as it shrivelled. And at lunch time, when they went down to the café with pink sunshades, she looked—she looked—

For them.

But they were not there.

No, they *were* there, but she could not *see* them.

Campari with ice. Red wine. Antipasto. Fresh peaches in a basket. The brandy bottle (his).

A green lizard (not gold) spangling across the baked earth. Cyclamen in pots on a wall.

Today I'll walk out and see the vineyards.

She did not.

She sat, long after Craig had gone back to the hotel. She sat looking, looking. Not seeing them. Seeing their *absence.*

Those nights, or that night, Craig and she ate their dinner in the usual restaurant.

The priest who emerged from a little side door by the church, at a quarter past twelve, listened to Chrissie's stammering request. He spoke enough English, and did not seem to mind her lack of anything but the most basic Italian, which mostly consisted of exclaiming *Bella!* and endlessly apologizing to or thanking him.

She had thought the church was locked, but it was not.

He let her go in, and in a panic of courtesy, Chrissie pulled off her sleeveless cardigan, and draped it over her head.

When she did this, he glanced at her, and she thought his face was sorry, sorry for her. She noted he had seen she was not a Catholic. So then she stood there, ashamed to have let him down.

And how graceful it was, when he genuflected before the altar and the Idea of God. Yes, she wished she had been a Catholic, and able to do it, not just for his sake, but her own, to offer this, and receive the undoubted blessing of an inner response.

It was a powerful church, dark amber out of the sun, the windows hanging in space, brass gleams cast at random, as in some cunning ancient painting. The stone floor and pillars induced a sense of heavy depth, as if under water. There was a triptych above the altar, birth, ministry, death and resurrection.

Chrissie went round and gazed at the few ornaments, the windows and paintings. Then she sat on a wooden seat for half an hour. She felt she was an impostor and should not be there. Part of her wanted to throw itself howling at the naked, nail-pierced feet of the Christ. But why? What could she ask for?

She had never been religious. This was ridiculous now. *She* was ridiculous, (as Craig had again told her, when she protested at todays's policy of having a sandwich lunch in the hotel bar). She did not have the affrontery to go running to Jesus.

In the end, she had to face the fact the church could not help her. She got up and went out by the other little side door the priest had taken when he left her. She did this, she believed, quite innocently.

Outside was the narrowest, dimmest alley.

For a moment, she might have been anywhere in Italy, even in time. The encroaching walls were cracked and high and somehow black even in the shadowed daylight. Chrissie thought that she must go left, to return herself to the square. But the alley looked twisted that way, almost deformed—impassable, and it stank of urine and some sort of trouble—she did not know what that was, but vaguely she heard, or thought she did, angry male voices. Her independence, which was so pathetic, had maybe been stated enough, when she left Craig at the hotel. So, she went the other way along the alley. The wrong way. And here the light came, a topaz flood, and then she walked out into a place that seemed to have formed between two cliffs of sunstruck primrose plaster. High above, a delicate iron balcony let loose a torrent of violet flowers all down the wall.

And under these, they were waiting for her.

There came a wash of terror. But adventure, joy, always made Chrissie afraid. She laughed, and Arrigo and Gina laughed back at her, soundlessly, their teeth like summer-resistant snow.

And then—they were—

They were touching

her—

caressing her ... they were covering her like a silk blanket.

Chrissie had not often been deliberately touched. In lovemaking, even then, the explorations of her flesh were, (she surmised) unimpressed, and accordingly swift and desultory.

But no one anyway ever could have touched her—like this. *Their* hands, sliding over her, *their* arms encircling her, *their* lips—their *tongues*—moving across her face, her neck, her skin—They pressed firmly against her. Every surface of her felt them on itself. And she could not particularly notice which was Arrigo, which Gina—it did not matter—they were, all three of them, One.

So warm, so electric. It was like sex, yet not like sex. It was another *kind* of sex? Perhaps, maybe—for it had its own glorious momentum, it own rising to summit after summit—

Don't let it ever stop.

She lay back on the wall, in their arms, holding them, feeling them against her, (part of them) these hot, satiny-smooth bodies, that were scented of fur and sand and honey and—Was she conscious? Yes—No—

Her eyes were shut. She could not open them. She spun upward, mile after mile, swimming with Arrigo and Gina in a sea of sun, desire and flame.

They did not kiss her. They did not seek to probe her body in any way. She was not penetrated. No, she was *permeated*. It was—*osmosis*.

Oh—God—

What *were* they? In her swimming blind delight, the questions darted round her, swimming too, like tiny pretty fish. Arrigo and Gina were not ghosts—for they were solid, she could feel and grasp them, as they her.

There had been another dream. Forgotten, now—with the questioning fish—it surfaced too. What had the dream shown her? Something visual—she had seen the square, and a banner floating there, as if in some renaissance festival. White, with golden words written over it, and what had the words said? Something spelled out in her own faulty Italian—what? What?

Who cared? Only this, with them. Only they—They—

Never let me go.

Never stop.

Don't leave me—

Take me with you—

On the banner, seen now over hills of the mind, through hazes of unthought, the words, hardening. She read them from the drowning sea.

Popolo di Mezzogiorno.

A cloud must have swallowed the sun. She tried to ignore how abruptly cold she was, chilled and shivering.

But the wall, reality, pushed hard into her back, and the purple flowers so near her face gave off a tang that all at once she did not like, a cat's-piss smell—and she was

alone.

Chrissie opened her eyes. A sob wrenched convulsively as sick out of her mouth. She coughed and swore. She raised her wrist, visibly shaking, and stared at her shaking watch. One minute after 2:00 p.m.

She drew the withered weed out of the glass that afternoon, as Craig slept like an exhausted rhinoceros. The stem was rotten, the rest of it parched and blackened. The scent, if anything, was slightly stronger.

The latest bottle, whisky this time, still two thirds full as only brought up here this afternoon, stood on the little desk between the windows.

Craig slept, but carefully she kept her back to him. She undid the whisky and crumbled into it the frond, which swirled in the clear brown liquid, for a moment like flakes from a fire, then melted, disappeared.

Chrissie did not know what the frond was, its exact nature or name. Only that it had fragilely forced its way through stone. She did know what it would do, approximately. It was no use making out she did not. So she would fail to be at all astounded at following developments and would need to take extra care, be cautious, and, in the theatrical sense, act. As she had acted for years with Craig, pretending to a light-hearted tolerance and respect that had long since died. And instead of a thick grey rhinoceros hide, like his own, that she had also tried to pretend she had, she must become soft and startled, emotional and desperate. Just those very things she had always had to keep inside, from about the age of thirteen.

After she had seen to the whisky, Chrissie took another shower. (He cursed and grumbled at her when she came out, for waking him, then went back to sleep.)

Having dressed she went down and had an espresso in the bar. There were a few people there by now; it was about four-thirty, and the light deepening, thickening, the lamp-like bottles turned to chunks of green and tawny shadow.

She engaged the barman in a little touristy banter. He flirted at her, kindly, nicely, seeing she would know enough not to push her luck, but would appreciate the civility.

"My husband's been getting so tired," she added sadly. "We so want to go to the city, see the red and white cathedral. But he just can't face it. And I'm afraid the food isn't agreeing with him. Such a shame. I *love* the food."

When she had finished the espresso, she went out for a stroll. In the lobby, an oldish, blond man was standing talking to the reception clerk. She heard the blond man say, "They won't listen, never will, won't believe what you tell them. About the streets, the square. Especially the square."

Chrissie thought he spoke in an accented English; how else could she understand? An American, perhaps.

As she crossed into the spotlight of levelling sun at the threshold, as if into a red-gold box, isolated, she heard the man say, "Only a couple of hours. Does it hurt to watch out, to take precautions, just from twelve till two? Little enough. Doctors say you should keep out of the midday sun now, anyway. For the skin. Too many bad rays getting through."

Chrissie found she had hesitated. Pretending now to examine the strap of her sandal.

"*Popolo,*" said the man. "Citizens of noon," the man said. "*Mezzogiorrio.*"

And then she realized he spoke in Italian, not English, and suddenly she could not understand him.

She stepped out into the street, where cats were lying on balconies and in doorways, and a woman was selling bunches of flowers from the hills.

The bell sounded in the square. Five o'clock.

Inside, upstairs, behind her, Chrissie visualized Craig rolling off the bed, pouring himself two or three stiff drinks before taking his shower.

Craig did not want dinner, he said, (he told her why not; the disgusting food) but she, being a wimp, would make a fuss if they did not go out.

They walked down to the restaurant, through the square.

(The families were strolling. Two handsome young men on Lambrettas entertained a batch of beautiful girls—*bella! bella!* Stars had appeared.) Craig's colour was not good. He looked a little older.

In the restaurant he pushed most of the food far from him across the plates.

"Filthy fucking muck," he said, too loudly. Around the room, faces glanced and away. The other diners looked almost fearful. But not precisely of Craig. Of something.

Although he did not eat, Craig drank copiously. He had the brandy, all the bottle.

His speech was slurred.

His little bluish pinkish eyes peered at Chrissie.

"What are you staring at me for? Eh? Fuck you, you stupid cunt bitch."

If he had made a public scene like this previously, and now and then it had come close, Chrissie would have curled together, shrivelled with embarrassment and terror. Tonight, she sat looking obediently away from Craig, her face stamped with a sort of compassion.

The other people in the restaurant would see how much he drank, how he behaved, his violence, the purple-red and porridge-sludge tones that alternated in his face. And they would observe how sorrowful Chrissie was, how meek, how she did her best, stayed quiet and unruffled. And yet so concerned—she had often pretended to solicitous concern before.

When Craig smashed his brandy glass—part accident, part dislocated rage—the manager came out with his son, a tanned and muscular youth in jeans and a white shirt.

"I regret, *signore*, I must ask you to—"

"Leave? My fucking pleasure, you nonce."

At the door, she slipped back.

"I'm so sorry. He's not himself. He's been feeling ill. He works too hard."

"*É ben difficile, signora.* But—it is nothing. Yourself, you are always welcome, while you remain."

But in his face, as well, even in the face of the burly and competent son, a shifting of unease, a *carefulness*.

Outside, suddenly Craig swung sideways and vomited raucously on to the cobbles.

This went on some while, during which Chrissie stood, a picture of anxious helplessness, wide-eyed, clutching her hands together. Calm, and unmoved.

Raising his now mozzarella-coloured face, wiping his mouth, "There's the advert for this crap joint," croaked Craig at the empty street. "That's what their food's good for, in that shithole."

But then he had to lean over and commence puking again, and for some time, his sounds were restricted by and to this activity.

IV

All night Craig vomited. At first he made it to the bathroom, returning, staggering, to crash on his bed. Later he told her to bring him the waste-paper basket, and presently he told her to empty it. This became the routine. The colours changed, however. Black appeared, and crimson.

Between the bouts of his sickness, Chrissie slept a little, lying on her bed. There was an awful smell in the room, but this time he did not object when she opened both windows.

Above her, in the faintly luminous night, she saw the stains in the ceiling were quite different after dark, yet still she could make nothing of them. And then she believed she had, and she followed the map of stains and came into a place of nothingness, crowded with unseen, incredibly tall trees, but then a fearsome noise began and she woke up and it was Craig being sick again.

(The sounds he made now were so alarming, she was half-surprised no one had come to knock on their door. If they did, she was primed and had her performance all ready.)

When first light began, Craig spoke to Chrissie, in what was left of his voice. "Get me a doctor." So she got off the bed and went out of the room, closing the door behind her. She had kept on her clothes from the previous evening, and now she ran her fingers through her hair which never, anyway, looked like anything, so why bother. Then she turned the sign round on the door handle, so that it read, in Italian, French and English, *Do not disturb*.

There was already movement in the hotel. Spectral maids pattered through the corridors with armfuls of linen. In the lobby, the doors stood open to a cool nacreous dawn and they were watering the flowers in tubs by the doors.

Outside, birds sang.

Chrissie went straight to the square, and sat at one of the tables left out, but its umbrella folded to a pencil, the doors of the café shut.

It was very early. She would have to wait.

She could smell the dew, the morning. She might never ever smell that again, or see a dawn or a night. She understood this quite well, and what she had renounced.

Each day, there would only be two hours of life. But a life of gold and crystal, a life of perfection. Spent—with Them.

All this they had promised her when they showed her the venomous frond. If only she would be brave enough. They had really wanted her. They had made that so obvious. Why did not matter. And armed with that she had been brave. Although, in fact, it had needed no bravery at all. Which was as well, since her courage had been entirely used up by the years of staying with him. To kill him—that had only been, ultimately, common sense.

Chrissie sat calmly, almost mindlessly, at her table, and when the café opened just after eight, various people came and put up her umbrella, and wiped the table, and brought her coffee and an orange.

She enjoyed them so much, the black bitter drink with its caffeine zing, the tart fruit—the last foods she would eat in this world.

She knew They did not eat, and when she became one of them, neither would she.

Were there others? Other *people of the noon*—perhaps. Possibly, when no longer visible to the susceptible human eye, they assumed, or returned to, some other form. Which was—? —diamanté lizards—gleaming smokes—that glitter which sometimes came, when glancing away from something bright, and was thought to be some reflex of the optic nerve—

Was she excited at the prospect before her? Oh, she was radiant. She thought of how she would change, her skin turning to copper and her straw hair to spun gold. She thought of their embrace. Their love.

She had never been loved. Had she ever, herself, loved? No. Not until now.

"Arrigo," she murmured, "and Gina. And... Chrissie..."

Men and women came and went around her and about the square. A cart rumbled by, a lorry. Mopeds. A girl who shouted. Children tumbling. A striding man with striding dogs. Her table was no longer approached, the waiters did not come to chivvy her, ask her what else she would have. They left her in her thrumming peace. As if they could see the shining cloud which contained her, as she waited for her lovers in the sunlight's unfolding sunflower.

At about ten to twelve, Chrissie rose. When she did so, a curtain seemed to hang down from the burning sky, which drew itself all round her. Beyond the curtain, the quietness throbbed faintly with the undertones of other things, separate existences.

The square had emptied entirely, no one was there any more, but for herself. All around, barricaded inside the glass windows of the cafés, she saw them, these others, at the tables, eating and drinking, playing cards. And in windows above the square, high up, she saw them too, their backs turned, their shutters closed. Already she had left them all.

Chrissie stood by the fountain. Its spray leapt up and over, over and up. She had brought nothing with her. She would need nothing ever again.

She knew, this time, she would see them arrive. The midday sun would bring them out, like flowers, like blisters in paint, like creatures from under a rock.

The bell rang from the church, cracked and irreversible.

They came up out of the rim of the fountain's bowl, and up from the ground. It was the way something might squeeze out of a tube, except that the tube was invisible. They were ectoplasmic, yet liquidly glassy. She thought of the wings of insects which, emerging from the chrysalis, must harden in the sun.

And then they were really there.

The light flared off them, through them, out of them, and heat radiated from them.

Chrissie smiled, and Arrigo and Gina smiled. Chrissie stretched out her hands, and as she did so, the sun flamed on her skin, the harmfully *bad rays* of twelve o'clock till two. And her skin was altered. It was peachy and translucent—Already, it began.

"I did it," Chrissie said to Arrigo and Gina. "I poisoned him with the plant." They smiled. "He'll probably be dead by now.

Chrissie thought abruptly, Perhaps not everyone uses the poison that way. Maybe they swallow it themselves. Or even sometimes it isn't poison, that isn't appropriate—a knife concealed in a wall, a razor-blade in a dustbin—we are all their potential victims, we susceptible ones. We won't heed the warnings. They can do their work through us, one way or another way—

But she was not scared, no not at all. For the first and last time in her life, Chrissie was exalted.

And then—what was it? Some new sound, some other awareness—Chrissie felt that after all, she and they were not quite alone in the noon square. And although she did not care, she looked over her shoulder. This was when she saw the two policemen, in their dark uniforms, with their snouting guns, standing across from her, at the entry of the street which led to the hotel.

Like Arrigo and Gina, the policemen wore sunglasses, very black, and as she had infallibly known it with Arrigo and Gina, Chrissie now knew that the policemen were staring directly at her. She turned again, away from them.

Arrigo and Gina smiled.

"Well," Chrissie said. "They must have found him—I thought it would happen in the night, someone coming in—I was all ready to act upset, frantic—but then it was morning and—oh, I forgot, didn't I, to empty out the last of the whisky—I thought it wouldn't matter. It can't now, can it? It's too late. See my hands—my hands are almost transparent, aren't they—" But no, she thought then, something in her stumbling, the motion-sickness of the fall, no, her hands—were just as always. Bony, opaque, white, thin and *thick*.

Chrissie began to feel the new feeling, which was of utter darkness, there in the sun. Darkness and a wild flash of anger. For the town had known, this nice Italian town, most of them. They had seen, and warned, and stood aside, protecting themselves, knowing that Chrissie was the dupe—was the one— who would be lost—

She thought how lions stalked a herd of deer, and how one deer would become hypnotized, or was singled out because it was already in some way impaired, and slow. How the lions brought the deer down. And then the rest of the herd settled, and began again to feed innocently on the grass, alongside the lions feeding on the meat of the dead deer.

Arrigo and Gina still smiled, but they did not touch her. No need for it now. Instead they took off their own sunglasses, as if to see her better.

Their eyes were not as she had imagined. They were small and round and brilliant blood-red beads, without pupil or white, set in swivelling scaley portholes. The eyes of lizards. And their strawberry tongues, (lizardlike) flicked in and out two or three times. *Tasting.*

"Oh," Chrissie said, blankly.

Arrigo and Gina dissolved. They shimmered away, they and their horrible radioactive beauty and their reptile eyes and their satisfaction.

And Chrissie once more looked back towards the policemen, who remained exactly where they were. Waiting, perhaps, as Chrissie did, to see whether or not she too could impossibly grow transparent and vanish, or if she was only a human English woman, who had premeditatedly and viciously murdered a man in the hotel, her motives clear as day, and who was too fucking stupid to have covered up her tracks.

COLD FIRE

From an idea by John Kaiine

We was ten mile out from Chalsapila, and it's a raw night. The sea mist brewing thick as wool. Then little tramp ship come alongside. I on the bridge with Cap'n. He my brother. Kinda. Jehosalee Corgen. Well. But sudden the tramper puts up her lights. She's gotten a lot of sail on for what she's at, maybee tracking tobaccer or hard liquor up and down. They take a need of that, in the little ports along Great Whale Sound.

—Fuckendam, say Corgen.—What this bitch go to want?

I shrug, don't I. How the hell I know. I amn't no sailor, I. He picks me up drunken at Chalsa, tooken me aboard. I can trim bit of sails, take a watch, that kinda stuff.

Now the tramper swim in close, making signal.

Across the black night water, Corgen and her cap'n speak.

Sounds threat-like ta me.

—What he say? ask Beau, the mate.

Afore I can offer, he goes up ter see.

Then so does I.

We stand there on the poop, with the great wing of foresails over, and lanterns flash, and I hear other cap'n tells Corgen—Hey, this good for ye and yor crew. Make lotta dolla.

—Don't need no more cargo, say Corgen.

—Nar, yer take this, no cargo, jus tow. Like horse with wagon.

—This gurl ain't no horse, say Corgen.

—Hey hey, she a good ship. Has the weight ta do it.

I think the guy on tramper he sound like a Rus. Looks too, big, goodlooken guy, and beard.

He say, —All ye do, tow dammen thing outa back and up. Get maybee nine hundred dolla. We given ye wodka too.

Shooting star is went over, like a silver angel spit.

Seems to me maybee guy on tramper is eying me real much. I go off. Then Beau too come back aways. —Govment, say Beau from mouth corner.—Seems we havta.

Corgen's busyness on sea never much legal. But govment boats turn a blind ey, ifn you make nice. So we'll do this, what so this is.

In a bit, tramper boys bring some stuff aboard, boxes, a crate, wodka in big cans like for kerosene. They gives ta Corgen where to go to pick up thing wants the towing, and he writes down careful. He sign a paper too. Then tramper turns off up the side of the night.

Boxes, stuff, full of food.

I hear Beau ask Corgen soon what the fuckdam we be go to carry.

—Chunk bludy ice, Corgen say.—Chunka ice and tow her up into bludy Artic.

—So high?

—Higher maybee. High as she go.

—For why in Christ's name?

Corgen shrug.—For nine hundred dolla.

Weather is clear, sea nearly smooth. Now we was sailing norard easterly, where the tramper say go. And all that pass us is fisher boats for the codfish, and the faint shadow that come and go of the land. First night ends and then a day, and when the sun low, making the sky red, Hammer up in look-out call he can see something new on the water. Men went go up rigging, to see, and so do I. Hanging there I can make out a kinda island, but it all put together of boats and rafts, with nets drifting, and there torchlights burn, so's as the red sea and sky getten black, this island what is no island, she go red.

—What there behind?

We crane forard like birds, stretch our necks. Behind the torch smokings stand something pale, like it was a misty pane of glass, so the darkness show through.

—A berg what that is.

—Nar. None of they here.

—A berg, I tells you. They come down this far, from Grenland. A great narrer one.

Like a piece of glass, like I say, so it is. A piece of the great ice, chipped offn sailing free, as the icebergs do.

Then come another ship, a big one she is, with no colours but with guns, and men on her deck all armed, officers and soldiers, only they ain't wearing any uniform, but you can see they are, the ways they's stood.

Corgen and Beau and Bacherly, they get rowed offn away.

We set ta wait. Don't go no closer.

Over on the island of boats men move around in the light and shadow, can't see what they do, that's all. The berg, if it a berg, none of us sure, goes fainter in the smokes.

Along of midnight, Corgen and the others they bring back.

Corgen has face like dried white fish. Other two ain't much pinker. They come up aboard. Corgen grabs me.

—Pete O Pete, say Corgen. —Christ. I never shoulda took this on. Thin luck, the days we leaves Chalsapila.

Then he puts his head down on my shoulder, like as when we was childa and ma was raw ter him.

The six other men on Corgen's bucket, they clusters around, and the over us sails nod, cos the wind's getting up from the south.

—Cap'n, what's to do?

He lifts his head. He look scared and sick.

—Never word'll come outa me, he say. —Shitten govment say we must, so we do. I can't tell you. You'll be to see it, morning come.

We stand round him, and his boys look like they have mutiny running in the back of their eyes. Then Corgen rechanges to his own self. He reach out and grip Hammer and Bacherly and shake pair of them so as the bones rattle under their clothes. —We got no choosing. Like birth and dying. No choosen. So we take it. Bruk the wodka out, Beau. We've a long haul to the North fuckdam pole.

Second night on the new course, two of Corgen's men jump over. You can see the land, can reach it if swim strong, and though that sea cold, men have their reasons.

Another man, Bacherly, he go over next night and not so lucky. Struck the side and stunned him. He's drunken, I guess. We pull him back aboard and empty him of water, but then he lie raving and shaken till Corgen speak to him. —I tell him, bite yer tongue or I'll throw ye back down.

Sight of land is gone by then. Bacherly is quiet, but sometimes he puke, or he cries.

The others is make to be brave. A coupla of them make pretend we don't tow no thing at all. Ando cusses a lot. He anyway allays do that.

None of them much goes aft to look. It don't matter if they looks, it amn't a danger—no moren towing it. They did tell us, when they brung it, and all the cables and chain was fixed and the hooks to hold all, they do tell us then, the ice on the berg is old and set so hard, thick as a stone wall, the officer say, ten feet forget it—this more twenty feet thick of ice. Can't stir.

Can't break. This why it must be took to go upways north, to the Pole, this why. Though it came, officer believe, from the Southron Pole below, all the wide mile down at the earth's end. From there. And all this time, the ice held. So now, cold as we go, now it shall never give way. He swears that too, on the Bible.

Since Chalsapila, when Corgen finds me in alley, I don't drink. Even the Rus blue and black wodka, sharp as spikes, I left it alone.

I saw to the work I can do, and I eat when others have their food, though they are keep back the food the tramper gave us for when this is done and over. Also I play them cards. Corgen gives me some money, so I can gamble on cards too and pay up when lose, which I do. Sometimes when I climb up to the yards, I tend the ties and canvas, but then I set a while, and look back along the ship to her stern, back to where the berg is. It is about half ship's length behind, seems to drift there. If was not for the iron cables, you should think it only followed us.

He said, the officer, the ice is twenty feet thick.

Yet I see through. Transpearant, the officer say, like crystal, this type of berg. Means nothing, still thick as five stone walls.

By see through it, I mean it's as like you look through frost on glass. I remember a gurl once, she wants her drink in a frost glass. Like that.

If any of the others see me, staring back, they never show at that time. Only Bacherly is sick, crying in the hold on his blankets. When I go to want to give him the hot soup he throws it down and he say I'm mad, to sail the ship. He say I never needed to go on, I coulda gone over side and ashore, I, like the other two that jumped over. He forget me that I can't swim.

But anyhow, strange though this is, I amn't afraid of it. What I am feeling as I look at it, I don't think to be fear. But each day or night then, either I'm up in the rigging, and watch toward the stern, or then I go up on the aft deck, and whoever is to be there at wheel, he give me a glance.

One say —Right glad I am that sail tween me and that sea.

One say —You insane, Pete Corgen. I allays knew ye was. Is drink rottened yor brain.

As him he drink from wodka can.

But I go on by to rail, and I stood there, and I look. The first night I am doing it, the moon's up, and the biggest brightest of the stars. Shines right through the ice, like the electric light in the bar shone through that gurl's frost glass.

I never am mad, as that man say. I be have seen them as are mad. I am not.

Now it seems, that first time, never I see it so good, not when it come, and they tied it to the ship. Perhaps then I couldn't. As when you young, the first time you truly see a gurl, you canna look proper at her, though she is to be all you ever think on.

But first night in moon's shine. Well.

Christ. Like fire it is. But dull in frost. Frozened. Yet beautiful.

Beautiful.

Once saw a metal forged, was steel. It went go that colour, afore the cooling starts. But this, this is tween the heat and the cool. White red. Red silver. How can I say?

The shape.

Well.

I have see a lizard once. Yet this now not really like this lizard, which was only small, a kind creature.

And this ain't kind. Nor small.

Well.

How can I say?

Well, let me say, first time I fuck a gurl, when I have seen her nakd, and there she is, my heart in my throat she so sweet and so.

There's no word.

And this, neither no word.

And still I must try explain.

Up in the column of the narrer ice the shape do stood, and it have the body of a lizard among the giant kind. The backbone is curving, flext like a curl of rope. And all covered with scale is it, like a great fish. And it is have wings. The wings are more like they of the butterfly. But tough, the wings, tough as sails, and have a pattern, but this like the kind of written book I canna read, the pattern. And it has legs, and forelegs like long arms, and on them like hands, both on the feet and the front feet, hands. And the hands do have to be with claws. Each claw look to be length my forearm. Then there is long neck, and the head.

What is head of it? Like horse, a little. But not like horse. No, like the lean head of race dog, long, and thin. It with two ears, set back. Ears are like dog ears. And the shut eyes like lizard's eys.

I don't know what it is, this thing, in the ice. But I say to you, long afore I see this, I've look in some books. What books say want go hard for me, and the pictures too, and yet, piece by piece, sometime I will read then. This name I bring out. Dragon.

Dragon, dull red as burnt fire and cloved over frost white, wings spread like a moth against a lighted candle, and the eys shut. Shut eyes. No moving. Still like dead. Dragon. Dragon.

This we tow.

The weather it held, with the sea in pleats and slow, and soft gray sky that has sun like a lemon slice, and by night a moon like a ghost.

Porpus teem through water, wet slick speckle, like cats. Then is later, and the packs of the flat ice drifting by, and above over us black head tarna flying.

All this while the dragon coil in the berg. No moving.

The twenty feet ice of the berg glister but never cracks. Each dayup, Corgen comes out with gun, and look over the berg ice, check.

I try say to him about the dragon in the ice.

Corgen won't say back. Three times I try. Third time he slap me hard in the mouth so down I fall. Beau pulls me away, but as I not any drink in me, I feel no will ter do nothing on this, only sad, like as when I child.

Nights though, he, me and Beau we eat in the cabin. The wodka is still plenty. The guys from the tramper, they brung over a lot. Good best stuff, best than any ever drunk.

Only tastes bit of kerosene, Corgen say. Who care for that?

They drink, try to make me, laugh at me that I won't.

They sing some nights. So I with them.

In the ice it never moving. Eyes shut.

I think what eyes did it had behind the close, hot metal colour lids. Were they like fire? Was fire what it breathed as the book say?

As Corgen won't speak, I ask of Beau, what did the officers on the other ship say of the dragon, when first they make Corgen and he to see it.

—They come out talk of prehistry, say Beau. —Say this like elephant thing in Rus, that was trapt in hard old ice. This one some kind dynosar. But I see them dead dynosars in a show once. This out there nothing like them.

—Is it died? I say.

—For Christ, Pete, how fuck am I go to know? Looks well dead to me.

But the one who dies around then is Bacherly. I find him, as we was getting well up to north, toward the world's top.

Dense white mist that day, and we to go very slowly cos for of the ice drifts, which you hear grunt and creak and squeak now near, and now far off, but never see till close. And I go down with mess of meatpotato, and Bacherly is there and he's dead, with a red smear on chin.

Corgen come and kicks him to wake up. Bacherly don't take notice. We havta put him over side, and Ando say the prayer.

Some of the others have gutache too. But Corgen say they are all time drunken and that this is why, can't hold Rus wodka, it too good for them.

Then he say soft to me, —Or it that thing in there.

Meaning the dragon in the ice.

He say, —Some shitten disease carry on it. Those guys from the military, they jaw on, say too cold for any germ. How the fuck they knows? Couldna wait to get rid, and we the fuckfools to do muck work for them.

The stillness is like a dream.

When mist melts, I see three storms, three, four mile off north and east, boiling. But these never come up with Corgen's bucket. As if afraid to.

Tward northard, that a strange place. Never had I been up so high. A terrible white place, with islands of ice that look to anchor, so steady they are stuck on the water. And the land what seem ter go to want draw near, white land, bare as a cracked china plate, but it's ice. And now we was to see animals about, the lolling seals and walrus. One time there is two like swords flash, fish with horns that fight in the sea. —Narhl, say Corgen.

He was been here afore and know such beasts.

We is both to forard, us, when he tell me that. He never at back of ship, save when at helm, or when he checks the berg.

We be have long days on this travel. I forgetten how many.

Then one day, just like that one I have describe, Corgen and I is by the rail, when he lean over, and I hear he's throw up. When back he come, he have a smear of red on his lip.

One or two other of his men are sick now days on days, and all the rest belly rotten. Only I am not.

—Pete, Corgen say. —You never taste that filthy Rus piss muck, say you never?

—The wodka? Nar, Corgen. I swore I'd never, after Chalsapila.

—Thank Christ, say Corgen. —Listen now, it's gotten be medcin in.

—What medcin?

—Don't you be bludy fool. What medcin ya think? To fuckkill us all. Govment do it. We haul thing up here, and all while drinken, and it gets hold. No bludy nine hundred dolla for us, but poisoned. Done for, the boatload ofn us.

I start to cry. He hits me. Then we hug hard, like long ago.

—Why they do it? I say.

—To sew up our mouths. Christ know they want that thing us be to tow kept safe and froze and none to find.

I turn my head, canna help that, look all the way of the ship, to where the ghostly berg she float there still on her cables, as if she follow us. And in the yeller blubber white amba of the ice, the dragon not moving, curven, and I see.

—Corgen, I say. —Corgen.

—Now, say Corgen. —Listen close. The men and I are up to go the cabin. Have a final drunk of the piss muck, feel good one last, then I use the gun. Cap'n's job. And me the last.

—Christ. Nar, nar. We lay over toward the west, some settled place, get help.

—Too late, Peter. And beside, what to do of that in some settled place? That lizard. No, we go in cabin, we already done for. You'll hear some shots is all. Soon done. Leave it be. We two do say our god's bye here. Ye never had a stomache for a ruckus. Keep yor head, ad, you'll make shore. Leave bludy ship. Take the boat. Leave ship and us and the thing. Sea is very calm and slow. You will make ter shore.

I never have words. Now neither, they don't come. He wring me in his arms, and then go, and the other men appearing and they go after, some even lifting a hand to me, and Beau give me a sorry grin, as they are leaving like for a new ship. The cabin door shuts.

I stand alone.

Above, over I the sails swing and sigh, and every side the pack ice grind in the waves. There's shout and cussing and a can thrown behind the door which make it to shake.

I stand alone till and I hear the shots. One, two, three. Then a bit. Then four. Which is he, my brother.

I set down on the planks and cry, all the ice and water and empty around me. He were never my brother in blood. Ma's son she allays beat, and I only her died brother's boy she beat too, but never me so hard and cruel as he. Hated me he shoulda. Never done that. My brother, Corgen.

The dark by this time is to be coming, and never is quite dark, nor never now quite day. But I go down to ship's end, and stare at the dragon in the ice. And I saw as I had when I look ahind just before Corgen go in to die, that its eys are have come open, open wide.

Its eyes not like fire, no, they look like an old piece silver I once see in a church, pale but tarnish of black, and shine behind.

Very slow, slow as think, they seem to move. The rest dead still, no breath, no trembler of leg or head. But just these eyes move this way and that way.

All Corgen and crew be stark dead, they, and this have awaken sure, and not dead, there alive in the white amba of the ice.

And then its eyes look down, at me, so far down on the planks of the ship. The eys are to stare. And I know it have never, in all the time of its living days afore seen a thing like I am. As I, in all my living, never saw a thing like it but in a book I proper couldna read.

All around the dark drop like the snow.

When I have the things set right, I beginning what now I must. So long a great while, the steel tooth works on the cabling, and the green sparks fly. I look up and they are reflect like thoughts in the old silver of the dragon's eyes.

All night I am take to cut the cords that bind the berg to the stern of Corgen's ship.

The big heat of cutting make me sweat, and make too the berg true sweat, and near the half dawn time, I see there are a crack all up the crystal ice, all splintery and furred white, and it leak, drip, drip, away in the cold sea.

The dragon watch all that.

No moving, but only the eys.

When part of the sky lift to the east, last of the iron cords smokes and screams off and crash down in the water. The berg shudder. There is wind now, blow fierce straight out of the sun, and drive Corgen's bucket over to larboard, to the west, and maybee we are to go to smash on the ice there. But I look back, and I see the berg drift now, free, and how the heat from the cutting I was made get ice to run down, and the sun catch on these flows, and sudden a chunk of the old, old ice fall out and into the water.

Then was a horrible circling tide that hides up in the ice packs, and hauls ship aways, with the wind too bending her, so she lie to her side, and the great berg go smaller and smaller. But I think of its eyes.

I go down in hold, where Bacherly died the first. I cover up me in his blude-mark blankets and sleep, for there's now no more of any kind I can be to do.

She run in, time later, on Spalt Island, where the codfishers have a camp town of huts, and they come take me from the ship to their fires. Later we bury my brother and his men in the deep inland snow. An old man he say words over them from the Bible. A young woman of the older peoples here, with hair black as oil, she rubs my hands in her square, hot, fat hands, to bring me warm. She's kind, the black haired woman.

The fishers go out and come in again in their boats with the nets thrashing with the codfish. But never have they to say that they see any odd thing.

Berg must of drift north and froze, or away again to south, or west or east, and burst like a frost glass on sharp wall of sun. Perhaps and too, what is in there maybee allays was dead, under the ice, its eyes only to open as sometimes a dead man's will, or he make groan or sigh, even though he dead as stone when you check him, but it's as you picken him up the final air go out. The men here say they have seen like this in shark. And too, it is like dead Beau done, yet he is rotten. But Corgen never did.

Long while since, I am on this island.

I am walking out to the land's edge, where ice thick as twenty feet. Stand there, I, and see the sky and the water. I think and think, but no word comes. Can such thing as a dragon come back from so far past? Such a thing as that, so pale metal red, so long shut in its prison of frost glass, just the sparks of the cutting free and the Artic sun's shine to warm it, just the tides to push it here or there, back into the cold on the world's roof, or down into the melt of the thaw. Or down otherways under the top of the sea.

The black haired woman kind to me, like they kind to the dead here. Ask no question.

I think all hour of all day. And night when I wait for to go sleep. Of Corgen shut in the snow and the dragon in the berg, and of that in me that is me, clove in the ice, gone out like a match. Forever and tomorrow and forever.

The black hair woman kind.

CRYING IN THE RAIN

There was a weather Warning that day, so to start with we were all indoors. The children were watching the pay-TV and I was feeding the hens on the shut-yard. It was about nine a.m. Suddenly my mother came out and stood at the edge of the yard. I remember how she looked at me: I had seen the look before, and although it was never explained, I knew what it meant. In the same way she appraised the hens, or checked the vegetables and salad in their grow-trays. Today there was a subtle difference, and I recognised the difference too. It seemed I was ready.

'Greena,' she said. She strode across to the hen-run, glanced at the disappointing hens. There had only been three eggs all week, and one of those had registered too high. But in any case, she wasn't concerned with her poultry just now. 'Greena, this morning we're going into the Centre.'

'What about the Warning, Mum?'

'Oh, that. Those idiots, they're often wrong. Anyway, nothing until noon, they said. All Clear till then. And we'll be in by then.'

'But, Mum,' I said, 'there won't be any buses. There never are when there's a Warning. We'll have to walk.'

Her face, all hard and eaten back to the bone with life and living, snapped at me like a rat-trap: 'So we'll *walk*. Don't go on and on, Greena. What do you think your legs are for?'

I tipped the last of the feed from the pan and started towards the stair door.

'And talking of legs,' said my mother, 'put on your stockings. And the things we bought last time.'

There was always this palaver. It was normally because of the cameras, particularly those in the Entry washrooms. After you strip, all your clothes go through the cleaning machine, and out to meet you on the other end. But there are security staff on the cameras, and the doctors, and they might see, take an interest. You had to wear your smartest stuff in order not to be ashamed of it, things even a Centre doctor could glimpse without repulsion. A stickler, my mother. I went into the shower and took one and shampooed my hair, and used powder bought in the Centre with the smell of roses, so all of me would be gleaming clean when I went through the shower and shampooing at the Entry. Then I dressed in my special underclothes, and my white frock, put on my stockings and shoes, and remembered to drop the carton of rose powder in my bag.

My mother was ready and waiting by the time I came down to the street doors, but she didn't upbraid me. She had meant me to be thorough.

The children were yelling round the TV, all but Daisy, who was seven and had been left in charge. She watched us go with envious fear. My mother shouted her away inside before we opened up.

When we'd unsealed the doors and got out, a blast of heat scalded us. It was a very hot day, the sky so far clear as the finest blue perspex. But of course, as there had been a weather Warning, there were no buses, and next to no one on the streets. On Warning days, there was anyway really nowhere to go. All the shops were sealed fast, even our three area pubs. The local train station ceased operating when I was four, eleven years ago.

Even the endless jumble of squats had their boards in place and their tarpaulins over.

The only people we passed on the burning dusty pavements were a couple of fatalistic tramps, in from the green belt, with bottles of cider or petromix; these they jauntily raised to us. (My mother tugged me on.) And once a police car appeared which naturally hove to at our side and activated its speaker.

'Is your journey really necessary, madam?'

My mother, her patience eternally tried, grated out furiously, 'Yes it is.'

'You're aware there's been a forecast of rain for these sections?'

'Yes,' she rasped.

'And this is your daughter? It's not wise, madam, to risk a child—'

'My daughter and I are on our way to the Centre. We have an appointment. Unless we're *delayed,'* snarled my mother, visually skewering the pompous policeman, only doing his job, through the Sealtite windows of the car, 'we should be inside before any rain breaks.'

The two policemen in their snug patrol vehicle exchanged looks.

There was a time we could have been arrested for behaving in this irresponsible fashion, my mother and I, but no one really bothers now. There was more than enough crime to go round. On our heads it would be.

The policeman who'd spoken to us through the speaker smiled coldly and switched it off—speaker and, come to that, smile.

The four official eyes stayed on me a moment, however, before the car drove off. That at least gratified my mother. Although the policeman had called me a child for the white under-sixteen tag on my wristlet, plainly they'd noticed I look much older and, besides, rather good.

Without even a glance at the sky, my mother marched forward. (It's true there are a few public weather-shelters but vandals have wrecked most of them.) I admired my mother, but I'd never been able to love her, not even to like her much. She was phenomenally strong and had kept us together, even after my father canced, and the other man, the father of Jog, Daisy and Angel. She did it with slaps and harsh tirades, to show us what we could expect in life. But she must have had her fanciful side once: for instance, the silly name she gave me, for green trees and green pastures and waters green as bottle-glass that I've only seen inside the Centre. The trees on the streets and in the abandoned gardens have always been bare, or else they have sparse foliage of quite a cheerful brown colour. Sometimes they put out strange buds or fruits and then someone reports it and the trees are cut down. They were rather like my mother, I suppose, or she was like the trees. Hard-bitten to the bone, enduring, tough, holding on by her root-claws, not daring to flower.

Gallantly she showed only a little bit of nervousness when we began to see the glint of the dome in the sunshine coming down High Hill from the old cinema ruin. Then she started to hurry quite a lot and urged mc to be quick. Still, she didn't look up once, for clouds.

In the end it was perfectly all right: the sky stayed empty and we got down to the concrete underpass. Once we were on the moving way I rested my tired feet by standing on one leg then the other like a stork I once saw in a TV programme.

As soon as my mother noticed she told me to stop it. There are cameras watching, all along the underpass to the Entry. It was useless to try persuading her that it didn't matter. She had never brooked argument and though she probably wouldn't clout me before the cameras she might later on. I remember I was about six or seven when she first thrashed me. She used a plastic belt, but took off the buckle. She didn't want to scar me. Not to scar Greena was a part of survival, for even then she saw something might come of me. But the belt hurt and raised welts. She said to me as I lay howling and she leaned panting on the bed, 'I won't have any back-answers. Not from you and not from any of you, do you hear me? There isn't time for it. You'll do as I say.'

After we'd answered the usual questions, we joined the queue for the washroom. It wasn't much of a queue, because of the Warning. We glided through the mechanical check, the woman operator even congratulating us on our low levels. 'That's section SEK, isn't it?' she said chattily. 'A very good area. My brother lives out there. He's over thirty and has three children.' My mother congratulated the operator in turn and proudly admitted our house was one of the first in SEK fitted with Sealtite. 'My kids have never played outdoors,' she assured the woman. 'Even Greena here scarcely went out till her eleventh birthday. We grow most of our own food.' Then, feeling she was giving away too much—you never knew who might be listening, there was always trouble in the suburbs with burglars and gangs —she clammed up tighter than the Sealtite.

As we went into the washroom a terrific argument broke out behind us. The mechanical had gone off violently. Some woman was way over the acceptable limit. She was screaming that she had to get into the Centre to see her daughter, who was expecting a baby—the oldest excuse, perhaps even true, though pregnancy is strictly regulated under a dome. One of the medical guards was bearing down on the woman, asking if she had Insurance.

If she had, the Entry hospital would take her in and see if anything could be done. But the woman had never got Insurance, despite having a daughter in the Centre, and alarms were sounding and things were coming to blows.

'Mum,' I said, when we passed into the white plastic-and-tile expanse with the black camera eyes clicking overhead and the Niagara rush of showers, 'who are you taking me to see?'

She actually looked startled, as if she still thought me so naïve that I couldn't guess she too, all this time, had been planning to have a daughter in the Centre. She glared at me, then came out with the inevitable.

'Never you mind. Just you hope you're lucky. Did you bring your talc?'

'Yes, Mum.'

'Here then, use these too. I'll meet you in the cafeteria.'

When I opened the carton I found 'Smoky' eye make-up, a cream lipstick that smelled of peaches, and a little spray of scent called *I Mean It*.

My stomach turned right over. But then I thought, So what. It would be frankly stupid of *me* to be thinking I was naïve. I'd known for years.

While we were finishing our hamburgers in the cafeteria, it did start to rain, outside. You could just *sense* it, miles away beyond the layers of protection and lead-glass. A sort of flickering of the sight. It wouldn't do us much harm in here, but people instinctively moved away from the outer suburb-side walls of the café, even under the plastic palm-trees in tubs. My mother stayed put.

'Have you finished, Greena? Then go to the Ladies and brush your teeth, and we'll get on. And spray that scent again.'

'It's finished, Mum. There was only enough for one go.'

'Daylight robbery,' grumbled my mother, 'you can hardly smell it.'

She made me show her the empty spray and insisted on squeezing hissing air out of it into each of my ears.

Beyond the cafeteria, a tree-lined highway runs down into the Centre. Real trees, green trees, and green grass on the verges. At the end of the slope, we waited for an electric bus painted a jolly, bright colour, with a rude driver. I used to feel that everyone in the Centre must be cheery and contented, bursting with optimism and the juice of kindness. But I was always disappointed. They know you're from outside at once, if nothing else gives you away, skin-tone is different from the pale underdome skin or chocolaty solarium Centre tan. Although you could never have got in here if you hadn't checked out as acceptable, a lot of people draw away from you on the buses or underground trains. Once or twice, when my mother and I had gone to see a film in the Centre no one would sit near us. But not everybody had this attitude. Presumably, the person my mother was taking me to see wouldn't mind.

'Let me do the talking,' she said as we got off the bus. (The driver had started extra quickly, half shaking our contamination off his platform, nearly breaking our ankles.)

'Suppose he asks me something?'

'He?' But I wasn't going to give ground on it now. 'All right. In that case, answer, but be careful.'

Parts of the Centre contain very old historic buildings and monuments of the inner city which, since they're inside, are looked after and kept up. We were now under just that sort of building. From my TV memories—my mother had made sure we had the educational TV to grow up with, along with lesson tapes and exercise ropes—the architecture looked late eighteenth or very early nineteenth, white stone, with top-lids on the windows and pillared porticos up long stairs flanked by black metal lions.

We went up the stairs and I was impressed and rather frightened.

The glass doors behind the pillars were wide open. There's no reason they shouldn't be, here. The cool-warm, sweet-smelling breezes of the dome-conditioned air blew in and out, and the real ferns in pots waved gracefully. There was a tank of golden fish in the foyer. I wanted to stay and look at them. Sometimes on the Centre streets you see well-off people walking their clean, groomed dogs and foxes. Sometimes there might be a silken cat high in a window. There were birds in the Centre parks, trained not to fly free anywhere else. When it became dusk above the dome, you would hear them tweeting excitedly as they roosted. And then all the lights of the city came on and moths danced round them. You could get proper honey in the Centre, from the bee-farms, and beef and milk from the cattle-grazings, and salmon, and leather and wine and roses.

But the fish in the tank were beautiful. And I suddenly thought, if I get to stay here—if I really *do*—but I didn't believe it. It was just something I had to try to get right for my mother, because I must never argue with her, ever.

The man in the lift took us up to the sixth floor. He was impervious; we weren't there, he was simply working the lift for something to do.

A big old clock in the foyer had said three p.m. The corridor we came out in was deserted. All the rooms stood open like the corridor windows, plushy hollows with glass furniture: offices. The last office in the corridor had a door which was shut.

My mother halted. She was pale, her eyes and mouth three straight lines on the plain of bones. She raised her hand and it shook, but it knocked hard and loud against the door.

In a moment, the door opened by itself.

My mother went in first.

She stopped in front of me on a valley-floor of grass-green carpet, blocking my view.

'Good afternoon, Mr Alexander. I hope we're not too early.'

A man spoke.

'Not at all. Your daughter's with you? Good. Please do come in.' He sounded quite young.

I walked behind my mother over the grass carpet, and chairs and a desk became visible, and then she let me step around her, and said to him, 'This is my daughter, Mr Alexander. Greena.'

He was only about twenty-two, and that was certainly luck, because the ones born in the Centre can live up until their fifties, their sixties even, though that's rare. (They quite often don't even cance in the domes, providing they were born there. My mother used to say it was the high life killed them off.)

He was tanned from a solarium and wore beautiful clothes, a cotton shirt and trousers. His wristlet was silver—I had been right about his age: the tag was red. He looked so fit and hygienic, almost edible. I glanced quickly away from his eyes.

'Won't you sit down?' He gave my mother a crystal glass of Centre gin, with ice-cubes and lemon slices. He asked me, smiling, if I'd like a milk-shake, yes, with real milk and strawberry flavour. I was too nervous to want it or enjoy it, but it had to be had. You couldn't refuse such a thing.

When we were perched in chairs with our drinks (he didn't drink with us) he sat on the desk, swinging one foot, and took a cigarette from a box and lit and smoked it.

'Well, I must say,' he remarked conversationally to my mother, 'I appreciate your coming all this way—after a Warning, too. It was only a shower I gather'

'We were inside by then,' said my mother quickly. She wanted to be definite—the flower hadn't been spoiled by rain.

'Yes, I know. I was in touch with the Entry.'

He would have checked our levels, probably. He had every right to, after all. If he was going to buy me, he'd want me to last a while.

'And, let me say at once, just from the little I've seen of your daughter, I'm sure she'll be entirely suitable for the work. So pretty, and such a charming manner.'

It was normal to pretend there was an actual job involved. Perhaps there even would be, to begin with.

My mother must have been putting her advert out since last autumn. That was when she'd had my photograph taken at the Centre. I'd just worn my nylon-lace panties for it; it was like the photos they take of you at the Medicheck every ten years. But there was always a photograph of this kind with such an advert. It was illegal, but nobody worried. There had been a boy in our street who got into the Centre three years ago in this same way. He had placed the advert, done it all himself. He was handsome, though his hair, like mine, was very fine and perhaps he would lose it before he was eighteen. Apparently that hadn't mattered.

Had my mother received any other offers? Or only this tanned Mr Alexander with the intense bright eyes?

I'd drunk my shake and not noticed.

Mr Alexander asked me if I would read out what was written on a piece of rox he gave me. My mother and the TV lessons had seen to it I could read, or at least that I could read what was on the rox, which was a very simple paragraph directing a Mr Cleveland to go to office 170B on the seventh floor arid a Miss O'Beal to report to the basement. Possibly the job would require me to read out such messages. But I had passed the test. Mr Alexander was delighted. He came over without pretence and shook my hand and kissed me exploringly on the left cheek. His mouth was firm and wholesome and he had a marvellous smell, a smell of money and safety. My mother had laboured cleverly on me. I recognised it instantly, and wanted it. Between announcements, they might let me feed the fish in the tank.

Mr Alexander was extremely polite and gave my mother another big gin, and chatted sociably to her about the latest films in the Centre, and the colour that was in vogue, nothing tactless or nasty, such as the cost of food inside, and out, or the SEO riots the month before, in the suburbs, when the sounds of the fires and the police rifles had penetrated even our sealed-tight home in SEK. He didn't mention any current affairs, either, the death-rate on the continent, or the trade-war with the USA—he knew our TV channels get edited. Our information was too limited for an all-round discussion.

Finally he said, 'Well, I'd better let you go. Thank you again. I think we can say we know where we stand, yes?' He laughed over the smoke of his fourth cigarette, and my mother managed her death's-head grin, her remaining teeth washed with gin and lemons. 'But naturally I'll be writing to you. I'll send you the details Express. That should mean you'll get them—oh, five days from today. Will that be all right?'

My mother said 'That will be lovely, Mr Alexander. I can speak for Greena and tell you how very thrilled she is. It will mean a lot to us. The only thing is, Mr Alexander, I do have a couple of other gentlemen—I've put them off of course. But I have to let them know by the weekend.'

He made a gesture of mock panic. 'Good God, I don't want to lose Greena. Let's say three and a half days, shall we? I'll see if I can't rustle up a special courier to get my letter to you extra fast.'

We said goodbye, and he shook my hand again and kissed both cheeks. A great pure warmth came from him, and a sort of power. I felt I had been kissed by a tiger, and wondered if I was in love.

At the Entry-exit, though it didn't rain again, my mother and I had a long wait until the speakers broadcast the All Clear. By then the clarified sunset lay shining and flaming in six shades of red and scarlet-orange over the suburbs.

'Look, Mum,' I said, because shut up indoors so much I didn't often get to see the naked sky, 'isn't it beautiful? It doesn't look like that through the dome.'

But my mother had no sympathy with vistas. Only the toxins in the air, anyway, make the colours of sunset and dawn so wonderful. To enjoy them is therefore idiotic, perhaps unlawful.

My mother had, besides, been very odd ever since we left Mr Alexander's office. I didn't properly understand that this was due to the huge glasses of gin he'd generously given her. At first she was fierce and energetic, keyed up, heroic against the polished sights of the Centre, which she had begun to point out to me like a guide. Though she didn't say so, she meant *Once you live here*. But then, when we had to wait in the exit lounge and have a lot of the rather bad coffee-drink from the machine, she sank in on herself, brooding. Her eyes became so dark, so bleak, I didn't like to meet them. She had stopped talking at me.

Though the rain-alert was over, it was now too late for buses. There was the added problem that gangs would be coming out on the streets, looking for trouble.

The gorgeous poisoned sunset died behind the charcoal sticks of trees and pyramids and oblongs of deserted buildings and rusty railings.

Fortunately, there were quite a few police-patrols about. My mother gave them short shrift when they stopped her. Generally they let us get on. We didn't look dangerous.

In SEK, the working street-lights were coming on and there were some ordinary people strolling or sitting on low broken walls, taking the less unhealthy air. They pop up like the rabbits used to, out of their burrows. We passed a couple of women we knew, outside the Sealtite house on the corner of our road. They asked where we'd come from. My mother said tersely we'd been at a friend's, and stopped in till the All Clear.

Although Sealtite, as the advert says, makes secure against anything but gelignite, my mother had by now got herself into an awful sort of rigid state. She ran up the concrete to our front door, unlocked it and dived us through. We threw our clothes into the wash-bin, though they hardly needed it as we'd been in the Centre most of the day. The TV was still blaring. My mother, dragging on a skirt and nylon blouse, rushed through into the room where the children were. Immediately there was a row. During the day Jog had upset a complete giant can of powdered milk. Daisy had tried to clear it up and they had meant not to tell our mother, as if she wouldn't notice one was missing. Daisy was only seven, and Jog was three, so it was blurted out presently. My mother hit all of them, even Angel. Daisy, who had been responsible for the house in our absence, she belted, not very much, but enough to fill our closed-in world with screaming and savage sobs.

After it was over, I made a pot of tea. We drank it black since we would have to economise on milk for the rest of the month.

The brooding phase had passed from my mother. She was all sharp jitters. She said we had to go up and look at the hens. The eggs were always registering too high lately. Could there be a leak in the sealing of the shut-yard?

So that was where we ended up, tramping through lanes of lettuce, waking the chickens who got agitated and clattered about. My mother wobbled on a ladder under the roofing with a torch. 'I can't see anything,' she kept saying.

Finally she descended. She leaned on the ladder with the torch dangling, still alight, wasting the battery. She was breathless.

'Mum . . . the torch is still on.'

She switched it off, put it on a post of the hen-run, and suddenly came at me. She took me by the arms and glared into my face.

'Greena, do you understand about the Alexander man? Well, do you?'

'Yes, Mum.'

She shook me angrily but not hard.

'You know why you have to?'

'Yes, Mum. I don't mind, Mum. He's really nice.'

Then I saw her eyes had changed again, and I faltered. I felt the earth give way beneath me. Her eyes were full of burning water. They were soft and they were frantic.

'Listen, Greena. I was thirty last week.'

'I know—'

'You shut up and listen to me. I had my medicheck. It's no good, Greena.

We stared at each other. It wasn't a surprise. This happened to everyone. She'd gone longer than most. Twenty-five was the regular innings, out here.

'I wasn't going to tell you, not yet. I don't have to report into the hospital for another three months. I'm getting a bit of pain, but there's the Insurance: I can buy that really good pain-killer, the new one.'

'Mum.'

'Will you be quiet? I want to ask you, you know what you have to do? About the kids? They're your sisters and your brother, you know that, don't you?'

'Yes. I'll take care of them.'

'Get him to help you. He will. He really wants you. He was dead unlucky, that Alexander. His legal girlfriend canced. Born in the Centre and everything and she pegged out at eighteen. Still, that was good for us. Putting you on the sterilisation programme when you were little, thank God I did. You see, he can't legally sleep with another girl with pregnancy at all likely. Turns out he's a high-deformity risk. Doesn't look it, does he?'

'Yes, Mum, I know about the pregnancy laws.'

She didn't slap me or even shout at me for answering back. She seemed to accept I'd said it to reassure her I truly grasped the facts. Alexander's predicament had anyway been guessable. Why else would he want a girl from outside?

'Now, Angel—' said my mother '—I want you to see to her the same, sterilisation next year when she's five. She's got a chance too: she could turn out very nice-looking. Daisy won't be any use to herself, and the boy won't. But you see you get a decent woman in here to take care of them. No homes. Do you hear? Not for my kids.' She sighed, and said again, *'He'll* help you. If you play your cards right, he'll do anything you want. He'll cherish you, Greena.' She let me go and said, grinning, 'We had ten applications. I went and saw them all. He's the youngest and the best.'

'He's lovely,' I said. 'Thanks, Mum.'

'Well, you just see you don't let me down.

'I won't. I promise. I promise, really.'

She nodded, and drew up her face into its sure, habitual shape, and her eyes dry into their Sealtite of defiance.

'Let's get down now. I'd better rub some anesjel into those marks on Daisy.'

We went down and I heard my mother passing from child to child, soothing and reprimanding them as she harshly pummelled the anaesthetic jelly into their hurts.

For a moment, listening on the landing, in the clamped house-dark, I felt I loved my mother.

Then that passed off. I began to think about Mr Alexander and his clothes and the brilliance of his eyes in his tanned healthy face.

It was wonderful, He didn't send a courier. He came out himself. He was in a small sealed armoured car like a TV alligator, but he just swung out of it and up the concrete into our house. (His bodyguard stayed negligently inside the car. He had a pistol and a mindless, attentive, lethal look.)

Mr Alexander brought me half a dozen perfect tawny roses, and a crate of food for the house, toys and TV tapes for the children, and even some gin for my mother. He presumably didn't know yet she only had three months left, but he could probably work it out. He made a fuss of her, and when she'd spoken her agreements into the portable machine, he kissed me on the mouth and then produced a bottle of champagne. The wine was very frothy, and the glassful I had made me feel giddy. 1 didn't like it, but otherwise our celebration was a success.

I don't know how much money he paid for me. I'd never want to ask him. Or the legal fiddles he must have gone through. He was able to do it, and that was all we needed to know, my mother, me. (She always kept the Insurance going and now, considerably swelled, the benefits will pass on to the children.)

She must have told him eventually about the hospital. I do know he saw to it personally that she had a private room and the latest in pain relief, and no termination until she was ready. He didn't let me see her after she went in. She'd said she didn't want it, either. She had already started to lose weight and shrivel up, the way it happens.

The children cried terribly. I thought it could never be put right, but in the end the agency he found brought us a nineteen-year-old woman who'd lost her own baby and she seemed to take to the children at once. The safe house, of course, was a bonus no one sane would care to ignore. The agency will keep an eye on things, but her levels were low, she should have at least six years. The last time I went there they all seemed happy. He doesn't want me to go outside again.

Six months ago, he brought me officially into the Centre.

All the trees were so *green* and the fish and swans sparkled in and on the water, and the birds sang, and he gave me a living bird, a real live tweeting, yellow, jumping bird in a spacious, glamorous cage; I love this bird and sometimes it sings. It may only live a year, he warned me, but then I can have another.

Sometimes I go to a cubicle in the foyer of one of the historic buildings and read out announcements over the speaker. They pay me in Centre credit discs, but I hardly need any money of my own.

The two rooms that are mine on Fairgrove Avenue are marvellous. The lights go on and off when you come in or go out, and the curtains draw themselves when it gets dark, or the blinds come down when it's too bright. The shower room always smells fresh, like a summer glade is supposed to, and perhaps once did. I see him four, five or six times every week, and we go to dinner and to films, and he's always bringing me real flowers and chocolates and fruit and honey. He even buys me books to read. Some days, 1 learn new words from the dictionary.

When he made love to me for the first time, it was a strange experience, but he was very gentle. It seemed to me I might come to like it very much, (and I was right), although in a way, it still seems rather an embarrassing thing to do.

That first night, after, he held me in his arms, and I enjoyed this. No one had ever held me caringly, protectingly, like that, ever before. He told me, too, about the girl who canced. He seemed deeply distressed, as if no one ever dies that way, but then, in Centres, under domes, death isn't ever certain.

All my mother tried to get was time, and when that ran out, control of pain and a secure exit. But my darling seems to think that his girl had wanted much, much more, and that I should want more too. And in a way that scares me, because I may not even live to be twenty, and then he'll break his heart again. But then again he'll probably find someone else. And maybe I'll be strong like my mother. I hope so. I want to keep my promise about the children. If I can get Angel settled, she can carry on after me. But I'll need ten or eleven years for that.

Something funny happened yesterday. He said, he would bring me a toy tomorrow—today. Yes, a toy, though I'm a woman, and his lover. I never had a toy. I love my bird best. I love him, too.

The most peculiar thing is, though, that I miss my mother. I keep on remembering what she said to me, her blows and injunctions. Going shopping with her, or to the cinema; how, when her teeth were always breaking, she got into such a rage.

I remember mistily when I was small, the endless days of weather Warnings when she, too, was trapped in the house, my fellow prisoner, and how the rain would start to pour down, horrible, sinister torrents that frightened me, although then I didn't know why. All the poisons and the radioactivity that have accumulated and go on gathering on everything in an unseen glittering, and which the sky somehow collects and which the rain washes down from the sky in a deluge. The edited pay-TV seldom reports the accidents and oversights which continually cause this. Sometimes an announcement would come on and tell everyone just to get indoors off the street, and no reason given, and no rain or wind even. The police cars would go about the roads sounding their sirens, and then they too would slink into holes to hide. But next day, usually there was the All Clear.

In the Centre, TV isn't edited. I was curious to see how they talked about the leaks and pollutions, here. Actually they don't seem to mention them at all. It can't be very important, underdome.

But I do keep remembering one morning, that morning of a colossal rain, when I was six or seven. I was trying to look out at the forbidden world, with my nose pressed to the Sealtite. All I could see through the distorting material was a wavering leaden rush of liquid. And then 1 saw something so alien I let out a squeal.

'What is it?' my mother demanded. She had been washing the breakfast dishes in half the morning ration of domestic filtered water, clashing the plates bad-temperedly. 'Come on, Greena, don't just make silly noises.'

I pointed at the Sealtite. My mother came to see.

Together we looked through the fall of rain, to where a tiny girl, only about a year old, was standing—*out on the street.* No knowing how she got there—strayed from some squat, most likely. She wore a pair of little blue shorts and nothing else, and she clutched a square of ancient blanket that was her doll. Even through the sealed pane and the rainfall you could see she was bawling and crying in terror.

'Jesus Christ and Mary the Mother,' said my own mother on a breath. Her face was scoured white as our sink. But her eyes were like blazing fires, hot enough to quench the rain.

And next second she was thrusting me into the TV room, locking me in, shouting, *Stay there! Don't you move or I'll murder you!*

Then I heard both our front doors being opened. Shut. When they opened again and shut again, I heard a high-pitched infantile roaring. The roar got louder and possessed the house. Then it fell quiet. I realised my mother had flown out into the weather and grabbed the lost child and brought her under shelter.

Of course, it was no use. When my mother carried her to the emergency unit next day, after the All Clear, the child was dying. She was so tiny. She held her blanket to the end and scorned my mother, the nurse, the kindly needle of oblivion. Only the blanket was her friend. Only the blanket had stayed and suffered with her in the rain.

When she was paying for the treatment and our own decontam, the unit staff said horrible things to my mother, about her stupidity until I started to cry in humiliated fear. My mother ignored me and only faced them out like an untamed vixen, snarling with her cracked teeth.

All the way home I whined and railed at her. Why had she exposed us to those wicked people with their poking instruments and boiling showers, the hurt and rancour, the downpour of words? (I was jealous too, I realise now, of that intruding poisonous child. I'd been till then the only one in our house.)

Go up to bed! shouted my mother. I wouldn't.

At last she turned on me and thrashed me with the plastic belt. Violent, it felt as if she thrashed the whole world, till in the end she made herself stop.

But now I'm here with my darling, and my lovely bird singing. I can see a corner of a green park from both my windows. And it never, never rains.

It's funny how I miss her, my mother, so much.

WE ALL FALL DOWN

*C**alling Antic . . . Calling Antic Base . . .*
(Citizen Data File: UK) *Letter.* . . . but the best thing is my flowers! The scent is glorious! How is your brother? Asthma's such a horrible . . .

(Bridgehead Gazette: East Sussex) *Man grows 20 foot rose bush.* Amateur gardener Peter Collis confessed yesterday, "Normally anything I try to grow dies. Like that conifer there" . . .

(Llanfycwn News: West Wales) *Mystery disease hits ancient woodland.* Historic woods dating back to the 10th Century are under attack by an unknown blight. Locals say they have seen trees falling, as if 'cut down by an invisible axe.' British Heritage has . . .

(Citizen Data File: Spain) *Pepperpaperblog.* . . . garden here's suddenly full of them. Can't believe it—the soil is lousy. Even growing up the walls—blood red. Smell is overpoweringly gorgeous . . .

(Comp.pp email: Ireland) The whole town looks like it's hung in red bunting. Dublin's the same I've heard . . .

(Comp. webpage: Sweden) We too have the roses, in the pines. Red and white . . .

(NICS Health Services report: General Europe) *Compound Duplication.* The high incidence of asthma, hay fever, and related allergies is causing increasing concern. Reduction in traffic density operating in large urban areas does not seem to influence the disturbing . . .

Calling Antic Base . . .

(News Bulletin: www.uk) *Happy Christmas!* Astonishment prevails in Great Britain and much of Europe as vast quantities of red roses are seen literally blooming in the winter frost. Termed a 'wonderful Christmas gift', they have cheered millions enduring the present severe weather, and poor economic . . .

(Checkpoint Worldcast) Strange weather—ordinary climate change, or atmospheric occlusion (A.O)? . . .

Toronto (Unclassified) Reports of sewers blocked. Also in Paris, France, Manhattan, and Bristol, UK . . .

Iran (International Web-Exchange) Desert blooms as roses break through dunes . . . Pictures show lush carpet of . . .

Cairo (Int.net web-exchange) Nile choked. Not since Biblical times . . .

(Classified) Ship lost V. of O. Survivors describe scarlet rose-like weed . . .

(From Our Own Correspondent: BBC Radio via Skylink) ". . . time in Africa, I'd see roses springing from the drought parched soils of the Andjaba . . ."

(Sunday Telegraph Gardening Supplement: UK) Europe is mourning the loss of the white rose, which today joined the other colour variants supposedly destroyed by the scarlet strain. Previous losers in this horticultural prize fight have been the peach, pink and yellow, and so-called 'mauve', 'black' and 'blue' varieties. Deaton Forde, president of the Rose Growers Consortium, told us, 'The red has become a ferocious specimen. Years of coping with climate change and human ignorance have caused its adaptation to a peak of strength that brooks no

WE ALL FALL DOWN 113

competitors.' This apparently includes any neighbouring flower. Even trees are liable . . .

(UK Classified) Thames Basin high-rise collapse due to action of RR . . .

(France Aller: Unlimited News Network) *State Troops in war of the Roses.* America is now battling with the Red Rose menace across 15 states. The anti-GM lobby maintains GM crops are responsible for a mutated . . . even army clearance still unable . . .

(Pan-India World Service) Update: Hospitals groan under weight of new admissions. Pollen count now off scale in High Delhi. The overwhelming scent causes also nausea and a sensation of choking . . . penetrates even sealed environment . . .

(The Independent: UK) Front page picture: A single red rose. Caption: *The Face Of Our Enemy?*

(Cit.Dat.File: Unknown) *Bubbleblog.* . . . things we cut and put in vases, sent to lovers . . . ending the world . . .

(Farweb.Skylink) A state of emergency was today declared in 44 European cities. Reports from West Africa, India and China indicate . . .

(Daily Chain: UK) A grain-less America is starving, its agriculture and meat industry . . .

(Compound data File: Classified) Government authorizes evacuation plans to Antipodes and South Pole . . .

(Classified) Airlift due. Please be ready. Hand-luggage up to 3 kilos. No disabled . . .

(Farweb.Skylink) Australia, formerly immune to RR strain, reports outbreaks. Communication out Melbourne, Sydney . . . Uluru, holy site of the Koori . . . Firefighters, in reversal of usual role, are burning plants . . . Smoke visible from space. Cue pictures . . .

(Classified) Contact with Russia has been los . . .

(Northern Seaboard: Canada Base) Overflight shows disturbance in ocean 10 kilometers south. Unlikely due to submarine life as whale populations are now . . .

(Classified) SS *Constant*, Western Pacific. Confirms plants now abundantly growing along the ocean surface. Samples reveal new and incomprehensible tolerance to salt water. Marine life, strangled by stems or eviscerated by thorns, lies dead or dying in the web . . .

(Outreach.sub: Unknown) One eyewitness says, 'The Sea was bright red for about 13 miles. Like something from Revelations . . .'

Calling Antic Base . . . come in . . . come in . . .

Ring-a-ring-a-roses, a pocket full of posies . . .

Not a plague song then. A prophecy . . .

A-tishoo, a –tishoo,

We all . . .

From Antic Base, Last Hope City (Antarctica) . . . they are here . . . we see them—like red veins in the face of the white ice . . . Not long now . . . God help us all . . . Signing off . . .

. . . fall down.

THE BEAUTIFUL AND DAMNED
BY F. SCOTT FITZGERALD

A man had collapsed in the airport. They were dealing with it in the usual efficient way. It had taken so long to get in through the front-line tome security, and they tried to hustle me on like the rest when I paused to see. I blazed my PI card. They backed away then and let me watch.

God, he was a handsome guy. I mean, he was truly beautiful, the man being lifted on to the trolly. Gold hair, unlined tan of skin, perfect weight—looked like he could run for the Olympian at St Max. But he was barely conscious now, though softly whimpering, and they'd already set up the float-drip to feed him pain relief and rehydration. His eyes were shut.

The nearest medic glanced at me. "Seen enough? Just stick around," she snapped. Her voice and eyes were full of controlled rage. She wasn't wearing a medi-mask, and she was rather special-looking herself.

I took the elevator up to the next stage of security, (heightened now) and another long wait. I was glad I'd brought a book.

They are pretty tight, the tomes. Enclosed runway and landing area, outer airlock, double inner airlock, frisker, and then every robo-check known to mankind, plus all the extra ones installed during the past seven months. Iris-reading, prints, bone-marrow stat. DNA, blood and phy stat, skull-template. Molecular shower. Absolvement.

Going the other way the treatment is even more complex. Four and three quarter hours as opposed to the three needed going in. But who's aiming to leave? Aside, of course, from people like me.

"Hi, Jack."

Good old Edmund Kovalchy. There he was, just the same as ever, twenty to twenty-five pounds overweight, and bald as a balloon.

He led me down the block and into the diner.

It was only around noon, not a lot of custom yet. And there wouldn't be, he assured me, until much later in the day, when citizens surfaced from the haze and made it here for a dunch. Only a couple of diehards sat at tables far off across the big shadowy room, an old woman with green hair scribbling on a notepad, a decanter and glass beside her, and a feller in one corner, who was working his way through the kind of breakfast I—and Ed—used to regularly take when we were twenty-four: double steak, triple egg, mushrooms, carrash, hashes, and a separate big bowl of fries.

"Each to his own poison."

"Sure," I said. The two people looked OK. "How are you doing, Edmund, my man?"

"Fine," he said, grinning. "Gained two extra pounds so the weight-winner tells me. Oh, and I reckon my very last scalp hair resigned last night. Found it on the pillow. Marianna said that deserved a coffee cake. So she's baking one. You are welcome to drop by around nine tonight, if you can make a break, sample the same."

We paused awhile, thinking respectfully of Marianna's coffee cake. Funny the way little things hold you.

But his eyes were sad.

Of course they were.

It was only a couple of weeks ago.

"How's she taking it, Ed?"

"She's a warrior, Jack. Y'know that."

"I know."

The service wheeled over, and we ordered sandwiches, some rye whiskey for Ed, and a tumbler of fresh orange for me. "Got to watch it till later."

"Sure, sure. Make up for it then."

"Like half the city," I said.

Maybe I shouldn't have, should have waited. But Ed is one of my oldest friends. We go back such a long way, sometimes I can barely count the dips in the road between now and then. But some of them were steep. And we made it, Ed and I, and Marianna.

"How is it?" he asked me, serious, looking up from his glass. "Any progress?"

"Not much."

"I thought not," he said. We're in the same business. His Corp clearance is *omega*. No need to lie, and in fact I couldn't. One of the reasons I was here to see him was to link him in, put him wise. I reached over and lay the little disc, only about the size of a quarter, next to the bottle. "For your eyes only."

"Yeah." He slid it into the secure pocket. "My eyes though, Jack, have seen a great many things in this city during the past sixteen weeks."

"Sure."

"What goes out on TV-wide?"

"Not a lot. They edit. To spare the Sensitive Viewer."

He let go a loud gout of laughter which startled me. I had every reason to think he might act unstable, hut somehow Ed, of anyone—I'd thought he would handle it. In another second he did. "Sorry, chum. Just makes me angry."

"It does." And it does. Some angry, some sad, and some very afraid.

"Aren't they doing a frigging thing?" Now his voice was soft, and his sad eyes fixed only on the whiskey.

"They are trying. But—"

I broke off. And he, not even turning, knew at once why I did.

"Some of them—one of them has come in," he said, "right?"

"That's right."

"Gal or guy?"

"Guy."

"Look like trouble?"

"Not yet."

"Christ," he said. "He's early. Most of 'em don't shift until late afternoon—why would they? How far is he along?"

"Looks a way."

Ed turned slowly and squinted back into the light where the doorway gave on the sidewalk. He took a brief visual camera shot of what I had seen, a man apparently around thirty-four, built of lean muscle, and with black hair hung to his collar. He was dressed OK, which sometimes they are not, some of them. Especially later, when plenty come out flaunting naked. The man laughed when he saw us looking. Then walked, easy, to our table.

"Hi, fellers."

"Sorry," Ed mumbled.

"'S OK. Don't blame you. And after all, you never know. You may still be able to stare at me next Thanksgiving."

As he strode off to the service bar, our sandwiches arrived. Only the woman with green hair stood up and left, walking out with the decanter of yellow wine half-full in her hand.

Gane's Journal X7

I was never the pretty one. Ugly duckling, me. Used to upset Mom more than me, I think. I think she made me self-conscious.

My nose was too big, and my mouth—fat, and my eyes not big enough, and my hair too fine and greasy. And diet all I would, still too heavy. The humiliation of the school scales. And then the weight-loser. Every other kid sloughing off the fat, and poor Gane. Hey, Gane's *gained* another pound!

Lay off the Chocostars, they told me. Never believed I didn't eat them anyway.

Metabolic weight, they said, when I was an anorexic twenty-year-old, losing my hair and weighing in at one hundred and seventy-six pounds.

You're too fat, said Mel, when he ditched me and I was thirty.

You fat cow, said Martin, when he left me the day after my fortieth birthday.

And then, last year. Fall. Then.

Just a little thing.

Hey, Ganey! You've finally cracked it!

In fall, seven pounds fall from me, like leaves.

"What shampoo is that, Gane? Say, your hair is *brilliant.*"

This, about two months before they fix on the dome.

After Ed and I split, I took a cab over to Memphis Street. The driver was full of it.

"Y'know what I think it is?" A prompting pause.

"What do you think it is?"

"It's these new pump aerosols."

"Right. How's that?"

"Well, buddy. Ya spray the darn things all over. Some folks gonna react. What ya expect."

I expect to hear the theory of every man I meet, who isn't creeping through a shadow or beating out his brain on a wall. And I've heard plenty. It's the ME block. It's terrorism-funded. It's extra-terrestrials. It's feral crops that have grown legs and glowing eyes, and run through the night snarling. It's vampires. So: Angry, sad, scared—and stupid. Just plain dumb.

The front for the Corp building on Memphis is a deli, and I climbed up the old paper-screws of fifty-one stairs to reach the office.

There's big security on the door, always was. But now too, another airlock, bullet-proof, bomb-proof, maybe.

Wilson sat behind his desk. He looked the same as ever too.

"Good to see you, Jack, despite the circumstance."

"Yeah, likewise."

I placed the second, larger, disc by his hand, and a robo-service whipped out the wall and squirrelled it away.

"How is it outside?"

I told him.

Wilson looked grim. "Since we got closed down, we've gotten a bit of a delay in here finding things out. That wasn't so at the start. Except we get all the news—unexpurgated—for the other three cities involved—"

He consulted his lappo-file as if to avoid my look when I said, dumb as the cabby, *"Three?"*

"Ah, you hadn't heard. Yeah, three now." He showed me the screen. "Here is the latest. Eastern seaboard. One hundred and eighty-seven confirmed, ninety pending. At this stage, that's enough. They'll be shutting down by this evening. Shut-down gets faster, has to. They were over a month with us, you can imagine the pink tape."

"Another city under a tome."

He looked at me. A cold-eyed bastard, Wilson, steel and mirror.

"What else, Jack, do we got?"

The *tomes,* it's jargon. Officially they are known as what they are, *domes.* Hygienic, air-proof, water-proof. Not another rainy day, some of them joked, when the first was lowered and cemented into place. Pure self-cleaning, germ-erasing air. And not a chance of a rogue airplane breaking through. Never a cloud without a silver . . .

Gane's Journal X7

"Good morning, Miss—uh—" said my regular physician, as I walked into his office.

"Carradene."

"Carradene? Now that's strange, we already have a Miss Carradene."

"I am she."

He smiled. "No you're not."

I did what I had to around the city. Had gotten through most of it before the deadline. Like Ed, and others, had told me, by then I began to see them coming out of their bolt-holes into the light of deepening afternoon. It reminded me of semi-nocturnal animals leaving their burrows. Dangerous animals, and the rest of the prey-animals then scatter off the veldt. The streets were certainly emptying. The vulnerable ones, whose employers still don't let them off early, club together for a taxi or a hire-bus. There is safety in numbers. Perhaps.

But of course it's less any kind of attack they're afraid of, than just the hell of foreseeing.

Did anyone think it would ever be like this?

Did anyone ever predict it could *happen* like this?

We've watched the movies, the shock-doccus, read— some of us—the history books.

There was an old guy sat on the sidewalk outside Ed's apartment block, drinking a can of Colby's. He looked up and shook his dirty grey locks at me and winked a bleary eye. "You an' me both, sir. The weak shall inherit."

"Sure, pops."

Marianna.

I used to have a big thing about her, when Ed and I were in our twenties. But she chose Ed, and a better guy she could not have found, if she had panned the whole state for gold.

And cook . . . God, could Marianna cook.

Yes, a cliché. But you see, she *liked* to cook. With her, it was performance art, it was art. And it even lasted. You never forgot. I have dated events sometimes from the food she made—the day of the Lobster with Oranges, the hour of the Cinnamon Cookie—

Ed used to tell me, these past thirty years, you kept your weight down, boy, because you never lived with anyone could cook like Marianna.

In fact, the past half year, I'd had something else to help me there. Better late than never.

She, though, never altered. Well, OK. She was older, around fifty-nine now I guessed, I'd never really known her age. Her hair had greyed but she blonded it at the salon. Her figure was lush but not out of shape. So, a few lines in the rose-petal of her face.

Sure. I still loved her. But now, in the way you love the best of your past. She had never been mine, and I was glad. I wouldn't have made her happy, and Ed—he had.

We had a drink on the balcony. It looked out along Walnut towards Bate Street, and over there now you could see the bars flashing like fallen suns in the black city hollows of the dark. Loud music rumbled and pulsed. But it was faint enough back here.

We talked about nothing, the old times, about when we'd gone to Greece, and to Italy, Venice, the lights on the Grande Canal, that kind of stuff. Pretending that this was just one more lit up night, meant for the young and beautiful, which once, (had we?) we had been too.

Then she brought the cake.

It was like a birthday.

She made me cut the first slice.

It was like I remembered. No one cooks like that. It's taxable. And Ed, fat happy Ed, best buddy—how had he *kept* himself to *just* two hundred and thirty pounds?

Over on the dresser was an enhanced photo of Marianna's dad, who died fifteen days ago. He had been eighty-six. At eighty-six, perhaps not so bad. But no, it had been. Bad.

But they'd be all right. They'd be fine. You could see it shine out of them, I thought, the way that other thing *burns* from the rest.

"What's wrong, honey?"

Marianna touched Ed's arm.

I hadn't noticed a thing, caught up in my inner dream, one eye still on the horizon of jangle-tangle disco lights.

"Nothing—just... I guess a bit of nut stuck in a tooth—"

"*Ed.* I *never* put in any nuts. I know your teeth—you can break a molar on cold butter!"

"OK, honey, no. I know you wouldn't. Just something—hey, excuse me, folks. I'll go seek the kindness of the dental floss."

Laughing he went, and laughing we let him go.

"Are you all right, Jack?" she said then to me, so tenderly.

"Sure, Marianna. Only I'm sorry I can't get you both out of here."

"When we just repainted the apartment? It's fine, Jack. Ed wouldn't go anyhow. He takes the job seriously. And he's so needed now. Isn't he?"

"You look wonderful," I said. "You look—"

"I look *old*," she said playfully. "And isn't that *exactly* as it should be at my age?"

Ed came back, wandering back smiling on to the balcony, his glass of wine still in his hand.

"Better, sweetheart?" she asked.

"Yeah, it was nothing. Only a bit of—well, honey, you *said* you didn't use any nuts."

Marianna decided there must have been nuts in the flour which no label had revealed. She blamed the tome shutdown, and said she'd have a word at the store.

Only about midnight, as he saw me down in the elevator to the cab I'd ordered via the Corp, did I ask him. "What was wrong in your mouth?"

"Guess it's nothing, feller."

"And? "

"Old tooth, right the way back, broken in a ball game and extracted, I was about fourteen. Seems to be . . ." he paused. He said, as the elevator doors undid, "growing back."

Outside, the cab and cab driver, and his side-rider in the passenger seat with his .29 special, catch off all through the ride. Beyond the windows the lightning of the lights, and the young lions out all over the streets, spilled like a river of gold and ice and ebony and diamond. Running, screaming, laughing, dancing, performing acrobatics, crying.

A flood of glamour. Going crazy. But the young and beautiful have always done that.

At the hotel the security netted me in and slammed shut the thick bullet-proof glass of the doors. The cab drove off fast as fire through oil. But next minute there was a paramedic vehicle coming on a siren shriek, and soon the doors undid again to let the medics through. The hotel receptionist had long, long pale hair, and when the trolly carried her out to the vehicle, this hair trailed along the floor. Someone whispered, "I didn't know—she doesn't look so different—Christ, we're in trouble—" She was very beautiful. And her eyes, crystal clear, green as glass, stared at me as they wheeled her by. "Wanna kiss me, gramps?" she murmured. Then smiled. "I guess you'd rather kiss the cunt of hell."

Gane's Journal X7

"Really, Miss Carradene. This is foolish, isn't it. Perhaps you are a friend, even a relative of the Miss Carradene who is on our books here. I can see a slight resemblance, I admit, in the PI image. But I'm afraid I can't treat you. I'm not your registered physician."

"They checked my PI at the desk."

"Yes, yes."

"So how did I get through if I'm not who I say?"

"I really don't know, Miss Carradene, but identity theft isn't unknown. Perhaps I should call the police."

I got up then and walked out of his office.

He'd always been fairly stupid, making a fuss and frightening me over my weight, when I couldn't do another thing about it. And although there was the big poster out in front, he apparently said that was all nonsense—I'd heard the assistant talking on her CP about this, she thought I couldn't hear. Well, a month before I wouldn't have.

Going back home, I bought myself another dress a couple more sizes smaller. I'd gotten a new hair cut too. No need to do much with my hair now though. This deep red colour. Thick silk.

I saw more of the posters. They were here and there. Anything unusual, consult your health centre.

But it was nothing to do with me, whatever that was. I'd only gone to him because I wanted a contraception shot. I had a date tonight. A really good one. (I'd been peri-meno for a while, but I didn't take risks.) I could buy the shot anyhow, at Fast-Hosp. I'd just do that.

I was just happy. Finally it was all paying off, the boring gruelling exercise, the strict starvation diet, the prayers and lit candles. Even that whole-body alternative vitamin.

I noticed some big tracks running by on the overhead, the kind of rail-vehicle they use for building work. Some copters too, off to the west and east, buzzing around on the sky's edge like big black flies.

But you live in the city, things go on. Don't they.

It was the start of the foundation for the dome—the tome. But I didn't know, and there was still another month before anyone properly did.

Alexander the Great wanted to conquer the world, so did Napoleon Bonaparte, and Adolf Hitler. A few others too, come to that, who didn't make it quite so far, or earn so much media attention.

You get your troops and you march. And you blast and burn and you kill. And then each bit of land, a village, a city, a country, a continent, belongs to you. But you've made a mess of it, getting there. A real mess. In the end all you can really say you are is a king of the dead.

The next day I saw to most of the remaining business. A couple of the cab drivers—I made certain I always used a different one—congratulated me. "How old are you? Fifties, I guess. No spring in your step. Like me. Look, see these brown spots on my hands. I count 'em every morning. All present and correct, yessir!"

And then the last one, that afternoon, a young attractive guy who said, "'S OK, mister. I ain't no problem. Look, here's my license. I'm twenty-nine years and four months legit, see? And look, see—broken tooth."

Something made me say—it had been one helluva day—"You could have broken that this morning. Still be like that, maybe.

And he swore at me. "You wan' my fuckin' wheels or ya don' t."

"I want them. Pardon my big mouth."

"Yeah," he said, letting me in. "Yeah. Ya wanna watch that big mouth of yours."

"Sure. You're absolutely right."

"My dad," he said. That was all. *My dad.* Another father.

Then, twenty miles on: "He was only forty-seven. Young enough. And fit as they go. Fitter'n me driving this tin can shit around and around. Used to play ball, my dad, for the Ruby League. Ya think—"

"Yeah. I'm sorry."

"Yeah," he said. "Just watch your mouth."

It isn't better for the fit ones anyway. I could have told him, but I was watching my mouth, as I damn well should have. As I had with Rosso Centi at the Overmile Building.

I'd seen the moment we met. Anyone would.

And he saw me see, by now practised.

"What do you think, Jack?"

"You tell me," I said. "If you want."

"I've joined the army," he said, as we pulled out chairs and sat, with the double-screen lappo-lux between us.

"Army . . . ?"

"The conquering horde, Jack. What else. I'm enlisted." Centi was sixty-seven, and he'd kept his hair, something Ed but not I had always envied. Only now that hair was a deep rich molasses brown. Dark eyes clear as a child's.

A couple of years ago, I'd have thought he'd been off for a plasti-job. But he hadn't, of course.

We completed the task with the screens, exchanged discs. A robo brought us coffee.

"I've always been healthy, stayed fit," he said, when we shook hands. "So I won't have long. See you next time, Jack. Wherever, ifever. Always nice to work with you."

Gane's Journal X7

That date was even better than I'd dreamed. Best first date I ever had.

Strange to say—or maybe not—I'd been attracted to a guy about my own age, well, a few years younger, fifty-two, fifty-three. And he, well he'd taken to me all right.

You get used to what you see in a mirror.

I'd gotten used to seeing this fat ugly thing that wasn't ever me. And somewhere in the deepest core of the *real* me, gotten used to always knowing I would one day *change*. Cinderella *goes* to the ball, doesn't she? Snow-White and Beauty get kissed *back* out of living death? And that girl in the mouldy catskin, she gets to throw it off.

My nose, my blubber lips—they had been only fat, obviously. They'd melted back to what they always must have been, there under the disguise of Ugly. A *slim* nose, a full but well-shaped mouth, all ready for a prince to kiss.

And two big blue-as-blue eyes.

And red haired, as if from the finest henna I'd never ever tried, silk hair falling grass-thick over my shoulders, to my new firm full breasts, and just touching my reinvented slender waist and those lovely dancer's hips. Legs—I had legs now, not chopped-off tree trunks. Ankles you can circle each with one strong hand.

Pretty. I'm so pretty.

He and I had dinner and went to a hotel. I'd never had so much sex in all my life. He was fit enough, a great lover, even for a guy younger than he was. Or maybe it was already kicking in.

I didn't need, had I known, the contraceptive shot. Shame, really, I could have saved the money. But then, for what.

He said, "I'm old enough to be your . . . uncle." Amused at the old line.

"Don't be worried," I said, "I'm—"

"Don't tell me now. God. Twenty-four?"

And, delirious from the wine and the love-making, and the glimpses I caught of myself in the mirrors, I thought, no, I *won't* tell you.

Because I was sixty-one.

But that had been the me before I changed.

After our first date there were several others. He had dough and we went to Flores Beach. And he said, "You've woken me up, Ganey. I never felt so good. I feel *young*. And look, are you proud of me? I've lost three inches off my waist—"

Later, when the dome went up, he'd stopped calling me. They all did, all the five men I'd gone with by then. The youngest one, he was about thirty—he stopped first. I don't know now if he knew, or if he—it's worse then. I wish with him I hadn't—but how could I know any of that?

The older ones, maybe I meet them sometimes on the street at night, when we party, and fuck against the walls in the neon lights, and throw bottles to try and smash the bulletproof glass shutters of the bars. They'll know *me,* but maybe I won't know them. Not like they are now.

Who wants to get old?
 Who'll buy? Anyone?
None of us?

It's in the small-print when we're born. When we're struggling through the challenged incapacity of infancy and childhood and the teenage years. It's the monster behind the glittering door.

Eighteen, twenty-one, twenty-five: the staircase top. Then down.

Nobody wants it, but nobody wants to die either. Unless you make them want it. No one.

Ed called me at a quarter to four in the morning, when outside, despite the noise-resistance of the hotel, I could just dimly hear the crash of music and of breaking things, and see, through a nip in the dark blind, a ripple of red light that was a burning car.

"Have to speak soft, Jack. I'm in the downstairs john with the CP. Sorry, sorry to wake you."

"Was awake, Ed." I didn't mention the noises had woken me, the *flames*. "Working."

"Sure. Sorry, pal."

"What is it? Is it the tooth?"

"Oh boy. If only. It's—it's my frigging *hair*, Jack." He says it on a screaming whisper. "All over my head, growing back. Thought this morning—shaved it. Just tidy up the wisps— But tonight—it itches me. And I can feel it now, like—it's like thick felt, a nap, all over my scalp."

"OK, OK, Ed."

"But I was just normal yesterday. I'd *gained* weight. The weight-winner the doc gave me *showed* it. But tonight I ate, deliberately, I ate like a hog. And I've lost six pounds, Jack."

We stay in silence. A silence rimmed, like the camp in the jungle, by watching unseen sounds and eyes of flame.

"Do you want me to fast-track you into Corp medicare, Ed? Get you a proper check? This may only be—"

"Jack, I can *see* it. My face. It's different. And Marianna—she can see it too, I can tell."

"Is she—"

"She doesn't say a word."

"But *how* is she?"

"Oh—no, she's—I think she's fine, Jack. Only. Only. We." He falters. The longest pause of all. "We had relations yesterday. We do, Jack, y'know. She and I."

"Listen. We both know this fucking shit gets passed by anything. By a sneeze in a crowded room. By a patch of damp from a sweaty palm on a handrail. A sobbed out *tear*. Even contact with a piece of clothing like a dry clean scarf. You pick it up—"

"I *know*. I know. I just—"

"I know, Ed. It's OK."

"Christ, it isn't. I put the light on in here, Jackie, and I can see my face. Even in four more hours it's firming up. It's smoothing off. I always have to stop on the twenty-fifth stair at work, just a quick breath. Only today . . . I didn't have to stop."

"Let me help. What can I do?"

"How do I know?"

"Come in to the medicare. Wilson's outfit is able—"

"It's all right." He sounds deadly calm now. "I've booked a session with the doc, did it earlier . . . thought he might reassure me. Tomorrow at 5 P.M. Only appointment he has left. Decent guy. He's just thirty. The other feller—the one Mari and I knew. The arthritis in his knee went, scan showed the bone had straightened, gone back into shape. That was all. He had to leave the practice. Last I heard he killed himself, ran his car into the West Bridge."

Tome.

It comes from two words, one of which obviously is *dome*. Each dome is city-wide, and takes in the suburbs too. They bulldoze out a kind of no man's land at the perimeter. Sure, some people lose their homes, the freeway's interrupted. They rehouse you, inside. And make new tunnels for the rail service. Airlocks, landing strips. But it's surprising how fast they can do it. When they have to.

Condition red.

But why the 't' and not the 'd'?

You guessed, possibly. T is for Tomb. A tomb-dome, a *tome*.

Because once it starts it isn't going to stop. One case, two cases, that is the same as one thousand, two million. And rising.

Soon to be billions. Like it was, and is, in those other two—*three* now—places.

So all you can do is wall it in, cover it over, put on the lid. Rev up the support services inside and the surveillance. Then monitor, and *care*. But care from a distance.

And censor the TV channels, to protect that Sensitive Viewer, whoever the fuck that can be.

Tome.

Entomed.

I was sitting in the waiting area, nicely air-conditioned and noise-proofed, with not unpleasant musak playing to keep us all serene, when the redhead walked in.

Long legs, perfect figure, hair swinging to the kind of waist you used to see only in old Technicolor movies. Only now, here and there, you see it quite a lot, especially once the afternoon advances.

A hush falls. A few of them put on their little portable masks. But most of them know the masks aren't a lot of use. It will get in at any crack, and probably it did already.

And anyway, maybe this is just one of those rare beings, a naturally stunningly physically beautiful human.

She speaks to the reception assistants, gives them her card. They process that.

The processing is auto, and there is a partition between the staff here and all the patients, exactly as there is now in there, where Ed is, talking to the doctor.

Even so, the assistants kind of huddle away.

She walks back from the desk and hesitates, looking for a seat that's far off from everyone.

What will it matter, the screens, the separation? Under the tome, with its ever-clean recycling air, the germs of all of us move in a never-ending dance, threading and rethreading, so every breath any of us inhales, *exhales,* is laced with minute unseeable beads of sombre potential.

There was outcry when the first tome went up, over and on.

But, like the cement and bomb-proof glass, it settled.

Perhaps this thing can be contained? Surely better to sacrifice X number trillion lives, and so save the greater number, whatever in the end that will be? And there is always, with these events, a percent of natural immunity, too. Not everyone, not all—

"Why don't you sit here?"

She glances at me. Oh, I must be already infected, even if I don't look it, not a smidge. And I'm parked well away from the rest.

"Thanks."

She sits on the seat next to mine.

After a moment she says, "I shouldn't have come here."

"Maybe not."

"Don't know if he'll even see me. My own physician kept refusing to believe I *was* me. I mean, I'm over sixty. He thought I was insane, or I'd stolen my identity. And then when he changed too—the practice shut."

"Yes."

She crosses her legs. Oh, those legs.

She's lovely. She's dead.

"I just want to ask them something. I—sort of want to know—how long I've got."

I said, "They can't always tell. Some have had it six months, or a year. No longer than a year, at least not so far that anyone knows. Others . . . It can be sooner."

"Somebody said the fitter you are the quicker . . ."

"It can do that. If you're fine to start with it has less to work on."

"Like—somebody young. Good-looking. I was obese, or so they said. I looked like shit." She gives a sudden silky laugh.

Nobody, even if that offends them, takes any apparent notice. They're all pretending she isn't here, or that everything is ordinary.

"And you said, you're sixty."

"Yes," she says.

"That's good. You'll probably go over ten months, a full year. That's the current notion. A friend of mine, his wife's father was eighty-six, partly blind, and very frail. He was going strong for more than eleven months. And he didn't get sick. He died in a fight."

I'm speaking, impartially, of Marianna's father. I had never been shown a recent image, how he'd become after changing. Only the old photo, the view of a tired old man. I hadn't seen him either, in the apartment, sixteen weeks back, cursing Marianna, this young handsome godlike naked man of thirty-five or six, with his shining hair and mouth full of flawless teeth and dirt. Young enough to be his daughter's son. Before Ed managed to throw the naked god out. Was that how Ed had gotten infected? Very likely.

Just a touch will do it.

I reach over and pat the girl's smooth hand, with its long strong oval nails. "It's OK. Hang in there. They're working on a cure."

And they are.

Only trouble is, they don't know what this thing is.

Looked at under all those microscopes, in all those cunningly lit dark rooms, that tiny golden evanescent spangle, now here, now gone.

Where has it come from? No one knows. Has it been created willfully, or in error, or has it only spontaneously come to be? No one can tell. Brought in or simply dropped from space, or risen up through millennia from the depths of the guts of the world, it bears no relation to anything known, or even to the premise of the unknown *possible*.

A door comes open up the long room.

Out steps Ed Kovalchy, smiling and quiet. The thick new cap of blond hair sheens on his head. It might not be anything. He might only be white already and regularly shave his scalp.

He walks briskly to me, sees the girl, and looks at her with his sad eyes.

"My name's Gane," she says, "that's Gainor Carradene. Nice to meet you." And she gets up after all and goes out. And Ed says to me, quiet under the musak, "Let's find a bar."

So we go find a bar, although by now it's almost 6 p.m., and on the streets the carnivores are gathering in their glowing pelts of murder.

All my life I read books, lots of them. Off a screen, between paper or cloth or leather covers. Always have. My weakness. My eyesight's always been good too, I don't even need spectacles now, in my fifty-sixth year.

So I have, in the course of reading, read about the great disasters, the wars and sieges, the plagues, when mankind, trapped in the pit of a single village or city or country or continent, roiled and rioted, went mad in an orgy of lust and venery, the last supper of hate, before the blackest death of all swept in to claim them.

And that's what happens now.

Once they know they have it, they leave the rules behind. They take off their clothes and their souls and hang them on a hook, and reach deep into the fire of life for one last several times.

Ed didn't care now. He had joined the legion. He sat and drank whiskey, all one bottle, and then he had some more.

He hadn't called Marianna. What could he say?

She knows. She knows.

The young think they won't get this, I mean the truly young ones, the ones who really not only look, but *are* eighteen, twenty, thirty. But they do get it. It just kills them much quicker. Snuffs them out between its amorphous golden fingers. And the children. Quicker still. They just drop. There's not much it can do there, only kill. Maybe it's kinder, then, that fast erasing, like a dab of white-out on a printed page.

It kills them all. It kills anything human, or one must presume *almost* anything, because there will be the cases of natural immunity, even if this far none have shown up.

Four cities down now; as of 8 a.m. today.

I heard that from Wilson over the scram CP not an hour ago. Over to the west, the latest conquest. Oh, and the first cases showing up in Europe too. One suspect (for one read one thousand) in the far East.

It has a name.

Everything has to have one, doesn't it.

"You're not drinking, Jack," Ed said, slurring a little. "G'on. Let's drink to long life."

In the middle of the bar dance-floor, where the neons are starting to flash orange and blue and white, a whirling girl with bare breasts that put the goddess of love to shame, arcs slowly over and falls to the ground.

None of the others take any notice except they dance around her for a while. But some minutes after, I see they just dance over her, trampling her into the earth. The floor's wet there, white-wet, blue-wet, orange.

*S*ymbiosis—Is an interaction between two differing organisms which come to live in physical association. This relationship is usually of advantage to both, i.e. as with Jentle's coral, whose bright color and luminescence, so attracting to prey, spring from the action of the minute boring worm Isrulum. However, as in this particular partnership, if other conditions become unsuitable, the worm will abandon the host it has colonized, at which both color and light are lost, and hollowed out and starved, the coral dies. From the Greek word *Sumbios*—a companion.

*P*arasite—Is an organism existing in or on another and living at the expense of said other. A parasite will normally colonize and destroy the host. From the Latin *Parasitus* via the Greek *Parasitos*—one who eats at another's table.

*V*irus—Is a submicroscopic infective agent (consisting of etc:) able to multiply only within the living walls of a host. From the Latin *Virus*—poison.

*N*obody even tries that hard now to stay clear, as I saw for myself first in the airport. The healthy ones are getting blasé, many of them. What can you do? The air is full of it, was so even before the tome. Every breath you take.
    Symparasic Virus.
    That is the name. SPV for short. Used in code once before everyone started to have to know.
    The initial cases went completely overlooked for months, longer, because of the peculiar action, the *method* the virus employs.
    Before it kills, it makes beautiful. It corrects any imperfections, restores movement and function to impaired limbs, anatomy, organs, dispenses with aging, reversing time to a level legitimately in balance with existing years—twenties for fifties early sixties, say, thirties for the ones over eighty. It banishes infirmity. Whatever is even cosmetically wrong it expunges and makes fine. Whatever is right it improves to the highest degree endurable. The infected, and by then dying victims, become glorious, and remain so until the last three to seven hours of their lives.
    Why? It's obvious isn't it. To make them enticing.
    SPV likes to colonize. To conquer. That is its sole blind and total ambition. And so each host grows enticing in order to lure further prey—to which the virus can then pass.
    That works more or less one hundred percent.

Because we love beautiful things, most of us. We love to look at them and hold them, and kiss them and fuck them, and at the worst, maybe we just pick up the clean scarf they dropped unknowing on the sidewalk, and sleep with it under the pillow...

It doesn't think, Symparasic. Doesn't need to. No more than the snow-ball rolling downhill that becomes an avalanche.

But I mentioned the last hours.

A comparatively swift death compared to the kind of stuff the human race has routinely suffered. But not enviable. Deliquescence. That word will do, I guess. That's enough. Enough for all the world, and for Ed, who was my friend. And Marianna maybe. And that little girl with her auburn-burning hair. Enough.

I got him home across the city. The cab driver was one of the night guys from the Corp. He too had his shotgun riding alongside in the passenger seat.

Marianna met me, calm and unruffled as she wouldn't ever have been if I'd just dragged her partner in from one of our youthful drunks of thirty years before.

Once she'd put him to bed, she said to me, "I guess he won't feel bad tomorrow—no hangover. Do I have that right?"

"No. He'll be fine."

"That's how it works, this *thing*."

"SPV. Yes, how it works. Anything goes wrong like that, it puts it right. Alcohol—even tainted food—toxins. Neutralizes them in a few hours."

We stood in the living room. Books on the walls, the music and TV centre, good colors, home comforts.

"If there's anything I can do, Marianna. Someone'll be out and see him tomorrow around noon. Henry, I think."

"OK," she said.

"I have to go back to—well, where I have to go. But I can be here again soon as I can if there is anything—"

"No, Jack," she said firmly. "Don't come again. Just—let us go now. We all just have to let go, don't we. It's all right, Jack." She smiled at me. "It's not *if,* after all, is it. Only *when.* The readiness," she added, with a sudden arch lift of her brows, "is all."

"Sure. But—"

"Oh Jack. Do you really think I had my hair bleached this month?"

I stared at her.

She said, "Do you know, I'm such a fool, when I first dropped four pounds I was pleased, thought it was the diet."

"Christ. Not you."

"Not me? *Why* not me? Why not *Ed?* It's all of us. Or—most of us. I said, didn't I, or Shakespeare did, the guy I quoted back there."

"Yes." I didn't know, even then, if I believed her, or would let myself. Don't now.

She came and kissed me, gentle, on the mouth. "I know I can't hurt you."

"No you can't. Not that way."

"Dear Jack. Trust me for this. Ed and I won't fetch up—like those others. Maybe we can even enjoy ourselves a little before—we have to end it. But that's what we'll do. Quietly, here. I know there are no shots, no cure. But there are tablets to make it decent, aren't there, so we can choose. Ed and I discussed it, weeks ago. Of course we did. That's what we'll do."

"Speak to Henry tomorrow. The tablets. He'll see to it you get the best."

"Yes, we will. Thank you, Jack. Good-bye, Jack. I'll tell Ed so-long for you. Nice—lovely, lovely, Jack, to know you."

When I went down, the cab was waiting by the sidewalk, and so was the girl with red hair, Gainor Gane Carradene.

"She's stable," said the Corp guy. "I checked her out. She's about a nine-monther and holding fine. Brain action's OK. Not pissed and not a crazy. What d'you want I do?"

"I'll speak to her."

"I'm right over here."

She and I walked up the block in the cindery dark between the clear white shine of two street lamps.

Over there, by now, the discos bellowed. Strobes like Northern Lights in the lower sky. Might have been another planet.

"Thanks for what you told me before," she said. "About the time I have left. You know that kind of stuff, I can see."

"How did you find me?"

"Followed you. You and the other guy."

"Why was that?"

"I don't know." She raised her beautiful face to look at one single brilliant star high in the aerial corridor between the buildings. "No, I do know. I wondered how you're not afraid of this—of what I've gotten inside me. Because you're not sick, are you—you don't have it?"

"I don't have Symparasic."

"So why aren't you afraid? Have they *found* something that can stop it—"

"I'm sorry. I told you, not yet."

"If you aren't cured and aren't sick—then are you immune?"

"Yes, Gane," I said. "In a way."

"So how?"

Her face turned to me now, her eyes—not sad or angry, not stupid or scared, or anything at all. Empty, her eyes. Waiting to be filled, only I couldn't fill them. Only the star that was somehow caught in both of them, only the star could do that.

"I have cancer, Gane. It's terminal. Another conquering colonizer, and too major an outfit for even SPV to fight it and win. They say TB is the same in its advanced stages, and one or

THE BEAUTIFUL AND DAMNED BY F. SCOTT FITZGERALD

two other of the big gun parasites. It tries, SPV, can't get a hold. And no, one won't cancel out the other. I'm on the same highway, Gane. We all are. We all always were."

Aboard the flight, once we were clear of the locks and covered take-off, out in the liquid night, the human girl came by with drinks and snacks. She looks like a movie star, she has it too. But no one minds. This is a Corp flight, and we all have it here, or something else that won't let it in. And we all know where we're headed and what to do about it. Readiness. Yes.

So it doesn't matter either when she sees what I'm reading, this wonderful novel, one of the best of the twentieth century. The title doesn't even faze her when she asks, then bends to look. "I read that in high school," she tells me, and passes on. And I look out the window and watch the city in the tome, one now among seven, soon one among a countless multitude, falling away behind me into the night. Then I go back into the book, which has less to do with any of this than any other thing I can think of. And its name? Everything has to have one. *The Beautiful and Damned* by F. Scott Fitzgerald.

THE ISLE IS FULL OF NOISES

... and if you gaze into the abyss, the abyss gazes also into you.
—*Nietzsche*

I

It is an island here, now.
    At the clearest moments of the day—usually late in the morning, occasionally after noon, and at night when the lights come on—a distant coastline is sometimes discernable. This coast is the higher area of the city, that part which still remains intact above water.
    The city was flooded a decade ago. The Sound possessed it. The facts had been predicted some while, and various things were done in readiness, mostly comprising a mass desertion.
    They say the lower levels of those buildings which now form the island will begin to give way in five years. But they were saying that too five years back.
    Also there are the sunsets. (Something stirred up in the atmosphere apparently, by the influx of water, some generation of heat or cold or vapour.) They start, or appear to do so, the sunsets, about three o'clock in the afternoon, and continue until

the sun actually goes under the horizon, which in summer can be as late a seven forty-five.

For hours the roof terraces, towerettes and glass-lofts of the island catch a deepening blood-and-copper light, turning to new bronze, raw amber, cubes of hot pink ice.

Yse lives on West Ridge, in a glass-loft. She has, like most of the island residents, only one level, but there's plenty of space. (Below, if anyone remembers, lies a great warehouse, with fish, even sometimes barracuda, gliding between the girders.)

Beyond her glass west wall, a freak tree has rooted in the terrace. Now nine years old, it towers up over the loft, and the surrounding towers and lofts, while its serpentine branches dip down into the water. Trees are unusual here. This tree, which Yse calls Snake (for the branches), seems unphased by the salt content of the water. It may be a sort of willow, a willow crossed with a snake.

Sometimes Yse watches fish glimmering through the tree's long hair, that floats just under the surface. This appeals to her, as the whole notion of the island does. Then one morning she comes out and finds, caught in the coils of her snake-willow, a piano.

Best to describe Yse, at this point, which is not easy. She might well have said herself, (being a writer by trade but also by desire) that she doesn't want you to be disappointed, that you should hold on to the idea that what you get at first, here, may not be what is to be offered later.

Then again, there is a disparity between what Yse seems to be, or is, and what Yse *also seems* to be, or *is*.

Her name, however, as she has often had to explain, is pronounced to rhyme with 'please'—more correctly, *pleeze:*

Eeze. Is it French? Or some sport from Latin-Spanish? God knows.

Yse is in her middle years, not tall, rather heavy, dumpy. Her fair, greying hair is too fine, and so she cuts it very short. *Yse* is also slender, taller, and her long hair, (still fair, still greying) hangs in thick silken hanks down her back. One constant, grey eyes.

She keeps only a single mirror, in the bathroom above the wash basin. Looking in it is always a surprise for Yse: Who on earth is that? But she never lingers, soon she is away from it and back to herself. And in this way too, she deals with Per Laszd, the lover she has never had.

Yse had brought the coffee-pot and some peaches on to the terrace. It is a fine morning, and she is considering walking along the bridgeway to the boat-stop, and going over to the cafés on East Heights. There are always things on at the cafés, psychic fairs, art shows, theatre. And she needs some more lamp oil.

Having placed the coffee and fruit, Yse looks up and sees the piano.

"*Oh,*" says Yse, aloud.

She is very, very startled, and there are good reasons for this, beyond the obvious oddity itself.

She goes to the edge of the terrace and leans over, where the tree leans over, and looks at the snake arms which hold the piano fast, tilted only slightly, and fringed by rippling leaves.

The piano is old, huge, a type of pianoforte, its two lids fast shut, concealing both the keys and its inner parts.

Water swirls round it idly. It is intensely black, scarcely marked by its swim.

And has it been swimming? Probably it was jettisoned from some apartment on the mainland (the upper city). Then, stretching out its three strong legs, it set off savagely for the island, determined not to go down.

Yse has reasons, too, for thinking in this way.

She reaches out, but cannot quite touch the piano.

There are tides about the island, variable, sometimes rough. If she leaves the piano where it is, the evening tide may be a rough one, and lift it away, and she will lose it.

She *knows* it must have swum here.

Yse goes to the table and sits, drinking coffee, looking at the piano. As she does this a breeze comes in off the Sound, and stirs her phantom long heavy soft hair, so it brushes her face and neck and the sides of her arms. And the piano makes a faint twanging, she thinks perhaps it does, up through its shut lids that are like closed eyes and lips together.

"What makes a vampire seductive?" Yse asks Lucius, at the Café Blonde. "I mean, irresistible?"

"His beauty," says Lucius. He laughs, showing his teeth. "I knew a vampire, once. No, make that twice. I met him twice."

"Yes?" asks Yse cautiously. Lucius has met them all, ghosts, demons, angels. She partly believes it to be so, yet knows he mixes lies with the truths; a kind of test, or trap, for the listener. "Well, what happened?"

"We walk, talk, drink, make love. He bites me. Here, see?" Lucius moves aside his long locks (luxurious, but greying, as are her own). On his coal-dark neck, no longer young, but strong as a column, an old scar.

"You told me once before," says Yse, "a shark did that."

"To reassure you. But it was a vampire."

"What did you do?"

"I say to him, Watch out, monsieur."

"And then?"

"He watched out. Next night, I met him again. He had yellow eyes, like a cat."

"He was undead?"

"The undeadest thing I ever laid."

He laughs. Yse laughs, thoughtfully. "A piano's caught in my terrace tree."

"*Oh* yeah," says Lucius, the perhaps arch liar.

"You don't believe me."

"What is your thing about vampires?"

"I'm writing about a vampire."

"Let me read your book."

"Someday. But Lucius—it isn't their charisma. Not their beauty that makes them irresistible—"

"No?"

"Think what they must be like . . . skin in rags, dead but walking. Stinking of the grave—"

"They use their hudja-magica to take all that away."

"It's how they make *us* feel."

"Yeah, Yse. You got it."

"What they can do to *us*."

"Dance all night," says Lucius, reminiscent. He watches a handsome youth across the café, juggling mirrors that flash unnervingly, his skin the colour of an island twilight.

"Lucius, will you help me shift the piano into my loft?"

"Sure thing."

"Not tomorrow, or next month. I mean, could we do it today, before sunset starts?"

"I love you, Yse. Because of you, I shall go to Heaven."

"Thanks."

"Shit piano," he says. "I could have slept in my boat. I could have paddled over to Venezule. I could have watched the thought of Venus rise through the grey brain of the sky. Piano huh, piano. Who shall I bring to help me? That boy, he looks strong, look at those mirrors go."

The beast had swum to shore, to the beach, through the pale, transparent urges of the waves, when the star Venus was in the brain-grey sky. But not here.

There.

In the dark before star-rise and dawn, more than two centuries ago. First the rifts, the lilts of the dark sea, and in them these mysterious thrusts and pushes, the limbs like those of some huge swimmer, part man and part lion and part crab—but also, a manta ray.

Then, the lid breaks for a second through the fans of water, under the dawn star's piercing steel. Wet as black mirror, the closed lid of the piano, as it strives, on three powerful beast-legs, for the beach.

This Island is an island of sands, then of trees, the sombre sullen palms that sweep the shore. Inland, heights, vegetation, plantations, some of coffee and sugar and rubber, and one of imported kayar. An invented island, a composite.

Does it crawl on to the sand, the legs still moving, crouching low like a beast? Does it rest on the sand, under the sway of the palm trees, as a sun rises?

The Island has a name, like the house which is up there, unseen, on the inner heights. Bleumaneer.

(*Notes:* Gregers Vonderjan brought his wife to Bleumaneer in the last days of his wealth . . . .)

The piano crouched stilly at the edge of the beach, the sea retreating from it, and the dark of night falling away . . .

It's sunset.

Lucius, in the bloody light, with two men from the Café Blonde (neither the juggler), juggle the black piano from the possessive tentacles of the snake-willow.

With a rattle, a shattering of sounds (like slung cutlery), it, fetches up on the terrace. The men stand perplexed, looking at it. Yse watches from her glass wall.

"Broke the cock thing."

"No way to move it. Shoulda tooka crane."

They prowl about the piano, while the red light blooms across its shade.

Lucius tries delicately to raise the lid from the keys. The lid does not move. The other two, they wrench at the other lid, the piano's top (pate, shell). This too is fastened stuck. (Yse had made half a move, as if to stop them. Then her arm fell lax.)

"Damn ol' thing. What she wan' this ol' thing for?"

They back away. One makes a kicking movement. Lucius shakes his head; his long locks jangle across the flaming sky.

"*Do* you want this, girl?" Lucius asks Yse by her glass.

"Yes." Shortly. "I said I did."

"'S all broke up. Won't play you none," sings the light-eyed man, Carr, who wants to kick the piano, even now his loose leg pawing in its jeans.

Trails of water slip away from the piano, over the terrace, like chains.

Yse opens her wide glass doors. The men carry the piano in, and set it on her bare wooden floor.

Yse brings them, now docile as their maid, white rum, while Lucius shares out the bills.

"Hurt my back," whinges Carr the kicker.

"Piano," says Lucius, drinking, "pian—o—O pain!"

He says to her at the doors (as the men scramble back into their boat), "That vampire I danced with. Where he bit me. Still feel him there, biting me, some nights. Like a piece of broken bottle in my neck. I followed him, did I say to you? I followed him and saw him climb in under his grave just before the sun came up. A marble marker up on top. It shifted easy as breathe, settles back like a sigh. But he was beautiful, that boy with yellow eyes. Made me feel like a king, with him. Young as a lion, with him. *Old* as him, too. A thousand years in a skin of smoothest suede."

Yse nods.

She watches Lucius away into the sunset, of which three hours are still left.

Yse scatters two bags of porous litter-chips, which are used all over the island, to absorb the spillages and seepages of the

Sound, to mop up the wet that slowly showers from the piano. She does not touch it. Except with her right hand, for a second, flat on the top of it.

The wood feels ancient and hollow, and she thinks it hasn't, perhaps, a metal frame.

As the redness folds over deeper and deeper, Yse lights the oil lamp on her work-table, and sits there, looking forty feet across the loft, at the piano on the sunset. Under her right hand now, the pages she has already written, in her fast untidy scrawl.

Piano-o. O pain.

Shush, says the Sound-tide, flooding the city, pulsing through the walls, struts and girders below.

Yse thinks distinctly, suddenly—it is always this way—about Per Laszd. But then another man's memory taps at her mind.

Yse picks up her pen, almost absently. She writes:

'Like those hallucinations which sometimes come at the edge of sleep, so that you wake, thinking two or three words have been spoken close to your ear, or that a tall figure stands in the corner ... like this, the image now and then appears before him.

'Then he sees her, the woman, sitting on the rock, her white dress and her ivory-coloured hair, hard-gleaming in a post-storm sunlight. Impossible to tell her age. A desiccated young girl, or unlined old woman. And the transparent sea lapping in across the sand ...

'But he has said, the Island is quite deserted now.'

2: Antoinelle's Courtship

Gregers Vonderjan brought his wife to Bleumaneer in the last days of his wealth.

In this way, she knew nothing about them, the grave losses to come, but then they had been married only a few months. She knew little enough about him, either.

Antoinelle was raised among staunch and secretive people. Until she was fourteen, she had thought herself ugly, and after that, beautiful. A sunset revelation had put her right, the westering glow pouring in sideways to paint the face in her mirror, on its slim, long throat. She found too she had shoulders, and cheekbones. Hands, whose tendons flexed in fans. With the knowledge of beauty, Antoinelle began to hope for something. Armed with her beauty she began to fall madly in love—with young officers in the army, with figures encountered in dreams.

One evening at a parochial ball, the two situations became confused.

The glamorous young man led Antoinelle out into a summer garden. It was a garden of Europe, with tall dense trees of twisted trunks, foliage massed on a lilac northern sky.

Antoinelle gave herself. That is, not only was she prepared to give of herself sexually, but to give herself up to this male person, of whom she knew no more than that he was beautiful.

Some scruple—solely for himself, the possible consequences—made him check at last.

"No—no—" she cried softly, as he forcibly released her and stood back, angrily panting.

The beautiful young man concluded (officially to himself), that Antoinelle was 'loose', and therefore valueless. She was not rich enough to marry, and besides, he despised her family.

Presently he had told his brother officers all about this girl, and her 'looseness'.

"She would have done anything," he said.

"She's a whore," said another, and smiled.

Fastidiously, Antoinelle's lover remarked, "No, worse than a whore. A whore does it honestly, for money. It's her work. This one simply does it."

Antoinelle's reputation was soon in tatters, which blew about that little town of trees and societal pillars, like the torn flag of a destroyed regiment.

She was sent in disgrace to her aunt's house in the country.

No one spoke to Antoinelle in that house. Literally, no one. The aunt would not, and she had instructed her servants, who were afraid of her. Even the maid who attended Antoinelle would not speak, in the privacy of the evening chamber, preparing the girl for the silent evening supper below, or the lumpy three-mattressed bed.

The aunt's rather unpleasant lap-dog, when Antoinelle had attempted, unwatched, to feed it a marzipan fruit, had only turned its rat-like head away. (At everyone else, save the aunt, it growled.)

Antoinelle, when alone, sobbed. At first in shame—her family had already seen to that, very ably, in the town. Next in frustrated rage. At last out of sheer despair.

She was like a lunatic in a cruel, cool asylum. They fed her, made her observe all the proper rituals. She had shelter and a place to sleep, and people to relieve some of her physical wants. There were even books in the library, and a garden to walk in on sunny days. But language—*sound*—they took away from her. And language is one of the six senses. It was as bad perhaps as blindfolding her. Additionally, they did not even speak to each other, beyond the absolute minimum, when she was by—coarse-aproned girls on the stair stifled their giggles, and passed with mask faces. And in much the same way too, Antoinelle was not permitted to play the aunt's piano.

Three months of this, hard, polished months, like stone mirrors which reflected nothing.

Antoinelle grew thinner, more pale. Her young eyes had hollows under them. She was like a nun.

The name of the aunt who did all this was Clemence—which means, of course, clemency—mild, merciful. (And the name of the young man in the town who had almost fucked Antoinelle, forced himself not to for his own sake, and then fucked instead her reputation, which was to say, her *life* . . . His name was Justus.)

On a morning early in the fourth month, a new thing happened.

Antoinelle opened her eyes, and saw the aunt sailing into her room. And the aunt, glittering with rings like knives, *spoke* to Antoinelle.

"Very well, there's been enough of all this. Yes, yes. You may get up quickly and come down to breakfast, Patice will see to your dress and hair. Make sure you look your best."

Antoinelle lay there, on her back in the horrible bed, staring like the dead newly awakened.

"Come along," said Aunt Clemence, holding the awful little dog untidily scrunched, "make haste now. What a child!" As if Antoinelle were the strange creature, the curiosity.

While, as the aunt swept out, the dog craned back and chattered its dirty teeth at Antoinelle.

And then, the third wonder, Patice was chattering, breaking like a happy stream at thaw, and shaking out a dress.

Antoinelle got up, and let Patice see to her, all the paraphernalia of the toilette, finishing with a light pollen of powder, even a fingertip of rouge for the matte pale lips, making them moist and rosy.

"Why?" asked Antoinelle at last, in a whisper.

"There is a visitor," chattered Patice, brimming with joy.

Antoinelle took two steps, then caught her breath and dropped as if dead on the carpet.

But Patice was also brisk; she brought Antoinelle round, crushing a vicious clove of lemon oil under her nostrils, slapping the young face lightly. Exactly as one would expect in this efficiently cruel lunatic asylum.

Presently Antoinelle drifted down the stairs, lightheaded, rose-lipped and shadow-eyed. She had never looked more lovely or known it less.

The breakfast was a ghastly provincial show-off thing. There were dishes and dishes, hot and cold, of kidneys, eggs, of cheeses and hams, hot breads in napkins, brioches, and chocolate. (It was a wonder Antoinelle was not sick at once.) All this set on crisp linen with flashing silver, and the fine china normally kept in a cupboard.

The servants flurried round in their awful, stupid (second-hand) joy. The aunt sat in her chair and Antoinelle in hers, and the man in his, across the round table.

Antoinelle had been afraid it was going to be Justus. She did not know why he would be there—to castigate her again, to apologise—either way, such a boiling of fear—or something—had gone through Antoinelle that she had fainted.

But it was not Justus. This was someone she did not know.

He had stood up as she came into the room. The morning was clear and well-lit, and Antoinelle had seen, with a dreary sagging of relief, that he was old. Quite old. She went on thinking this as he took her hand in his large one and shook it as if carelessly playing with something, very delicately. But his hand was manicured, the nails clean and white-edged. There was one ring, with a dull colourless stone in it.

Antoinelle still thought he was quite old, perhaps not so old as she *had* thought.

When they were seated, and the servants had doled out to them some food and drink, and gone away, Antoinelle came to herself rather more.

His hair was not grey but a mass of silvery blond. A lot of hair, very thick, shining, which fell, as was the fashion then, just to his shoulders. He was thick-set, not slender, but seemed immensely strong. One saw this in ordinary, apparently unrelated things—for example the niceness with which he helped himself now from the coffee-pot. Indeed, the dangerous playfulness of his handshake with a woman; he could easily crush the hands of his fellow men.

Perhaps he was not an old man, really. In his forties, (which would be the contemporary age of fifty-five or -six.) He was losing his figure, as many human beings do at that age, becoming either too big or too thin. But if his middle had spread, he was yet a presence, sprawled there in his immaculately white ruffled shirt, the broad-cut coat, his feet in boots of Spanish leather propped under the table. And to his face, not much really had happened. The forehead was both wide and high, scarcely lined, the nose aquiline as a bird's beak, scarcely thickened, the chin undoubled and jutting, the mouth narrow and well-shaped. His eyes, set in the slightest rouching of skin, were large, a cold clear blue. He might actually be only just forty (that is, fifty). A fraction less.

Antoinelle was not to know, in his youth, the heads of women had turned for Gregers Vonderjan like tulips before a gale. Or that, frankly, now and then they still did so.

The talk, what was that about all this while? Obsequious pleasantries from the aunt, odd anecdotes he gave, to do with ships, land, slaves and money. Antoinelle had been so long without hearing the speech of others, she had become nearly word-deaf, so that most of what he said had no meaning for her, and what the aunt said even less.

Finally the aunt remembered an urgent errand, and left them.

They sat, with the sun blazing through the windows. Then Vonderjan looked right at her, at Antoinelle, and suddenly her face, her whole body, was suffused by a savage burning blush.

"Did she tell you why I called here?" he asked, almost indifferently.

Antoinelle, her eyes lowered, murmured childishly, thoughtlessly, "No—she—she hasn't been speaking to me—"

"Hasn't she? Why not? Oh," he said, "that little business in the town."

Antoinelle, to her shock, began to cry. This should have horrified her—she had lost control—the worst sin, as her family had convinced her, they thought.

He knew, this man. He knew. She was ashamed, and yet unable to stop crying, or to get up and leave the room.

She heard his chair pushed back, and then he was standing over her. To her slightness, he seemed vast and overpowering.

He was clean, and smelled of French soap, of tobacco, and some other nuance of masculinity, which Antoinelle at once intuitively liked. She had scented it before.

"Well, you won't mind leaving her, then," he said, and he lifted her up out of her chair, and there she was in his grip, her head drooping back, staring almost mindlessly into his large, handsome face. It was easy to let go. She did so. She had in fact learnt nothing, been taught nothing by the whips and stings of her wicked relations. "I called here to ask you," he said, "to be my wife."

"But . . ." faintly, "I don't know you."

"There's nothing to know. Here I am. Exactly what you see. Will that do?"

"But . . ." more faintly still, "why would you want me?"

"You're just what I want. And I thought you would be."

"But," nearly inaudible, "I was—disgraced."

"We'll see about that. And the old she-cunt won't talk to you, you say?"

Antoinelle, innocently not even knowing this important word (which any way he referred to in a foreign argot), only shivered. "No. Not till today."

"Now she does because I've bid for you. You'd better come with me. Did the other one, the soldier-boy, have you? It doesn't matter, but tell me now."

Antoinelle threw herself on the stranger's chest—she had not been told, or heard his name. "No—no—" she cried, just as she had when Justus pushed her off.

"I must go slowly with you then," said this man. But nevertheless, he moved her about, and leaning over, kissed her.

Vonderjan was an expert lover. Besides, he had a peculiar quality, which had stood him, and stands others like him, in very good stead. With those he wanted in the sexual way, providing they were not unwilling to begin with, he could spontaneously communicate some telepathic echo of his needs, making them theirs. This Antoinelle felt at once, as his warm lips moved on hers, his hot tongue pierced her mouth, and the fingers of the hand which did not hold her tight, fire-feathered her breasts.

In seconds her ready flames burst up. Businesslike, Vonderjan at once sat down, and holding her on his lap, placed his hand, making nothing of her dress, to crush her centre in an inexorable rhythmic grasp, until she came in gasping spasms against him, wept, and wilted there in his arms, his property.

When the inclement aunt returned with a servant, having left, she felt, sufficient time for Vonderjan to ask, and Antoinelle sensibly to acquiesce, she found her niece tear-stained and dead white in a chair, and Vonderjan drinking his coffee, and smoking a cigar, letting the ash fall as it wished on to the table linen.

"Well then," said the aunt, uncertainly.

Vonderjan cast her one look, as if amused by something about her.

"Am I to presume—may I—is everything—"

Vonderjan took another puff and a gout of charred stuff hit the cloth, before he mashed out the burning butt of the cigar on a china plate.

"Antoinelle," exclaimed the aunt, "what have you to say?"

Vonderjan spoke, not to the aunt, but to his betrothed. "Get up, Anna. You're going with me now." Then, looking at the servant (a look the woman said after was like that of a basilisk), "Out, you, and put some things together, all the lady will need for the drive. I'll supply the rest. Be quick."

Scarlet, the aunt shouted, "Now sir, this isn't how to go on."

Vonderjan drew Antoinelle up, by his hand on her elbow. *He* had control of her now, and she need bother with nothing. She turned her drooping head, like a tired flower, looking only at his boots.

The aunt was ranting. Vonderjan, with Antoinelle in one arm, went up to her. Though not a small woman, nor slight like her niece, he dwarfed her, made of her a pygmy.

"Sir—there is her father to be approached—you must have a care—"

Then she stopped speaking. She stopped because, like Antoinelle, she had been given no choice. Gregers Vonderjan had clapped his hand over her mouth, and rather more than that. He held her by the bones and flesh of her face, unable to pull away, beating at him with her hands, making noises but unable to do more, and soon breathing with difficulty.

While he kept her like this, he did not bother to look at her, his broad body only disturbed vaguely by her flailing, weak blows. He had turned again to Antoinelle, and asked her if there was anything she wished particularly to bring away from the house.

Antoinelle did not have the courage to glance at her struggling and apoplectic aunt. She shook her head against his shoulder, and after a little shake of his own (at the aunt's face) he let the woman go. He and the girl walked out of the room and out of the house, to his carriage, leaving the aunt to progress from her partial asphyxia to hysterics.

He had got them married in three days by pulling such strings as money generally will. The ceremony did not take place in the town, but all the town heard of it. Afterwards Vonderjan went back there, without his wife, to throw a lavish dinner party, limited to the male gender, which no person invited dared not attend, including the bride's father, who was trying to smile off, as does the deathshead, the state it has been put into.

At this dinner too was Justus. He sat with a number of his friends, all of them astonished to be there. But like the rest, they had not been able, or prepared, to evade the occasion.

Vonderjan treated them all alike, with courtesy. The food was of a high standard—a cook had been brought from the city—and there were extravagant wines, with all of which Gregers Vonderjan was evidently familiar. The men got drunk, that is, all the men but for Vonderjan, who was an established drinker, and consumed several bottles of wine, also brandy and schnapps, without much effect.

At last Vonderjan said he would be going. To the bowing and fawning of his wife's relatives he paid no attention. It was Justus he took aside, near the door, with two of his friends. The young men were all in full uniform, smart as polish, only their bright hair tousled, and faces flushed by liquor.

"You mustn't think my wife holds any rancour against you," Vonderjan announced, not loudly, but in a penetrating tone. Justus was too drunk to catch himself up, and only idiotically nodded. "She said, I should wish you a speedy end to your trouble."

"What trouble's that?" asked Justus, still idiotically.

"He has no troubles," added the first of his brother officers, "since you took that girl off his hands."

The other officer (the most sober, which was not saying much—or perhaps the most drunk, drunk enough to have gained the virtue of distance), said, "Shut your trap, you fool. Herr Vonderjan doesn't want to hear that silly kind of talk."

Vonderjan was grave. "It's nothing to me. But I'm sorry for your Justus, naturally. I shouldn't, as no man would, like to be in his shoes."

"What shoes are they?" Justus belatedly frowned.

"I can recommend to you," said Vonderjan, "an excellent doctor in the city. They say he is discreet."

"What?"

"What is he saying—"

"The disease, I believe they say, is often curable, in its earliest stages."

Justus drew himself up. He was almost the height of Vonderjan, but like a reed beside him. All that room, and waiters on the stair besides, were listening. "I am not—I have no—*disease*—"

Vonderjan shrugged. "That's your argument, I understand. You should leave it off perhaps, and seek medical advice, certainly before you consider again any courtship. Not all women are as soft-hearted as my Anna."

"What—what?"

"Not plain enough? From what you showed her she knew you had it, and refused you. Of course, you had another story."

As Vonderjan walked through the door, the two brother officers were, one silent, and one bellowing. Vonderjan half turned, negligently. "If you don't think so, examine his prick for yourselves."

Vonderjan did not tell Antoinelle any of this, but a week later, in the city, she did read in a paper that Justus had mysteriously been disgraced, and had then fled the town after a duel.

Perhaps she thought it curious.

But if so, only for a moment. She had been absorbed almost entirely by the stranger, her strong husband.

On the first night, still calling her Anna, up against a great velvet bed, he had undone her clothes and next her body, taking her apart down to the clockwork of her desires. Her cry of pain at his entry turned almost at once into a wavering shriek of ecstasy. She was what he had wanted all along, and he what she had needed. By morning the bed was stained with her virginal blood, and by the blood from bites she had given him, not knowing she did so.

Even when, a few weeks after, Vonderjan's luck began to turn like a sail, he bore her with him on his broad wings. He said nothing of his luck. He was too occupied wringing from her again and again the music of her lusts, forcing her arching body to contortions, paroxysms, screams, torturing her to willing death in blind red afternoons, in candlelit darkness, so that by daybreak she could scarcely move, would lie there in a stupor in the bed, unable to rise, awaiting him like an invalid or a corpse, and hungry always for more.

3

Lucius paddles his boat to the jetty, lets it idle there, looking up.

Another property of the flood-vapour, the stars by night are vast, great liquid splashes of silver, ormolu.

The light in Yse's loft burns contrastingly low.

That sweet smell he noticed yesterday still comes wafting down, like thin veiling, on the breeze. Like night-blooming jasmine, perhaps a little sharper, almost like oleanders.

She must have put in some plant. But up on her terrace, only the snake tree is visible, hooping over into the water.

Lucius smokes half a roach slowly.

Far away the shoreline glimmers, where some of the stars have fallen off the sky.

"What you doing, Yse, Yse-do-as-she-please?"

Once he'd thought he saw her moving, a moth-shadow crossing through the stunned light, but maybe she is asleep, or writing.

It would be simple enough to tie up and climb the short wet stair to the terrace, to knock on her glass doors. (How are you, Yse? Are you fine?) He had done that last night. The blinds were all down, the light low, as now. But through the side of the transparent loft he had beheld the other shadow standing there on her floor. The piano from the sea. No one answered.

That flower she's planted, it is sweet as candy. He'd never known her do a thing like that. Her plants always died, killed, she said, by the electrical vibrations of her psyche when she worked.

Somewhere out on the Sound a boat hoots mournfully.

Lucius unships his paddles, and wends his craft away along the alleys of water, towards the cafés and the bigger lights.

Whenever she writes about Per Laszd, which, over twenty-seven years, she has done a lot, the same feeling assails her: slight guilt. Only slight, of course, for he will never know. He is a man who never reads anything that has nothing to do with what he does. That was made clear in the beginning. She met him only twice, but has seen him, quite often, then and since, in newspapers, in news footage, and on network TV. She has been able therefore to watch him change, from an acidly, really too-beautiful young man, through his thirties and forties (when some of the silk of his beauty frayed, to reveal something leaner and more interesting, stronger and more attractive), to a latening middle age, where he has gained weight, but lost none of his masculine grace, nor his mane of hair which—only perhaps due to artifice—has no grey in it.

She was in love with him, obviously, at the beginning. But it has changed, and become something else. He was never interested in her, even when she was young, slim and appealing. She was not, she supposed, his 'type'.

In addition, she rather admired what he did, and how he did it, with an actor's panache and tricks.

People who caught her fancy she had always tended to put into her work. Inevitably Per Laszd was one of these. Sometimes he appeared as a remote Figure, on the edge of the action of other lives. Sometimes he took the centre of the stage, acting out invented existences, with his perceived actor's skills.

She had, she found though, a tendency to punish him in these rôles. He must endure hardships and misfortunes, and often, in her work, he was dead by the end, and rarely of old age.

Her guilt, naturally, had something to do with this—was she truly punishing him, not godlike, as with other characters, but from a petty personal annoyance that he had never noticed her, let alone had sex with her, or a single real conversation. (When she had met him, it had both times been in a crowd. He spoke generally, politely including her, no more than that. She was aware he had been arrogant enough, if he had wanted to, to have demandingly singled her out.)

But really she felt guilty at the liberties she took of necessity, with him, on paper. How else could she write about him? It was absurd to do otherwise. But describing his conjectured nakedness, both physical and intellectual, even spiritual (even supposedly 'in character'), her own temerity occasionally dismayed Yse. How dared she? But then, how dare ever to write anything, even about a being wholly invented.

A mental shrug. *Alors* . . . well, well. And yet . . .

Making him Gregers Vonderjan, she felt, was perhaps her worst infringement. Now she depicted him (honestly) burly with weight and on-drawing age, although always hastening to add the caveat of his handsomeness, his power. Per himself, as she had seen, was capable of being majestic, yet also mercurial. She tried to be fair, to be at her most fair, when examining him most microscopically, or when condemning him to the worst fates. (But, now and then, did the pen slip?)

Had he ever sensed those several dreadful falls, those calumnies, those *deaths?* Of course not. Well, well. There, there. And yet . . .

How wonderful that vine smells tonight, Yse thinks, sitting up in the lamp-dusk. Some neighbour must have planted it. What a penetrating scent, so clean and fresh yet sweet.

It was noticeable last night, too. Yse wonders what the flowers are, that let out this aroma. And in the end, she stands up, leaving the pen to lie there, across Vonderjan and Antoinelle.

Near her glass doors, Yse thinks the vine must be directly facing her, over the narrow waterway under the terrace, for here its perfume is strongest.

But when she raises the blinds and opens the doors, the scent at once grows less. Somehow it has collected instead in the room. She gazes out at the other lofts, at a tower of shaped glass looking like ice in a tray. Are the hidden gardens there?

The stars are impressive tonight. And she can see the hem of the star-spangled upper city.

A faint sound comes.

Yse knows it's not outside, but in her loft, just like the scent.

She turns. Looks at the black piano.

Since yesterday (when it was brought in), she hasn't paid it that much attention. (Has she?) She had initially stared at it, tried three or four times to raise its lids—without success. She had thought of rubbing it down, once the litter-chips absorbed the leaking water. But then she had not done this. Had not touched it very much.

Coming to the doors, she has circled wide of the piano.

Did a note sound, just now, under the forward lid? How odd, the two forelegs braced there, and the final leg at its end, more as if it balanced on a tail of some sort.

Probably the keys and hammers and strings inside are settling after the wet, to the warmth of her room.

She leaves one door open, which is not perhaps sensible. Rats have been known to climb the stair and gaze in at her under the night blinds, with their calm clever eyes. Sometimes the criminal population of the island can be heard along the waterways, or out on the Sound, shouts and smashing bottles, cans thrown at brickwork or impervious, multi-glazed windows.

But the night's still as the stars.

Yse goes by the piano, and through the perfume, and back to her desk, where Per Laszd lies helplessly awaiting her on the page.

4: Bleumaneer

Jeanjacques came to the Island in the stormy season. He was a mix of black and white, and found both peoples perplexing, as he found himself.

The slave-trade was by then defused, as much, perhaps, as it would ever be. He knew there were no slaves left on the Island, that is, only freed slaves remained. (His black half lived with frenzied anger, as his white half clove to sloth. Between the two halves, he was a split soul.)

There had been sparks on the rigging of the ship, and all night a velour sky fraught with pink lightning. When they reached the bay next morning, it looked nearly colourless, the sombre palms were nearly grey, and the sky cindery, and the sea only transparent, the beaches white.

The haughty black master spoke in French.

"They call that place *Blue View.*"

"Why's that?"

"Oh, it was for some vogue of wearing blue, before heads began to roll in Paris."

Jeanjacques said, "What's he like?"

"Vonderjan? A falling man."

"How do you mean?"

"Have you seen a man fall? The instants before he hits the ground, before he's hurt—the moment when he thinks he is still flying."

"He's lost his money, they were saying at Sugarbar."

"They say so."

"And his wife's a girl, almost a child."

"Two years he's been with her on his Island."

"What's she like?"

"White."

"What else?"

"To me, nothing. I can't tell them apart."

There had been a small port, but now little was there, except a rotted hulk, some huts and the ruins of a customs house, thatched with palm, in which birds lived.

For a day he climbed with the escorting party, up into the interior of the Island. Inside the forest it was grey-green-black, and the trees gave off sweat, pearling the banana leaves and plantains. Then they walked through the wild fields of cane, and the coffee trees. Dark figures still worked there, and tending the kayar. But they did this for themselves. What had been owned had become the garden of those who remained, to do with as they wanted.

The black master had elaborated, telling Jeanjacques how Vonderjan had at first sent for niceties for his house, for china and Venetian glass, cases of books and wine. Even a piano had been ordered for his child-wife, although this, it seemed, had never arrived.

The Island was large and overgrown, but there was nothing, they said, very dangerous on it.

Bleumaneer, *Blue View*, the house for which the Island had come to be called, appeared on the next morning, down a dusty track hedged by rhododendrons of prehistoric girth.

It was white walled, with several open courts, balconies. Orange trees grew along a columned gallery, and there was a Spanish fountain (dry), on the paved space before the steps. But it was a medley of all kinds of style.

"Make an itinerary and let me see it. We'll talk it over, what can be sold."

Jeanjacques thought that Vonderjan reminded him most of a lion, but a lion crossed with a golden bull. Then again, there was a wolf-like element, cunning and lithe, which slipped through the grasslands of their talk.

Vonderjan did not treat Jeanjacques as what he was, a valuer's clerk. Nor was there any resentment or chagrin. Vonderjan seemed indifferent to the fix he was in. Did he even care that such and such would be sorted out and taken from him—that glowing canvas in the salon, for example, or the rose-mahogany cabinets, and all for a third of their value, or less, paid in banknotes that probably would not last out another year. Here was a man, surely, playing at life, at living. Convinced of it and of his fate, certainly, but only as the actor is, within his part.

Jeanjacques drank cloudy orjat, tasting its bitter orange-flowers. Vonderjan drank nothing, was sufficient, even in this, to himself.

"Well. What do you think?"

"I'll work on, and work tonight, present you with a summary in the morning."

"Why waste the night?" said Vonderjan.

"I must be ready to leave in another week, sir, when the ship returns."

"Another few months," said Yonderjan, consideringly, "and maybe no ship will come here. Suppose you missed your boat?"

He seemed to be watching Jeanjacques through a telescope, closely, yet far, far away. He might have been drunk, but there was no smell of alcohol to him. Some drug of the Island, perhaps?

Jeanjacques said, "I'd have to swim for it."

A man came up from the yard below. He was a white servant, shabby but respectable. He spoke to Vonderjan in some European gabble.

"My horse is sick," said Vonderjan to Jeanjacques. "I think I shall have to shoot it. I've lost most of them here. Some insect, which bites."

"I'm sorry."

"Yes." Then, lightheartedly, "But none of us escape, do we."

Later, in the slow heat of the afternoon, Jeanjacques heard the shot crack out, and shuddered. It was more than the plight of the unfortunate horse. Something seemed to have hunted Vonderjan to his Island and now picked off from him all the scales of his world, his money, his horses, his possessions.

The clerk worked at his tally until the sun began to wester about four in the evening. Then he went up to wash and dress, because Vonderjan had said he should dine in the salon, with his family. Jeanjacques had no idea what he would find. He was curious, a little, about the young wife—she must by now be seventeen or eighteen. Had there been any children? It was always likely, but then again, likely too they had not survived.

At five, the sky was like brass, the palms that lined the edges of all vistas like blackened brass columns, bent out of shape, with brazen leaves that rattled against each other when any breath blew up from the bay. From the roof of the house it was possible also to make out a cove, and the sea. But it looked much more than a day's journey off. Unless you jumped and the wind blew you.

Another storm mumbled over the Island as Jeanjacques entered the salon. The long windows stood wide, and the dying light flickered fitfully like the disturbed candles.

No one took much notice of the clerk, and Vonderjan behaved as if Jeanjacques had been there a year, some acquaintance with no particular purpose in the house, neither welcome nor un.

The 'family', Jeanjacques saw, consisted of Vonderjan, his wife, a housekeeper, and a young black woman, apparently Vrouw Vonderjan's companion.

She was slender and fine, the black woman, and sat there as if a slave-trade had never existed, either to crucify or enrage her. Her dress was of excellent muslin, ladyishly low cut for the evening, and she had ruby ear-drops. (She spoke at least three languages that Jeanjacques heard, including the patois of the

Island, or house, which she exchanged now and then with the old housekeeper.)

But Vonderjan's wife was another matter altogether.

The moment he looked at her, Jeanjacques' blood seemed to shift slightly, all along his bones. And at the base of his skull, where his hair was neatly tied back by a ribbon, the roots stretched themselves, prickling.

She was not at all pretty, but violently beautiful, in a way far too large for the long room, or for any room, whether spacious or enormous. So pale she was, she made her black attendant seem like a shadow cast by a flame. Satiny coils and trickles of hair fell all round her in a deluge of gilded rain. Thunder was the colour of her eyes, a dark that was not dark, some shade that could not be described visually but only in other ways. All of her was a little like that. To touch her limpid skin would be like tasting ice-cream. To catch her fragrance like small bells heard inside the ears in fever.

When her dress brushed by him as she first crossed the room, Jeanjacques inadvertently recoiled inside his skin. He was feeling, although he did not know it, exactly as Justus had felt in the northern garden. Though Justus had not known it, either. But what terrified these two men was the very thing which drew other men, especially such men as Gregers Vonderjan. So much was plain.

The dinner was over, and the women got up to withdraw. As she passed by his chair, Vonderjan, who had scarcely spoken to her throughout the meal (or to anyone), lightly took hold of his wife's hand. And she looked down at once into his eyes.

Such a look it was. Oh God, Jeanjacques experienced now all his muscles go to liquid, and sinking, and his belly sinking down into his bowels; which themselves turned over heavily as a serpent. But his penis rose very quickly, and pushed hard as a rod against his thigh.

For it was a look of such explicit sex, trembling so colossally it had grown still, and out of such an agony of suspense, that he was well aware these two lived in a constant of the condition, and would need only to press together the length of their bodies, to ignite like matches in a galvanic convulsion.

He had seen once or twice similar looks, perhaps. Among couples kept strictly, on their marriage night. But no, not even then.

They said nothing to each other. Needed nothing to say. It had been said.

The girl and her black companion passed from the room, and after them the housekeeper, carrying a branch of the candles, whose flames flattened as she went through the doors on to the terrace. (*Notes:* This will happen again later.)

Out there, the night was now very black. Everything beyond the house had vanished in it, but for the vague differential between the sky and the tops of the forest below. There were no stars to be seen, and thunder still moved restlessly. The life went from Jeanjacques' genitals as if it might never come back.

"Brandy," said Vonderjan, passing the decanter. "What do you think of her?"

"Of whom, sir?"

"My Anna." (Playful; who else?)

Jeanjacques visualized, in a sudden unexpected flash, certain objects used as amulets, and crossing himself in church.

"An exquisite lady, sir."

"Yes," said Vonderjan. He had drunk a lot during dinner, but in an easy way. It was evidently habit, not need. Now he said again, "Yes."

Jeanjacques wondered what would be next. But of course nothing was to be next. Vonderjan finished his cigar, and drank down his glass. He rose, and nodded to Jeanjacques. "Bon nuit."

How could he even have forced himself to linger so long? Vonderjan demonstrably must be a human of vast self-control.

Jeanjacques imagined the blond man going up the stairs of the house to the wide upper storey. An open window, drifted with a gauze curtain, hot, airless night. Jeanjacques imagined Antoinelle, called Anna, lying on her back in the bed, its nets pushed careless away, for what bit Vonderjan's horses to death naturally could not essay his wife.

"No, I shan't have a good night," Jeanjacques said to Vonderjan in his head. He went to his room, and sharpened his pen for work.

In the darkness, he heard her. He was sure that he had. It was almost four in the morning by his pocket watch, and the sun would rise in less than an hour.

Waveringly she screamed, like an animal caught in a trap. Three times, the second time the loudest.

The whole of the inside of the house shook and throbbed and scorched from it.

Jeanjacques found he must get up, and standing by the window, handle himself roughly until, in less than thirteen seconds, his semen exploded on to the tiled floor.

Feeling then slightly nauseous, and dreary, he slunk to bed and slept gravely, like a stone.

Antoinelle sat at her toilette mirror, part of a fine set of silver-gilt her husband had given her. She was watching herself as Nanetta combed and brushed her hair.

It was late afternoon, the heat of the day lying down but not subsiding.

Antoinelle was in her chemise; soon she would dress for the evening dinner.

Nanetta stopped brushing. Her hands lay on the air like a black slender butterfly separated in two. She seemed to be listening.

"More," said Antoinelle.

"Yes."

The brush began again.

Antoinelle often did not rise until noon, frequently later. She would eat a little fruit, drink coffee, get up and wander about in flimsy undergarments. Now and then she would read a novel, or Nanetta would read one to her. Or they would play cards, sitting at the table on the balcony, among the pots of flowers.

Nanetta had never seen Antoinelle do very much, and had never seen her agitated or even irritable.

She lived for night.

He, on the other hand, still got up mostly at sunrise, and no later than the hour after. His man, Stronn, would shave him. Vonderjan would breakfast downstairs in the courtyard, eating meat and bread, drinking black tea. Afterwards he might go over the accounts with the secretary. Sometimes the whole of the big house heard him shouting (except for his wife, who was generally still asleep). He regularly rode (two horses survived), round parts of the Island, and was gone until late afternoon, talking to the men and women in the fields, sitting to drink with them, rum and palm liquor, in the shade of plantains. He might return about the time Antoinelle was washing herself, powdering her arms and face, and putting on a dress for dinner.

A bird trilled in a cage, hopped a few steps, and flew up to its perch to trill again.

The scent of dust and sweating trees came from the long windows, stagnant yet energizing in the thickening yellow light.

Nanetta half turned her head. Again she had heard something far away. She did not know what it was.

"Shall I wear the emerald necklace tonight?" asked Antoinelle, sleepily. "What do you think?"

Nanetta was used to this. To finding an answer.

"With the white dress? Yes, that would be effective."

"Put up my hair. Use the tortoiseshell combs."

Nanetta obeyed deftly.

The satiny bright hair was no pleasure to touch, too electric, stickily clinging to the fingers—full of each night's approaching storm. There would be no rain, not yet.

Antoinelle watched as the black woman transformed her. Antoinelle liked this, having only to be, letting someone else put her together in this way. She had forgotten by now, but never liked, independence. She wanted only enjoyment, to be made and remade, although in a manner that pleased her, and which, after all, demonstrated her power over others.

When she thought about Vonderjan, her husband, her loins clenched involuntarily, and a frisson ran through her, a shiver of heat. So she rationed her thoughts of him. During their meals together, she would hardly look at him, hardly speak, concentrating on the food, on the light of the candles reflecting in things, hypnotizing herself and prolonging, unendurably, her famine, until at last she was able to return into the bed, cool by then, with clean sheets on it, and wait, giving herself up to darkness and to fire.

How could she live in any other way?

Whatever had happened to her? Had the insensate cruelty of her relations pulped her down into a sponge that was ultimately receptive only to this? Or was this her true condition, which had always been trying to assert itself, and which, once connected to a suitable partner, did so, evolving also all the time, spreading itself higher and lower and in all directions, like some amoeba?

She must have heard stories of him, his previous wife, and of a black mistress or two he had had here. But Antoinelle was not remotely jealous. She had no interest in what he did when not with her, when not about to be, or actually in her bed with her. As if all other facets, both of his existence and her own, had now absolutely no meaning at all.

About the hour Antoinelle sat by the mirror, and Vonderjan, who had not gone out that day, was bathing, smoking one of

THE ISLE IS FULL OF NOISES

the cigars as the steam curled round him, Jeanjacques stood among a wilderness of cane fields beyond the house.

That cane was a type of grass tended always to amaze him, these huge stripes of straddling stalks, rising five feet or more above his head. He felt himself to be a child lost in a luridly unnatural wood, and besides, when a black figure passed across the view, moving from one subaqueous tunnel to another, they now supernaturally only glanced at him, cat-like, from the sides of their eyes.

Jeanjacques had gone out walking, having deposited his itinerary and notes with Vonderjan in a morning room. The clerk took narrow tracks across the Island, stood on high places from which (as from the roof), coves and inlets of the sea might be glimpsed.

The people of the Island had been faultlessly friendly and courteous, until he began to try to question them. Then they changed. He assumed at first they only hated his white skin, as had others he had met, who had refused to believe in his mixed blood. In that case, he could not blame them much for the hatred. Then he understood he had not assumed this at all. They were disturbed by something, afraid of something, and he knew it.

Were they afraid of her—of the white girl in the house? Was it that? And why were they afraid? Why was he himself afraid—because afraid of her he was. Oh yes, he was terrified.

At midday he came to a group of hut-houses, patchily colour-washed and with palm-leaf roofs, and people were sitting about there in the shade, drinking, and one man was splitting rosy gourds with a machete, so Jeanjacques thought of a guillotine a moment, the red juice spraying out and the *thunk* of the blade going through. (He had heard they had split imported melons in Marseilles, to test the machine. But he was a boy when he heard this tale, and perhaps it was not true.)

Jeanjacques stood there, looking on. Then a black woman got up, fat and not young, but comely, and brought him half a gourd, for him to try the dripping flesh.

He took it, thanking her.

"How is it going, Mother?" he asked her, partly in French, but also with two words of the patois, which he had begun to recognize. To no particular effect.

"It goes how it go, monsieur."

"You still take a share of your crop to the big house?" She gave him the sidelong look. "But you're free people, now."

One of the men called to her sharply. He was a tall black leopard, young and gorgeous as a carving from chocolate. The woman went away at once, and Jeanjacques heard again that phrase he had heard twice before that day. It was muttered somewhere at his back. He turned quickly, and there they sat, blacker in shade, eating from the flesh of the gourds, and drinking from a bottle passed around. Not looking at him, not at all.

"What did you say?"

A man glanced up. "It's nothing, monsieur."

"Something came from the sea, you said?"

"No, monsieur. Only a storm coming."

"It's the stormy season. Wasn't there something else?"

They shook their heads. They looked helpful, and sorry they could not assist, and their eyes were painted glass.

Something has come from the sea.

They had said it too, at the other place, further down, when a child had brought him rum in a tin mug.

What could come from the sea? Only weather, or men. Or the woman. She had come from there.

They were afraid, and even if he had doubted his ears or his judgment, the way they would not say it straight out, that was enough to tell him he had not imagined this.

Just then a breeze passed through the forest below, and then across the broad leaves above, shaking them. And the light changed a second, then back, like the blinking of the eye of God.

They stirred, the people. It was as if they saw the wind, and the shape it had was fearful to them, yet known. Respected.

As he was walking back by another of the tracks, he found a dead chicken laid on a banana leaf at the margin of a field. A propitiary offering? Nothing else had touched it, even a line of ants detoured out on to the track, to give it room.

Jeanjacques walked into the cane fields and went on there for a while. And now and then other human things moved through, looking sidelong at him.

Then, when he paused among the tall stalks, he heard them whispering, whispering, the stalks of cane, or else the voices of the people. Had they followed him? Were they aggressive? They had every right to be, of course, even with his kind. Even so, he did not want to be beaten, or to die. He had invested such an amount of his life and wits in avoiding such things.

But no one approached. The whispers came and went.

Now he was here, and he had made out, from the edge of this field, Vonderjan's house with its fringe of palms and rhododendrons (Blue View), above him on the hill, only about half an hour away.

In a full hour, the sun would dip. He would go to his room and there would be water for washing, and his other clothes laid out for the dinner.

The whispering began again, suddenly, very close, so Jeanjacques spun about, horrified.

But no one was there, nothing was there.

Only the breeze, that the black people could see, moved round among the stalks of the cane, that was itself like an Egyptian temple, its columns meant to be a forest of green papyrus.

"It's black," the voices whispered. "Black."

"Like a black man," Jeanjacques said hoarsely.

"Black like black."

Again, God blinked his eyelid of sky. A figure seemed to be standing between the shafts of green cane. It said, "Not black like men. So black we filled with terror of it. Black like black of night is black."

"Black like black."

"Something from the sea."

Jeanjacques felt himself dropping, and then he was on his knees, and his forehead was pressed to the powdery plant-drained soil.

He had not hurt himself. When he looked up, no one was in the field that he could see.

He got to his feet slowly. He trembled, and then the trembling, like the whispers, went away.

The storm rumbled over the Island. It sounded tonight like dogs barking, then baying in the distance. Every so often, for no apparent reason, the flames of the candles flattened, as if a hand had been laid on them.

There was a main dish of pork, stewed with spices. Someone had mentioned there were pigs on the Island, although the clerk had seen none, perhaps no longer wild, or introduced and never wild.

The black girl, who was called Nanetta, had put up her hair elaborately, and so had the white one, Vonderjan's wife. Round her slim pillar of throat were five large green stars in a necklace like a golden cake-decoration.

Vonderjan had told Jeanjacques that no jewelry was to be valued. But here at least was something that might have seen him straight for a while. Until his ship came in. But perhaps it never would again. Gregers Vonderjan had been lucky always, until the past couple of years.

A gust of wind, which seemed to do nothing else outside, abruptly blew wide the doors to the terrace.

Vonderjan himself got up, went by his servants, and shut both doors. That was, started to shut them. Instead he was standing there now, gazing out across the Island.

In the sky, the dogs bayed.

His heavy bulky frame seemed vast enough to withstand any night. His magnificent mane of hair, without any evident grey, gleamed like gold in the candlelight. Vonderjan was so strong, so nonchalant.

But he stood there a long while, as if something had attracted his attention.

It was Nanetta who asked, "Monsieur—what is the matter?"

Vonderjan half turned and looked at her, almost mockingly, his brows raised.

"Matter? Nothing."

She has it too, Jeanjacques thought. He said, "The blacks were saying, something has come from the sea."

Then he glanced at Nanetta. For a moment he saw two rings of white stand clear around the pupil and iris of her eyes. But she looked down, and nothing else gave her away.

Vonderjan shut the doors. He swaggered back to the table. (He did not look at his wife, nor she at him. They kept themselves intact, Jeanjacques thought, during proximity, only by such a method. The clerk wondered, if he were to find Antoinelle alone, and stand over her, murmuring Vonderjan's name, over and over, whether she would fall back, unable to resist, and come, without further provocation and in front of him. And at the thought, the hard rod tapped again impatiently on his thigh.)

"From the sea, you say. What?"

"I don't know, sir. But they were whispering it. Perhaps Mademoiselle knows?" He indicated Nanetta graciously, as if giving her a wanted opening.

She was silent.

"I don't think," said Vonderjan, "that she does."

"No, monsieur," she said. She seemed cool. Her eyes were kept down.

Oddly—Jeanjacques thought—it was Antoinelle who suddenly sprang up, pushing back her chair, so it scraped on the tiles.

"It's so hot," she said.

And then she stood there, as if incapable of doing anything else, of refining any desire or solution from her own words.

Voriderjan did not look at her, but he went slowly back and undid the doors. "Walk with me on the terrace, Anna."

And he extended his arm.

The white woman glided across the salon as if on runners. She seemed weightless—*blown*. And the white snake of her little narrow hand crawled round his arm and out on to the sleeve, to rest there. Husband and wife stepped out into the rumbling night.

Jeanjacques sat back and stared across the table at Nanetta.

"They're most devoted," he said. "One doesn't often see it, after the first months. Especially where the ages are so different. What is he, thirty, thirty-two years her senior?"

Nanetta raised her eyes and now gazed at him impenetrably, with the tiniest, most fleeting smile.

He would get nothing out of her. She was a lady's maid, and he a jumped-up clerk, but both of them had remained slaves. They were calcined, ruined, defensive, and armoured.

Along the terrace he could see that Vonderjan and the woman were pressed close by the house, where a lush flowering vine only partly might hide them. Her skirts were already pushed askew, her head thrown sideways, mouth open and eyes shut. He was taking her against the wall, thrusting and heaving into her.

Jeanjacques looked quickly away, and began to whistle, afraid of hearing her cries of climax.

But now the black girl exclaimed, "Don't whistle, don't do that, monsieur!"

"Why? Why not?"

She only shook her head, but again her eyes—the black centres were silver-ringed. So Jeanjacques got up and walked out of the salon into Vonderjan's library across the passage, where now the mundane papers concerning things to be sold, lay on a table.

But it has come, it has come through the sea, before star-rise and dawn, through the rifts and fans of the transparent water, sliding and swimming like a crab.

It has crawled on to the sand, crouching low, like a beast, and perhaps mistaken for some animal.

A moon (is it a different moon each night? Who would know?), sinking, and Venus in the east.

Crawling into the tangle of the trees, with the palms and parrot trees reflecting in the dulled mirror of its lid, its carapace. Dragging the hind limb like a tail, pulling itself by the front legs, like a wounded boar.

Through the forest, with only the crystal of Venus to shatter through the heavy leaves of sweating bronze.

Bleumaneer, La Vue Bleu, Blue Fashion, Blue View, seeing through a blue eye to a black shape, which moves from shadow to shadow, place to place. But always nearer.

Something is in the forest.

Nothing dangerous. How can it hurt you?

5

Yse is buying food in the open air market at Bley. Lucius had seen her, and now stands watching her, not going over.

She has filled her first bag with vegetables and fruit, and in the second she puts a fish and some cheese, olive oil and bread.

Lucius crosses through the crowd, by the place where the black girl called Rosalba is cooking red snapper on her skillet, and the old poet paints his words in coloured sand.

As Yse walks into a liquor store, Lucius follows.

"You're looking good, Yse."

She turns, gazing at him—not startled, more as if she doesn't remember him. Then she does. "Thank you. I feel good today."

"And strong. But not *this* strong. Give me the vegetables to carry, Yse."

"O.K. That's kind."

"What have you done to your hair?"

Yse thinks about this one. "Oh. Someone put in some extra hair for me. You know how they do, they hot-wax the strands on to your own."

"It looks fine."

She buys a box of wine bottles.

"You're having a party?" Lucius says.

"No, Lucius. I don't throw parties. You know that."

"I know that."

"Just getting in my stores. I'm working. Then I needn't go out again for a while, just stay put and write."

"You've lost some weight," Lucius says, "looks like about twenty-five pounds."

Now she laughs. "*No.* I wish. But you know I do sometimes, when I work. Adrenaline."

He totes the wine and the vegetables, and they stroll over to the bar on the quay, to which fresh fish are being brought in from the Sound. (The bar is at the top of what was, once, the Aquatic Museum. There are still old cases of bullet-and-robber-proof glass, with fossils in them, little ancient dragons of the deeps, only three feet long, and coelacanths with needle teeth.)

Lucius orders coffee and rum, but Yse only wants a mineral water. Is she dieting? He has never known her to do this. She has said, dieting became useless after her forty-third year.

Her hair hangs long, to her waist, blonde, with whiter blonde and silver in it. He can't see any of the wax-ends of the extensions, or any grey either. Slimmer, her face, hands and shoulders have fined right down. Her skin is excellent, luminous and pale. Her eyes are crystalline, and outlined by soft black pencil he has never seen her use before.

She says sharply, "For a man who likes men, you surely know how to look a woman over, Lucius."

"None better."

"Well don't."

"I'm admiring you, Yse."

"Well, still don't. You're embarrassing me. I'm not used to it any more. If I ever was."

There is, he saw an hour ago—all across the market—a small white surgical dressing on the left side of her neck. Now she absently touches it, and pulls her finger away like her own mother would do. They say you can always tell a woman's age from her hands. Yse's hands look today like those of a woman of thirty-five.

"Something bite you, Yse?"

"An insect. It itches."

"I came by in the boat," he says, drinking his coffee, leaving the rum to stand in the glass. "I heard you playing that piano."

"You must have heard someone else somewhere. I can't play. I used to improvise, years ago. But then I had to sell my piano back then. This one . . . I haven't been able to get the damn lid up. I'm frightened to force it in case everything breaks."

"Do you want me to try?"

"Thanks—but maybe not. You know, I don't think the keys can be intact. How can they be? And there might be rats in it."

"Does it smell of rats?"

"Oddly, it smells of flowers. Jasmine, or something. Mostly at night, really. A wonderful smell. Perhaps something's growing inside it."

"In the dark."

"Night-blooming Passia," Yse says, as if quoting.

"And you write about that piano," says Lucius.

"Did I tell you? Good guess then. But it's not about a piano. Not really. About an Island."

"Where is this island?"

"Here." Yse sets her finger on a large note-book that she has already put on the table. (Often she will carry her work about with her, like a talisman. This isn't new.)

But Lucius examines the blank cover of the book as if scanning a map. "Where else?" he says.

Now Yse taps her forehead. *(In my mind.)* But somehow he has the impression she has also tapped her left ear, directly above the bite—as if the island was in there too. *Heard* inside her ear. Or else, heard, felt—inside the *bite*.

"Let me read it," he says, *not* opening the note-book.

"You can't."

"Why not?"

"My awful handwriting. No one can, until I type it through the machine and there's a disc."

"You write so bad to hide it," he says.

"Probably."

"What's your story really about?"

"I told you. An Island. And a vampire."

"And it bit you in the neck."

Again, she laughs. "*You're* the one a vampire bit, Lucius. Or has it gone back to being a shark that bit you?"

"All kinds have bit me. I bite them, too."

She's finished her water. The exciting odour of cooking spiced fish drifts into the bar, and Lucius is hungry. But Yse is getting up.

"I'll carry your bag to the boat-stop."

"Thanks, Lucius."

"I can bring them to your loft."

"No, that's fine."

"What did you say about a vampire," he asks her as they wait above the sparkling water for the water-bus, "not what they are, what they *do* to you—what they make you feel?"

"I've known you over five years, Lucius—"

"Six and a half years."

"Six and a half then. I've never known you very interested in my books."

The breeze blows off the Sound, flattening Yse's shirt to her body. Her waist is about five inches smaller, her breasts formed, and her whole shape has changed from that of a small barrel to a curvy egg-timer. Woman-shape. Young woman-shape.

He thinks, uneasily, will she begin to menstruate again, the hormones flowing back like the flood of the Sound tides through the towers and lofts of the island? Can he scent, through her cleanly-showered, soap and shampoo smell, the hint of fresh blood?

"Not interested, Yse. Just being nosy."

"All right. The book is about, among others, a girl, who is called Antoinelle. She's empty, or been made empty, because what she wants is refused her—so she's like a soft, flaccid, open bag, and she wants and wants. And the soft wanting emptiness pulls him—the man—inside. She drains him of volition, and of his good luck. But he doesn't care. He also wants this. Went out looking for it. He explains that in the next section, I think . . .

"So she's your vampire."

"No. But she makes a vampire possible. She's like a blue-print—like compost, for the plant to grow in. And the heat there, and the decline, that lovely word *desuetude*. And empty spaces that need to be continually *filled*. Nature abhors a vacuum. Darkness abhors it too, and rushes in. Why else do you think it gets dark when the sun goes down?"

"Night," he says flatly.

"Of course not." She smiles. "Nothing so ordinary. It's the black of outer space rushing to fill the empty gap the daylight filled. Why else do they call it *space?*"

She's clever. Playing with her words, with quotations and vocal things like that.

Lucius can see the tired old rusty boat chugging across the water.

(Yse starts to talk about the planet Vulcan, which was discovered once, twice, a hundred or a hundred and fifty years ago, and both times found to be a hoax.)

The bus-boat is at the quay. Lucius helps Yse get her food and wine into the boat. He watches as it goes off around this drowned isle we have here, but she forgets to wave.

In fact, Yse has been distracted by another thought. She had found a seashell lying on her terrace yesterday. This will sometimes happen, if an especially high tide has flowed in.

She's thinking about the seashell, and the idea has come to her that, if she put it to her left ear, instead of hearing the sound of the sea (which is the rhythm of her own blood, moving), she might hear a piano playing.

Which is how she might put this into the story.

By the time the bus-boat reaches West Ridge, sunset is approaching. When she has hauled the bags and wine to the doors of her loft, she stands a moment, looking. The snake-willow seems carved from vitreous. The alley of water is molten. But that's by now commonplace.

Even out here, before she opens her doors, she can catch the faint overture of perfume from the plant which may—must—be growing in the piano.

She dreamed last night she followed Per Laszd for miles, trudging till her feet ached, through endless lanes of shopping mall, on the mainland. He would not stop, or turn, and periodically he disappeared. For some hours too she saw him in conversation with a slender, dark-haired woman. When he vanished yet again, Yse approached her. "Is he your lover?" *"No,"* chuckled the incredulous woman. *"Mine? No."* In the end Yse had gone on again, seen him ahead of her, and at last given up, turned her back, walked away briskly, not wanting him to know she had pursued him such a distance. Then only did she feel his hands thrill lightly on her shoulders—

At the shiver of memory, Yse shakes herself.

She's pleased to have lost weight, but not so surprised. She hasn't been eating much, and change is always feasible. The extensions cost a lot of money. Washing her hair is now a nuisance, and probably she will have them taken out before too long.

However, seeing her face in the mirror above the wash basin, she paused this morning, recognizing herself, if only for a moment.

A red gauze cloud drifts from the mainland.

Yse undoes her glass doors, and in the shadow, there that other shadow stands on its three legs. It might be anything but what it is, as might we all.

6: Her Piano

On the terrace below the gallery of orange trees, above the dry fountain, Gregers Vonderjan stood checking his gun.

Jeanjacques halted. He felt for a moment irrationally afraid—as opposed to the other fears he had felt here.

But the gun, plainly, was not for him.

It was just after six in the morning. Dawn had happened not long ago, the light was transparent as a window-pane.

"Another," said Vonderjan enigmatically. (Jeanjacques had noticed before, the powerful and self-absorbed were often obscure, thinking everyone must already know their business, which of course shook the world.)

". . . Your horses."

"My horses. Only two now, and one on its last legs. Come with me if you like, if you're not squeamish.

I am, extremely, Jeanjacques thought, but he went with Vonderjan nevertheless, slavishly.

Vonderjan strode down steps, around corners, through a grove of trees. They reached the stables. It was vacant, no one about but for a single man, some groom.

Inside the stall, two horses were together, one lying down. The other, strangely uninvolved, stood aloof. This upright one was white as some strange pearly fish-animal, its eyes almost blue, Jeanjacques thought, but perhaps that was a trick of the pure light. The other horse, the prone one, half lifted its head, heavily.

Vonderjan went to this horse. The groom did not speak. Vonderjan kneeled down.

"Ah, poor soldier—" then he spoke in another tongue, his birth-language, probably. As he murmured, he stroked the streaked mane away from the horse's eyes, tenderly, like a father, caressed it till the weary eyes shut, then shot it, quickly through the skull. The legs kicked once, strengthlessly, a reflex. It had been almost gone already.

Jeanjacques went out and leaned on the mounting-block. He expected he would vomit, but did not.

Vonderjan presently also came out, wiping his hands, like Pilate.

"Damn this thing, death," he said. The anger was wholesome, *whole*. For a moment a real man, a human being, stood solidly by Jeanjacques, and Jeanjacques wanted to turn and fling his arms about this creature, to keep it with him. But then it vanished, as before.

The strong handsome face was bland—or was it *blind?*

"None of us escape death."

That cliché once more, masking the *horror*—but what *was* the horror? And was the use of the cliché only acceptance of the harsh world, precisely what Vonderjan must have set himself to learn?

"Come to the house. Have a brandy," said Vonderjan.

They went back, not the way they had come, but using another flight of stairs. Behind them the groom was clearing the beautiful dead horse like debris or garbage. Jeanjacques refused to look over his shoulder.

Vonderjan's study had no light until great storm-shutters were undone. It must face, like the terrace, towards the sea.

The brandy was hot.

"All my life," said Vonderjan, sitting down on his own writing-table, suddenly unsolid, his eyes wide and unseeing, "I've had to deal with fucking death. You get sick of it. Sick to death of it."

"Yes."

"I know you saw some things in France."

"I did."

"How do we live with it, eh? Oh, you're a young man. But when you get past forty. Christ, you feel it, breathing on the back of your neck. Every death you've seen. And I've seen plenty. My mother, and my wife. I mean, my first wife, Uteka. A beautiful woman, when I met her. Big, if you know what I mean. White skin and raven hair, red-gold eyes. A Viking woman."

Jeanjacques was mesmerized, despite everything. He had never heard Vonderjan expatiate like this, not even in imagination.

They drank more brandy.

Vonderjan said, "She died in my arms."

"I'm sorry—"

"Yes. I wish I could have shot her, like the horses, to stop her suffering. But it was in Copenhagen, one summer. Her people everywhere. One thing, she hated sex."

Jeanjacques was shocked despite himself.

"I found other women for that," said Vonderjan, as if, indifferently, to explain.

The bottle was nearly empty. Vonderjan opened a cupboard and took out another bottle, and a slab of dry, apparently stale bread on a plate. He ripped off pieces of the bread and ate them.

It was like a curious Communion, bread and wine, flesh, blood. (He offered none of the bread to Jeanjacques.)

"I wanted," Vonderjan said, perhaps two hours later, as they sat in the hard stuffed chairs, the light no longer windowpane pure, "a woman who'd take that, from me. Who'd want me pushed and poured into her, like the sea, like they say a mermaid wants that. A woman who'd take. I heard of one. I went straight to her. It was true."

"Don't all women—" Jeanjacques faltered, drunk and heart racing, "take—?"

"No. They give. Give, give, give. They give too bloody much."

Vonderjan was not drunk, and they had consumed two bottles of brandy, and Vonderjan most of it.

"But she's—she's taken—she's had your *luck*—" Jeanjacques blurted.

"Luck. I never wanted my luck."

"But you—"

"Wake up. I had it, but who else did? Not Uteka, my wife. Not my wretched mother. I hate cruelty," Vonderjan said quietly. "And we note, this world's very cruel. We should punish the world if we could. We should punish God if we could. Put Him on a cross? Yes. Be damned to this fucking God."

The clerk found he was on the ship, coming to the Island, but he knew he did not want to be on the Island. Yet of course, it was now too late to turn back. Something followed through the water. It was black and shining. A shark, maybe.

When Jeanjacques came to, the day was nearly gone and evening was coming. His head banged and his heart galloped. The dead horse had possessed it. He wandered out of the study (now empty but for himself) and heard the terrible sound of a woman, sick-moaning in her death-throes: Uteka's ghost. But then a sharp cry came; it was the other one, Vonderjan's second wife, dying in his arms.

As she put up her hair, Nanetta was thinking of whispers. She heard them in the room, echoes of all the other whispers in the house below.

Black—it's black—not black like a man is black... black as black is black...

Beyond the fringe of palms, the edge of the forest trees stirred, as if something quite large were prowling about there. Nothing else moved.

She drove a gold hairpin through her coiffure.

He was with her, along the corridor. It had sometimes happened he would walk up here, in the afternoons. Not for a year, however.

A bird began to shriek its strange stupid warning at the forest's edge, the notes of which sounded like *"J'ai des lits! J'ai des lits!"*

Nanetta had dreamed this afternoon, falling asleep in that chair near the window, that she was walking in the forest, barefoot, as she had done when a child. Through the trees behind her something crept, shadowing her. It was noiseless, and the forest also became utterly still with tension and fear. She had not dared look back, but sometimes, from the rim of her eye, she glimpsed a dark, pencil-straight shape, that might only have been the ebony trunk of a young tree.

Then, pushing through the leaves and ropes of a wild fig, she saw it, in front of her not at her back, and woke, flinging herself forward with a choking gasp, so that she almost fell out of the chair.

It was black, smooth. Perhaps, in the form of a man. Or was it a beast? Were there eyes? Or a mouth?

In the house, a voice whispered, "Something is in the forest."

A shutter banged without wind.

And outside, the bird screamed *I have beds! I have beds!*

The salon: it was sunset and thin wine light was on the rich man's china, and the Venice glass, what was left of it.

Vonderjan considered the table, idly, smoking, for the meal had been served and consumed early. He had slept off his brandy in twenty minutes on Anna's bed, then woken and had her a third time, before they separated.

She had lain there on the sheet, her pale arms firm and damask with the soft nap of youth.

"I can't get up. I can't stand up."

"Don't get up. Stay where you are," he said. "They can bring you something on a tray."

"Bread," she said, "I want soft warm bread, and some soup. And a glass of wine."

"Stay there," he agreed again. "I'll soon be back."

"Come back quickly," she said. And she held out the slender, strong white arms, all the rest of her flung there and limp as a broken snake.

So he went back and slid his hand gently into her, teasing her, and she writhed on the point of his fingers, the way a doll would, should you put your hand up its skirt.

"Is that so nice? Are you sure you like it?"

"Don't stop."

Vonderjan had thought he meant only to tantalize, perhaps to fulfill, but in the end he unbuttoned himself, the buttons he had only just done up, and put himself into her again, finishing both of them with swift hard thrusts.

So, she had not been in to dine. And he sat here, ready for her again, quite ready. But he was used to that. He had, after all, stored all that, during his years with Uteka, who, so womanly in other ways, had loved to be held and petted like a child, and nothing more. Vonderjan had partly unavoidably felt that the disease, which invaded her body, had somehow been given entrance to it because of this omitting vacancy, which she had not been able to allow him to fill—as night rushed to engulf the sky once vacated by a sun.

This evening the clerk looked very sallow, and had not eaten much. (Vonderjan had forgotten the effect brandy could have.) The black woman was definitely frightened. There was a type of magic going on, some ancient fear-ritual that unknown forces had stirred up among the people on the Island. It did not interest Vonderjan very much, nothing much did, now.

He spoke to the clerk, congratulating him on the efficiency of his lists and his evaluation, and the arrangements that had been postulated, when next the ship came to the Island.

Jeanjacques rallied. He said, "The one thing I couldn't locate, sir, was a piano."

"Piano?" Puzzled, Vonderjan looked at him.

"I had understood you to say your wife—that she had a piano—"

"Oh, I ordered one for her years ago. It never arrived. It was stolen, I suppose, or lost overboard, and they never admitted to it. Yes, I recall it now, a pianoforte. But the heat here would soon have ruined it anyway."

The candles abruptly flickered, for no reason. The light was going, night rushing in.

Suddenly something, a huge impenetrable shadow, ran by the window.

The woman, Nanetta, screamed. The housekeeper sat with her eyes almost starting out of her head. Jeanjacques cursed. *"What was that?"*

As it had run by, fleet, leaping, a mouth gaped a hundred teeth—like the mouth of a shark breaking from the ocean. Or had they mistaken that?

Did it have eyes, the great black animal which had run by the window?

Surely it had eyes—

Vonderjan had stood up, and now he pulled a stick from a vase against the wall—as another man might pick up an umbrella, or a poker—and he was opening wide the doors, so the women shrank together and away.

The light of day was gone. The sky was blushing to black. Nothing was there.

Vonderjan called peremptorily into the darkness. To Jeanjacques the call sounded meaningless, gibberish, something like *Hooh! Hoouah!* Vonderjan was not afraid, possibly not even disconcerted or intrigued.

Nothing moved. Then, below, lights broke out on the open space, a servant shouted shrilly in the patois.

Vonderjan shouted down, saying it was nothing. "Go back inside." He turned and looked at the two women and the man in the salon. "Some animal." He banged the doors shut.

"It—looked like a lion," Jeanjacques stammered. But no. It had been like a shark, a fish, which bounded on two or three legs, and stooping low.

The servants must have seen it too. Alarmed and alerted, they were still disturbed, and generally calling out now. Another woman screamed, and then there was the crash of glass.

"Fools," said Vonderjan, without any expression or contempt. He nodded at the housekeeper. "Go and tell them I say it's all right."

The woman dithered, then scurried away—by the house door; avoiding the terrace. Nanaetta too had stood up and her eyes had their silver rings. They, more even than the thing which ran across the window, terrified Jeanjacques.

"What was it? Was it a wild pig?" asked the clerk, aware he sounded like a scared child.

"A pig. What pig? No. Where could it go?"

"Has it climbed up the wall?" Jeanjacques rasped.

The black woman began to speak the patois in a singsong and the hair crawled on Jeanjacques' scalp.

"Tell her to stop it, can't you."

"Be quiet, Nanette," said Vonderjan.

She was silent.

They stood there.

Outside the closed windows, in the closed dark, the disturbed noises below were dying off.

Had it had eyes? Where had it gone to?

Jeanjacques remembered a story of Paris, how the guillotine would leave its station by night, and patrol the streets, searching for yet more blood. And during a siege of antique Rome, a giant phantom wolf had stalked the seven hills, tearing out the throats of citizens. These things were not real, even though they had been witnessed and attested, even though evidence and bodies were left in their wake. And, although unreal, yet they existed. They grew, such things, out of the material of the rational world, as maggots appeared spontaneously in a corpse, or fungus formed on damp.

The black woman had been keeping quiet. Now she made a tiny sound.

They turned their heads.

Beyond the windows—dark blotted dark, night on night.

"It's there."

A second time Vonderjan flung open the doors, and light flooded, by some trick of reflection in their glass, out across the place beyond.

It crouches by the wall, where yestereve the man carnally had his wife, where a creeper grows, partly rent away by their movements.

"In God's sight," Vonderjan says, startled finally, but not afraid.

He walks out, straight out, and they see the beast by the wall does not move, either to attack him or to flee.

Jeanjacques can smell roses, honeysuckle. The wine glass drops out of his hand.

Antoinelle dreams, now.

She is back in the house of her aunt, where no one would allow her to speak, or to play the piano. But she has slunk down in the dead of night, into the sitting-room, and rebelliously lifted the piano's lid.

A wonderful sweet smell comes up from the keys, and she strokes them a moment, soundlessly. They feel . . . like skin. The skin of a man, over muscle, young, hard, smooth. Is it Justus she feels? (She knows this is very childish. Even her sexuality, although perhaps she does not know this, has the wanton ravening quality of the child's single-minded demands.)

There is a shell the inclement aunt keeps on top of the piano, along with some small framed miniatures of ugly relatives.

Antoinelle lifts the shell, and puts it to her ear, listens to hear the sound of the sea. But instead, she hears a piano playing, softly and far off.

The music, Antoinelle thinks, is a piece by Rameau, for the harpsichord, transposed.

She looks at the keys. She has not touched them, or not enough to make them sound.

Rameau's music dies away.

Antoinelle finds she is playing four single notes on the keys, she does not know why, neither the notes, nor the word they spell, mean anything to her.

And then, even in the piano-dream, she is aware her husband, Gregers Vonderjan, is in the bed with her, lying behind her, although in her dream she is standing upright.

They would not let her speak or play the piano—they would not let her have what she must have, or make the sounds that she must make.

Now *she* is a piano.

He fingers her keys, gentle, next a little rough, next sensually, next with the crepitation of a feather. And, at each caress, she sounds, Antoinelle, who is a piano, a different note.

His hands are over her breasts. (In the dream too, she realizes, she has come into the room naked.) His fingers are on her naked breasts, fondling and describing, itching the buds at their centres. Antoinelle is being played. She gives off, note by note and chord by chord, her music.

Still cupping, circling her breasts with his hungry hands, somehow his scalding tongue is on her spine. He is licking up and up the keys of her vertebrae, through her silk-thin skin.

Standing upright, he is pressed behind her. While lying in the bed, he has rolled her over, crushing her breasts into his hands beneath her, lying on her back, his weight keeping her pinned, breathless.

And now he is entering her body, his penis like a tower on fire.

She spreads, opens, melts, dissolves for him. No matter how large, and he is now enormous, she will make way, then grip fierce and terrible upon him, her toothless springy lower mouth biting and cramming itself full of him, as if never to let go.

They are swimming strongly together for the shore.

How piercing the pleasure at her core, all through her now, the hammers hitting with a golden quake on every nerve-string.

And then, like a beast (a cat? A lion?), he has caught her by the throat, one side of her neck.

As with the other entry, at her sex, her body gives way to allow him room. And, as at the very first, her virgin's cry of pain changes almost at once into a wail of delight.

Antoinelle begins to come (to enter, to arrive).

Huge thick rollers of deliciousness, purple and crimson, dark and blazing, tumble rhythmically as dense waves upwards, from her spine's base to the windowed dome of her skull.

Glorious starvation couples with feasting, itching with rubbing, constricting, bursting, with implosion, the architecture of her pelvis rocks, punches, roaring and spinning in eating movements and swallowing gulps—

If only this sensation might last and last.

It lasts. It lasts.

Antoinelle is burning bright. She is changing into stars. Her stars explode and shatter. There are greater stars she can make. She is going to make them. She does so. And greater. Still she is coming, entering, arriving.

She has screamed. She has screamed until she no longer has any breath. Now she screams silently. Her nails gouge the bed-sheets. She feels the blood of her virginity falling drop by drop. She is the shell and her blood her sounding sea, and the sea is rising up and another mouth, the mouth of night, is taking it all, and she is made of silver for the night which devours her, and this will never end.

And then she screams again, a terrible divine scream, dredged independently up from the depths of her concerto of ecstasy. And vaguely, as she flies crucified on the wings of the storm, she knows the body upon her body (its teeth in her throat), is not the body of Vonderjan, and that the fire-filled hands upon her breasts, the flaming stem within her, are black, not as black is black, but black as outer space, which she is filling now with her millions of wheeling, howling stars.

7

The bird which cries *Shadily! Shadily!* flies over the island above the boiling afternoon lofts, and is gone, back to the upper city mainland, where there are more trees, more shade.

In the branches of the snake-willow, a wind-chime tinkles, once.

Yse's terrace is full of people, sitting and standing, with bottles, glasses, cans, and laughing. Yse has thrown a party. Someone, drunk, is dog-paddling in the alley of water.

Lucius, in his violet shirt, looks at the people. Sometimes Yse appears. She's slim and ash-pale, with long, shining hair, about twenty-five. Closer, thirty-five, maybe.

"Good party, Yse. Why you throw a party?"

"I had to throw something. Throw a plate, or myself away. Or something."

Carr and the fat man, they got the two lids up off the piano by now. It won't play, everyone knew it wouldn't. Half the notes will not sound. Instead, a music centre, straddled between the piano's legs, rigged via Yse's generator, uncoils the blues.

And this in turn has made the refrigerator temperamental. Twice people have gone to neighbours to get ice. And in turn these neighbours have been invited to the party.

A new batch of lobsters bake on the griddle. Green grapes and yellow pineapples are pulled apart.

"I was bored," she says. "I couldn't get on with it, that vampire story."

"Let me read it."

"You won't decipher my handwriting."

"Some. Enough."

"You think so? All right. But don't make criticisms, don't tell me what to do, Lucius, all right?"

"Deal. How would *I* know?"

He sits in the shady corner (*Shadily!* the bird cried mockingly *(J'ai des lits)* from Yse's roof), and now he reads. He can read her handwriting, it's easier than she thinks.

Sunset spreads an awning.

Some of the guests go home, or go elsewhere, but still crowds sit along the wall, or on the steps, and in the loft people are dancing now to a rock band on the music centre.

"Hey this piano don't play!" accusingly calls Big Eye, a late learner.

Lucius takes a polite puff of a joint someone passes, and passes it on. He sits thinking.

Sunset darkens, claret colour, and now the music centre plays Mozart.

Yse sits down by Lucius on the wall.

"Tell me, Yse, how does he get all his energy, this rich guy. He's forty, you say, but you say that was like fifty, then. And he's big, heavy. And he porks this Anna three, four times a night, and then goes on back for more."

"Oh that. Vonderjan and Antoinelle. It's to do with obsession. They're obsessive. When you have a kink for something, you can do more, go on and on. Straight sex is never like that. It's the perversity—so-called perversity. That revs it up."

"Strong guy, though."

"Yes."

"Too strong for you?"

"Too strong for me."

Lucius knew nothing about Yse's 'obsession' with Per Laszd. But by now he knows there is something. There has never been a man in Yse's life that Lucius has had to explain to that he, Lucius, is her friend only. Come to that, not any women in her life, either. But he has come across her work, read a little of it—never much—seen this image before, this big blond man. And the sex, for always, unlike the life of Yse, her books are full of it.

Lucius says suddenly, "You liked him but you never got to have him, this feller."

She nods. As the light softens, she's not a day over thirty, even from two feet away.

"No. But I'm used to that."

"What is it then? You have a bone to pick with him for him getting old?"

"The real living man you mean? He's not old. About fifty-five, I suppose. He looks pretty wonderful to me still."

"You see him?" Lucius is surprised.

"I see him on TV. And he looks great. But he was—well, fabulous when he was younger. I mean actually like a man out of a fable, a myth." She's forgotten, he thinks, that she never confided like this in Lucius. Still though, she keeps back the name.

Lucius doesn't ask for the name.

A name no longer matters, if it ever did.

"You never want to try another guy?"

"Who? Who's offering?" And she is angry, he sees it. Obviously, he is no use to her that way. But then, did she make a friendship with Lucius for just that reason?

"You look good, Yse."

"Thank you." Cold. Better let her be. For a moment. A heavenly, unearthly scent is stealing over the evening air.

Lucius has never seen the plant someone must have put in to produce this scent. Nothing grows on the terrace but for the snake-willow, and tonight people, lobster, pineapple, empty bottles.

"This'll be a mess to get straight," he says.

"Are you volunteering?"

"Just condoling, Yse."

The sunset totally fades. Stars light up. It's so clear, you can see the Abacus Tower, like a Christmas tree, on the mainland.

"What colour are his eyes, Yse?"

". . . Eyes? Blue. It's in the story."

"No, girl, the other one."

"Which—? Oh, *that* one. The vampire. I don't know. Your vampire had yellow eyes, you said."

"I said, he made me feel like a king. But the sex was good, then it was over. Not as you describe it, extended play."

"I did ask you not to criticise my work."

"No way. It's sexy. But tell me his eyes' colour?"

"Black, maybe. Or even white. The vampire is like the piano."

"Yeah. I don't see that. Yse, why is it a piano?"

"It could have been anything. The characters are the hotbed, and the vampire grows out of that. It just happens to form as a piano—a sort of piano. Like dropping a glass of wine, like a cloud—the stain, the cloud, just happen to take on a shape, randomly, that seems to resemble some familiar thing."

"Or is it because you can play it?"

"Yes, that too."

"And it's an animal."

"And a man. Or male. A male body."

"Black as black is black. Not skin-black."

"Blacker. As black as black can be."

He says quietly, "La Danse aux Vampires."

A glass breaks in the loft and wine spills on the wooden floor—shapelessly? Yse doesn't bat an eyelash.

"You used to fuss about your things."

"They're only things."

"We're all only things, Yse. What about the horses?"

"You mean Vonderjan's horses. This is turning into a real interrogation. All right. The last one, the white one like a fish, escapes, and gallops about the Island."

"You don't seem stuck, Yse. You seem to know plenty enough to go on."

"Perhaps I'm tired of going on."

"Looked in the mirror?"

"What do you mean?"

"Look in the mirror, Yse."

"Oh that. It's not real. It won't last."

"I never saw a woman could do that before, get fifteen years younger in a month. Grow her hair fifty times as thick and twenty times longer. Lose forty pounds without trying, and nothing *loose*. How do you *feel*, Yse?"

"All right."

"But do you feel good?"

"I feel all right."

"It's how they make you feel, Yse. You said it. They're not beautiful, they don't smell like flowers or the sea. They come out of the grave, out of beds of earth, out of the cesspit shit at the bottom of your soul's id. It's how they make you feel, what they can do to change you. Hudja-magica. Not them. What they can do to *you*."

"You are crazy, Lucius. There've been some funny smokes on offer up here tonight."

He gets up.

"Yse, did I say, the one I followed, when he went into his grave under the headstone, he say to me, *You come in with me, Luce. Don't mind the dark. I make sure you never notice* it."

"And you said no."

"I took to my hot heels and ran for my fucking life."

"Then you didn't love him, Lucius."

"I loved my fucking life."

She smiles, the white girl at his side. Hair and skin so ivory pale, white dress and shimmering eyes, and who in hell is she?

"Take care, Yse."

"Night, Lucius. Sweet dreams."

The spilled wine on the floor has spilled a random shape that looks like a screwed-up sock.

Her loft is empty. They have all gone.

She lights the lamp on her desk, puts out the others, sits, looking at the piano from the Sound, forty feet away, its hind lid and its forelid now raised, eyes and mouth.

Then she gets up and goes to the piano, and taps out on the keys four notes.

Each one sounds.

D, then E, then A. And then again D.

It would be *mort* in French, *dood* in Dutch, *tod* in German. Danish, Czech, she isn't sure . . . but it would not work.

I saw in the mirror.

PianO. O, pain.
But, it doesn't hurt.

8: Danse Macabre

A wind blew from the sea, and waxy petals fell from the vine, scattering the lid of the piano as it stood there, by the house wall.

None of them spoke.

Jeanjacques felt the dry parched cinnamon breath of Nanetta scorching on his neck, as she waited behind him. And in front of him was Vonderjan, examining the thing on the terrace.

"How did it get up here?" Jeanjacques asked, stupidly. He knew he was being stupid. The piano was supernatural. It had run up here.

"Someone carried it. Hew else?" replied Vonderjan.

Did he believe this? Yes, it seemed so.

Just then a stifled cry occurred above, detached itself and floated over them. For a moment none of them reacted to it; they had heard it so many times and in so many forms.

But abruptly Vonderjan's blond head went up, his eyes wide. He turned and strode away, half running. Reaching a stair that went to the gallery above, he bounded up it.

It was the noise his wife made, of course. But she made it when he was with her (inside her). And he had been here—

Neither Nanetta nor Jeanjacques went after Gregers Vonderjan, and neither of them went any nearer the piano.

"Could someone have carried it up here?" Jeanjacques asked the black woman, in French.

"Of course." But as she said this, she vehemently shook her head.

They moved away from the piano.

The wind came again, and petals fell again across the blackness of its carapace.

Jeanjacques courteously allowed the woman to precede him into the salon, then shut both doors quietly.

"What is it?"

She looked up at him sleepily, deceitfully.

"You called out."

"Did I? I was asleep. A dream . . ."

"Now I'm here," he said.

"No," she said, moving a little way from him. "I'm so sleepy. Later."

Vonderjan stood back from the bed. He gave a short laugh, at the absurdity of this. In the two years of their sexual marriage, she had never before said anything similar to him. (And he heard Uteka murmur sadly, "Please forgive me, Gregers. Please don't be angry.")

"Very well."

Then Antoinelle turned and he saw the mark on her neck, glowing lushly scarlet as a flower or fruit, in the low lamplight.

"Something's bitten you." He was alarmed. He thought at once of the horses dying. "Let me see."

"Bitten me? Oh, yes. And I scratched at it in my sleep, yes, I remember."

"Is that why you called out, Anna?"

She was amused and secretive.

Picking up the lamp, he bent over her, staring at the place.

A little thread, like fire, still trickled from the wound, which was itself very small. There was the slightest bruising. It did not really look like a bite, more as if she had been stabbed on purpose by a hat-pin.

Where he had let her put him off sexually, he would not let her do so now. He went out and came back, to mop up the little wound with alcohol.

"Now you've made it sting. It didn't before."

"You said it itched you."

"Yes, but it didn't worry me."

"I'll close the window."

"Why? It's hot, so hot—"

"To keep out these things which bite."

He noted her watching him. It was true she was mostly still asleep, yet despite this, and the air of deception and concealment which so oddly clung to her, for a moment he saw, in her eyes, that he was old.

When her husband had gone, Antoinelle lay on her front, her head turned, so the blood continued for a while to soak into her pillow.

She had dreamed the sort of dream she had sometimes dreamed before Vonderjan came into her life. Yet this had been much more intense. If she slept, would the dream return? But she slept quickly, and the dream did not happen.

Two hours later, when Vonderjan came back to her bed, he could not at first wake her. Then, although she seemed to welcome him, for the first time he was unable to satisfy her. She writhed and wriggled beneath him, then petulantly flung herself back. "Oh finish then. I can't. I don't want to."

But he withdrew gently, and coaxed her. "What's wrong, Anna? Aren't you well tonight?"

"Wrong? I want what you usually give me."

"Then let me give it to you."

"No. I'm too tired."

He tried to feel her forehead. She seemed too warm. Again, he had the thought of the horses, and he was uneasy. But she pulled away from him. "Oh, let me sleep, I must sleep."

Before returning here, he had gone down and questioned his servants. He had asked them if they had brought the piano up on to the terrace, and where they had found it.

They were afraid, he could see that plainly. Afraid of unknown magic and the things they beheld in the leaves and on the wind, which he, Vonderjan, could not see and had never believed in. They were also afraid of a shadowy beast, which apparently they too had witnessed, and which he thought he had seen. And naturally, they were afraid of the piano, because it was out of its correct situation, because (and he already knew this perfectly well), they believed it had stolen by itself out of the forest, and run up on the terrace, and *was* the beast they had seen.

At midnight, he went back down, unable to sleep, with a lamp and a bottle, and pushed up both the lids of the piano with ease.

Petals showered away. And a wonderful perfume exploded from the inside of the instrument, and with it a dim cloud of dust, so he stepped off.

As the film cleared, Vonderjan began to see that something lay inside the piano. The greater hind lid had shut it in against the piano's viscera of dulcimer hammers and brass-wire strings.

When all the film had smoked away, Vonderjan once more went close and held the lamp above the piano, leaning down to look, as he had with his wife's bitten throat.

An embalmed mummy was curled up tight in the piano.

That is, a twisted knotted thing, blackened as if by fire, lay folded round there in a preserved and tarry skin, tough as any bitumen, out of which, here and there, the dull white star of a partial bone poked through.

This was not large enough, he thought, to be the remains of a normal adult. Yet the bones, so far as he could tell, were not those of a child, nor of an animal.

Yet, it was most like the burnt and twisted carcass of a beast.

He released and pushed down again upon the lid. He held the lid flat, as if it might lunge up and open again. Glancing at the keys, before he closed them away too, he saw a drop of vivid red, like a pearl of blood from his wife's neck, but it was only a single red petal from the vine.

Soft and loud. In his sleep, the clerk kept hearing these words. They troubled him, so he shifted and turned, almost woke, sank back uneasily. *Soft and loud*—which was what *Pianoforte* meant . . .

Jeanjacques' mother, who had been accustomed to thrash him, struck him round the head. A loud blow, but she was soft with grown men, yielding, pliant. And with him, too, when grown, she would come to be soft and subserviently polite. But he never forgot the strap, and when she lay dying, he had gone nowhere near her. (His white half, from his father, had also made sure he went nowhere near his sire.)

Nanetta lay under a black, heavily-furred animal, a great cat, which kneaded her back and buttocks, purring. At first she was terrified, then she began to like it. Then she knew she would die.

Notes: The black keys are the black magic. The white keys are the white magic. (Both are evil.) Anything black, or white, must respond.

Even if half-black, half-white.

Notes: The living white horse has escaped. It gallops across the Island. It reaches the sea and finds the fans of the waves, snorting at them, and canters through the surf along the beaches, fish-white, and the sun begins to rise.

Gregers Vonderjan dreams he is looking down at his dead wife (Uteka), in the rain, as he did in Copenhagen that year she died. But in the dream she is not in a coffin, she is uncovered, and the soil is being thrown on to her vulnerable face. And he is sorry, because for all his wealth and personal magnitude, and power, he could not stop this happening to her. When the Island sunrise wakes him at Bleumaneer, the sorrow does not abate. He wishes now she had lived, and was here with him. (Nanetta would have eased him elsewhere, as she had often done in the past. Nanetta had been kind, and warm-blooded enough.) (Why speak of her as if she too were dead?)

Although awake, he does not want to move. He cannot be bothered with it, the eternal and repetitive affair of getting up, shaving and dressing, breakfasting, looking at the accounts, the lists the clerk has made, his possessions, which will shortly be gone.

How has he arrived at this? He had seemed always on a threshold. There is no time left now. The threshold is that of the exit. It is all over, or soon will be.

Almost all of them had left. The black servants and the white, from the kitchen and the lower rooms. The white housekeeper, despite her years and her pernickety adherences to the house. Vonderjan's groom—he had let the last horse out, too, perhaps taken it with him.

Even the bird had been let out of its cage in Antoinelle's boudoir, and had flown off.

Stronn stayed, Vonderjan's man. His craggy indifferent face said, *So, have they left?*

And the young black woman, Nanetta, she was still there, sitting with Antoinelle on the balcony, playing cards among the Spanish flowers, her silver and ruby earrings glittering.

"Why?" said Jeanjacques. But he knew.

"They're superstitious," Vonderjan, dismissive. "This sort of business has happened before."

It was four in the afternoon. Mornings here were separate. They came in slices, divided off by sleep. Or else, one slept through them.

"Is that—is the piano still on the terrace? Did someone take it?" said Jeanjacques, giving away the fact he had been to look, and seen the piano was no longer there. Had he dreamed it?

"Some of them will have moved it," said Vonderjan. He paced across the library. The windows stood open. The windows here were open so often, anything might easily get in.

The Island sweated, and the sky was golden lead.

"Who would move it?" persisted Jeanjacques.

Vonderjan shrugged. He said, "It wasn't any longer worth anything. It had been in the sea. It must have washed up on the beach. Don't worry about it."

Jeanjacques thought, if he listened carefully, he could hear beaded piano notes, dripping in narrow streams through the house. He had heard them this morning, as he lay in bed, awake, somehow unable to get up. (There had seemed no point in getting up. Whatever would happen would happen, and he might as well lie and wait for it.) However, a lifetime of frantic early arisings, of hiding in country barns and thatch, and up chimneys, a lifetime of running away, slowly curdled his guts and pushed him off the mattress. But by then it was past noon.

"Do they come back?"

"What? What did you say?" asked Vonderjan.

"Your servants. You said, they'd made off before. Presumably they returned."

"Yes. Perhaps."

Birds called raucously (but wordlessly) in the forest, and then grew silent.

"There was something inside that piano," said Vonderjan, "a curiosity. I should have seen to it last night, when I found it."

"What—what was it?"

"A body. Oh, don't blanch. Here, drink this. Some freakish thing. A monkey, I'd say. I don't know how it got there, but they'll have been frightened by it."

"But it smelled so sweet. Like roses—"

"Yes, it smelled of flowers. That's a funny thing."

"Sometimes the dead do smell like that. Just before the smell changes."

"I never heard of that."

"No. It surprised me years ago, when I encountered it myself."

Something fell through the sky—an hour. And now it was sunset.

Nanetta had put on an apron and cooked food in the kitchen. Antoinelle had not done anything to assist her, although, in her childhood, she had been taught how to make soups and bake bread, out of a sort of bourgeois pettiness.

In fact, Antoinelle had not even properly dressed herself. Tonight she came to the meal, which the black woman had meticulously set out, in a dressing-robe, tied about her waist by a brightly-coloured scarf. The neckline drooped, showing off her long neck and the tops of her round young breasts, and the flimsy improper thing she wore beneath. Her hair was also undressed, loose, gleaming and rushing about her with a water-wet sheen.

Stronn too came in tonight, to join them, sitting far down the table, and with a gun across his lap.

"What's that for?" Vonderjan asked him.

"The blacks are saying there's some beast about on the Island. It fell off a boat and swam ashore."

"You believe them?"

"It's possible, mijnheer, isn't it. I knew of a dog that was thrown from a ship at Port-au-Roi, and reached Venice."

"Did you indeed."

Vonderjan looked smart, as always. The pallid topaz shone in his ring, his shirt was laundered and starched.

The main dish they had consisted of fish, with a kind of ragoût, with pieces of vegetable, and rice.

Nanetta had lit the candles, or some of them. Some repeatedly went out. Vonderjan remarked this was due to something in the atmosphere. The air had a thick, heavy saltiness, and for once there was no rumbling of thunder, and constellations showed, massed above the heights, once the light had gone, each star framed in a peculiar greenish circle.

After Vonderjan's exchange with the man, Stronn, none of them spoke.

Without the storm, there seemed no sound at all, except that now and then, Jeanjacques heard thin little rills of musical notes.

At last he said, "What is that I can hear?"

Vonderjan was smoking one of his cigars. "What?"

It came again. Was it only in the clerk's head? He did not think so, for the black girl could plainly hear it too. And oddly, when Vonderjan did not say anything else, it was she who said to Jeanjacques, "They hang things on the trees—to honour gods—wind gods, the gods of darkness."

Jeanjacques said, "But it sounds like a piano."

No one answered. Another candle sighed and died.

And then Antoinelle—*laughed*.

It was a horrible, terrible laugh. Rilling and tinkling like the bells hung on the trees of the Island, or like the high notes of any piano. She did it for no apparent reason, and did not refer to it once she had finished. She should have done, she should have begged their pardon, as if she had belched raucously.

Vonderjan got up. He went to the doors and opened them on the terrace and the night.

Where the piano had rested itself against the wall, there was nothing, only shadow and the disarrangement of the vine, all its flower-cups broken and shed.

"Do you want some air, Anna?"

Antoinelle rose. She was demure now. She crossed to Vonderjan, and they moved out on to the terrace. But their walking together was unlike that compulsive, gliding inevitability of the earlier time. And, once out in the darkness, they *only* walked, loitering up and down.

She is mad, Jeanjacques thought. This was what he had seen in her face. That she was insane, unhinged and dangerous, her loveliness like vitriol thrown into the eyes of anyone who looked at her.

Stronn poured himself a brandy. He did not seem unnerved, or particularly *en garde,* despite the gun he had lugged in.

But Nanetta stood up. Unhooking the ruby ear-drops from her earlobes, she placed them beside her plate. As she went across the salon to the inner door, Jeanjacques noted her feet, which had been shod in city shoes, were now bare. They looked incongruous, those dark velvet paws with their nails of tawny coral, extending long and narrow from under her light gown; they looked lawless, in a way nothing of the rest of her did.

When she had gone out, Jeanjacques said to Stronn, "Why is she barefoot?"

'Savages."

Old rage slapped the inside of the clerk's mind, like his mother's hand. Though miles off, he must react. "Oh," he said sullenly, "barbaric, do you mean? You think them barbarians, though they've been freed."

Stronn said, "Unchained is what I mean. Wild like the forest. That's what it means, that word, savage—forest."

Stronn reached across the table and helped himself from Vonderjan's box of cigars.

On the terrace, the husband and wife walked up and down. The doors stayed wide open.

Trees rustled below, and were still.

Jeanjacques too got up and followed the black woman out, and beyond the room he found her, still in the passage. She was standing on her bare feet, listening, with the silver rings in her eyes.

"What can you hear?"

"You hear it too."

"Why are your feet bare?"

"So I can go back. So I can run away."

Jeanjacques seized her wrist and they stood staring at each other in a mutual fear, of which each one made up some tiny element, but which otherwise surrounded them.

"What—" he said.

"Her pillow's red with blood," said Nanetta. "Did you see the hole in her neck?"

"No."

"No. It closes up like a flower—a flower that eats flies. But she bled. And from her other place. White bed was red bed with her blood."

He felt sick, but he kept hold of the wand of her wrist.

"There *is* something."

"You know it too."

Across the end of the passageway, then, where there was no light, something heavy and rapid, and yet slow, passed by. It was all darkness, but a fleer of pallor slid across its teeth. And the head of it one moment turned, and, without eyes, as it had before, it gazed at them.

The black girl sagged against the wall, and Jeanjacques leaned against and into her. Both panted harshly. They might have been copulating, as Vonderjan had with his wife.

Then the passage was free. They felt the passage draw in a breath.

"Was in my room," the girl muttered, "was in my room that is too small anything so big get through the door. I wake, I see it there."

"But it left you alone."

"It not want me. Want *her*."

"The white bitch."

"Want her, have her. Eat her alive. Run to the forest," said Nanetta, in the patois, but now he understood her, "run to the forest." But neither of them moved.

"*N*o, no, please, Gregers. Don't be angry.'

The voice is not from the past. Not Uteka's. It

comes from a future now become the present.

"You said you have your courses. When did that prevent you before? I've told you, I don't mind it."

"No. Not this time."

He lets her go. Lets go of her.

She did not seem anxious, asking him not to be angry. He is not angry. Rebuffed, Vonderjan is, to his own amazement, almost relieved.

"Draw the curtains round your bed, Anna. And shut your window."

"Yes, Gregers."

He looks, and sees her for the first time tonight, how she is dressed, or not dressed.

"Why did you come down like that?"

"I was hot . . . does it matter?"

"A whore in the brothel would put on something like that." The crudeness of his language startles him. (Justus?) He checks. "I'm sorry, Anna. You meant nothing. But don't dress like that in front of the others."

"Nanetta, do you mean?"

"I mean, of course, Stronn. And the Frenchman."

Her neck, drooping, is the neck of a lily drenched by rain. He cannot see the mark of the bite.

"I've displeased you."

Antoinelle can remember her subservient mother (the mother who later threw her out to her aunt's house), fawning in this way on her father. (Who also threw her out.)

But Vonderjan seems uninterested now. He stands looking instead down the corridor.

Then he takes a step. Then he halts and says, "Go along to your room, Anna. Shut the door."

"Yes, Gregers."

In all their time together, they have never spoken in this way, in such platitudes, ciphers. Those things used freely by others.

He thinks he has seen something at the turn of the corridor. But when he goes to that junction, nothing is there. And then he thinks, of course, what *could* be there?

By then her door is shut.

Alone, he walks to his own rooms, and goes in.

The Island is alive tonight. Full of stirrings and displacements.

He takes up a bottle of Hollands, and pours a triple measure.

Beyond the window, the green-ringed eyes of the stars stare down at Bleumaneer, as if afraid.

When she was a child, a little girl, Antoinelle had sometimes longed to go to bed, in order to be alone with her fantasies, which (then), were perhaps 'ingenuous'. Or perhaps not.

She had lain curled up, pretending to sleep, imagining that she had found a fairy creature in the garden of her parents' house.

The fairy was always in some difficulty, and she must rescue it—perhaps from drowning in the bird bath, where sparrows had attacked it. Bearing it indoors, she would care for it, washing it in a tea-cup, powdering it lightly with scented dust stolen from her mother's box, dressing it in bits of lace, tied at the waist with strands of brightly coloured embroidery silk. Since it was seen naked in the tea-cup, it revealed it was neither male nor female, lacking both breasts and penis (she did not grossly investigate it further), although otherwise it appeared a full-grown specimen of its kind. But then, at that time, Antoinelle had never seen either the genital apparatus of a man or the mammalia of an adult woman.

The fairy, kept in secret, was dependent totally upon Antoinelle. She would feed it on crumbs of cake and fruit. It drank from her chocolate in the morning. It would sleep on her pillow. She caressed it, with always a mounting sense of urgency, not knowing where the caresses could lead—and indeed they never led to anything. Its wings she did not touch. (She had been told, the wings of moths and butterflies were fragile.)

Beyond Antoinelle's life, all Europe had been at war with itself. Invasion, battle, death, these swept by the carefully closed doors of her parents' house, and by Antoinelle entirely. Through a combination of conspiracy and luck, she learned nothing of it, but no doubt those who protected her so assiduously reinforced the walls of Antoinelle's self-involvement. Such lids were shut down on her, what else was she to do but make music with herself—*play* with herself...

Sometimes in her fantasies, Antoinelle and the fairy quarrelled. Afterwards they would be reconciled, and the fairy would hover, kissing Antoinelle on the lips. Sometimes the fairy got inside her nightdress, tickling her all over until she thought she would die. Sometimes she tickled the fairy in turn with a goose-feather, reducing it to spasms identifiable (probably) only as hysteria.

It never flew away.

Yet, as her own body ripened and formed, Antoinelle began to lose interest in the fairy. Instead, she had strange waking dreams of a flesh-and-blood soldier she had once glimpsed under the window, who, in her picturings, had to save her—not from any of the wild armies then at large—but from an escaped bear... and later came the prototypes of Justus, who kissed her until she swooned.

Now Antoinelle had gone back to her clandestine youth. Along, in the room, its door shut, she blew out the lamp. She threw wide her window. Standing in the darkness, she pulled off her garments and tossed them down.

The heat of the night was like damp velvet. The tips of her breasts rose like tight buds that wished to open.

Her husband was old. She was young. She felt her youngness, and remembered her childhood with an inappropriate nostalgia.

Vonderjan had thought something might get in at the window. She sensed this might be true.

Antoinelle imagined that something climbed slowly up the creeper.

She began to tremble, and went and lay down on her bed.

She lay on her back, her hands lying lightly over her breasts, her legs a little apart.

Perhaps after all Vonderjan might ignore her denials and come in. She would let him. Yes, after all she had stopped menstruating. She would not mind his being here. He liked so much to do things to her, to render her helpless, gasping and abandoned, his hands on her making her into his instrument, making her utter sounds, noises, making her come over and over. And she too liked this best. She liked to do nothing, simply to be made to respond, and so give way. In some other life she might have become the ideal fanatic, falling before the Godhead in fits whose real, spurious nature only the most sceptical could ever suspect. Conversely, partnered with a more selfish and less accomplished lover, with an ignorant Justus, for example, she might have been forced to do more, learned more, liked less. But that now was hypothetical.

A breeze whispered at the window. (What does it say?)

That dream she had had. What had that been? Was it her husband? No, it had been a man with black skin. But she had seen no one so black. A blackness without any translucence, with no blood inside it.

Antoinelle drifted, in a sort of trance.

She had wandered into a huge room with a wooden floor. The only thing in it was a piano. The air was full of a rapturous smell, like blossom, something which bloomed yet burned.

She ran her fingers over the piano. The notes sounded clearly, but each was a voice. A genderless yet sexual voice, crying out as she touched it—now softly, excitedly, now harsh and demanding and desperate.

She was lying on the beach below the Island. The sea was coming in, wave by wave—glissandi—each one the ripples of the wire harp-strings under the piano lid, or keys rippling as fingers scattered touches across them.

Antoinelle had drained Gregers Vonderjan of all he might give her. She had sucked him dry of everything but his blood. It was his own fault, exalting in his power over her, wanting to make her a doll that would dance on his fingers' end, penis's end, *power's* end.

Her eyes opened, and, against the glass windows, she saw the piano standing, its lids lifted, its keys gleaming like appetite, black and white.

Should she get up and play music on it? The keys would feel like skin.

Then she knew that if she only lay still, the piano would come to *her*. She was *its* instrument, as she had been Vonderjan's.

The curtain blew. The piano shifted, and moved, but as it did so, its shape altered. Now it was not only a piano, but an animal.

(*Notes:* Pianimal.)

It was a beast. And then it melted and stood up, and the form it had taken now was that of a man.

Stronn walked around the courtyard, around its corners, past the dry Spanish fountain. Tonight the husks of flowers scratched in the bowl, and sounded like water. Or else nocturnal lizards darted about there.

There was only one light he could see in Gregers Vonderjan's big house, the few candles left undoused in the salon.

The orange trees on the gallery smelled bitter-sweet. Stronn did not want to go to bed. He was wide awake. In the old days, he might have had a game of cards with some of the blacks, or even with Vonderjan. But those times had ceased to be.

He had thought he heard the white horse earlier, its shod hoofs going along the track between the rhododendrons. But now there was no sign of it. Doubtless one of the people on the Island would catch the horse and keep it. As for the other animal, the one said to have escaped from a passing ship, Stronn did not really think it existed, or if it did, it would be something of no great importance.

Now and then he heard the tinkling noise of hudja bells the people had hung on the banana trees. Then a fragment like piano music, but it was the bells again. Some nights the sea breathed as loudly up here as in the bay. Or a shout from one of the huts two miles off might seem just over a wall.

He could hear the vrouw, certainly. But he was used to hearing that. Her squeaks and yowls, fetching off as Vonderjan shafted her. But she was a slut. The way she had come in tonight proved it, in her bedclothes. And she had never given the meester a son, not even tried to give him a child, like the missus (Uteka) had that time, only she had lost it, but she was never very healthy.

A low thin wind blew along the cane fields, and Stronn could smell the coffee trees and the hairy odour of kayar.

He went out of the yard, carrying his gun, thinking he was still looking for the white horse.

A statue of black obsidian might look like this, polished like this.

The faint luminescence of night, with its storm choked within it, is behind the figure. Starlight describes the outline of it, but only as it turns, moving towards her, do details of its forward surface catch any illumination.

Yet too, all the while, adapting to the camouflage of its environment, it grows subtly more human, that is, more recognizable.

For not entirely—remotely—human is it.

Does she comprehend?

From the head, a black pelt of hair waterfalls away around it, folding down its back like a cloak—

The wide flat pectorals are coined each side three times. It is six-nippled, like a panther.

Its legs move, columnar, heavily muscled and immensely vital, capable of great leaps and astonishing bounds, but walking, they give it the grace of a dancer.

At first there seems to be nothing at its groin, just as it seems to have no features set into its face . . . except that the light had slid, once, twice, on the long rows of perfect teeth.

But now it is at the bed's foot, and out of the dark it has evolved, or made itself whole.

A man's face.

The face of a handsome Justus, and of a Vonderjan in his stellar youth. A face of improbable mythic beauty, and opening in it, like two vents revealing the inner burning core of it, eyes of grey ice, which each blaze like the planet Venus.

She can see now, it has four upper arms. They too are strong and muscular, also beautiful, like the dancer's legs.

The penis is large and upright, without a sheath, the black lotus bulb on a thick black stem. No change of shade. (No light, no inner blood.) Only the mercury-flame inside it, which only the eyes show.

Several of the side teeth, up and down, are pointed sharply. The tongue is black. The inside of the mouth is black. And the four black shapely hands, with their twenty long, flexible fingers, have palms that are black as the death of light.

It bends towards Antoinelle. It has the smell of night and of the Island, and of the sea. And also the scent of hot-house flowers, that came out of the piano. And a carnivorous smell, like fresh meat.

It stands there, looking at her, as she lies on the bed.

And on the floor, emerging from the pelt that falls from its head, the long black tail strokes softly now this way, now that way.

Then the first pair of hands stretch over on to the bed, and after them the second pair, and fluidly it lifts itself and *pours* itself forward up the sheet, and up over the body of the girl, looking down at her as it does so, from its water-pale eyes. And its smooth body rasps on her legs, as it advances, and the big hard firm organ knocks on her thighs, hot as the body is cool.

He walked behind her, obedient and terrified. The Island frightened him, but it was more than that. Nanetta was now like his mother (when she was young and slim, dominant and brutal). Once she turned, glaring at him, with the eyes of a lynx. *"Hush."* "But I—" he started to say, and she shook her head again, raging at him without words.

She trod so noiselessly on her bare feet, which were the indigo colour of the sky in its darkness. And he blundered, try as he would.

The forest held them in its tentacles. The top-heavy plantains loomed, their blades of black-bronze sometimes quivering. Tree limbs like enormous plaited snakes rolled upwards. Occasionally, mystically, he thought, he heard the sea.

She was taking him to her people, who grasped what menaced them, its value if not its actual being, and could keep them safe.

Barefoot and stripped of her jewels, she was attempting to go back into the knowingness of her innocence and her beginnings. But he had always been over-aware and a fool.

They came into a glade of wild tamarinds—could it be called that? A *glade?* It was an aperture among the trees, but only because trees had been cut down. There was an altar, very low, with frangi-pani flowers, scented like confectionary, and something killed that had been picked clean. The hudja bells chimed from a nearby bough, the first he had seen. They sounded like the sistra of ancient Egypt, as the cane fields had recalled to him the notion of a temple.

Nanetta bowed to the altar and went on, and he found he had crossed himself, just as he had done when a boy in church.

It made him feel better, doing that, as if he had quickly thrown up and got rid of some poison in his heart.

V'au l'eau, Vonderjan thought. Which meant, going downstream, to wrack and ruin.

He could not sleep, and turned on his side to stare out through the window. The stars were so unnaturally clear. Bleumaneer was in the eye of the storm, the aperture at its centre. When this passed, weather would resume, the ever-threatening presence of tempest.

He thought of the white horse, galloping about the Island, down its long stairways of hills and rock and forest, to the shore.

Half asleep, despite his insomnia, there was now a split second when he saw the keys of a piano, descending like the levels of many black and white terraces.

Then he was fully awake again.

Vonderjan got up. He reached for the bottle of schnapps, and found it was empty.

Perhaps he should go to her bed. She might have changed her mind. No, he did not want her tonight. He did not want anything, except to be left in peace.

It seemed to him that after all he would be glad to be rid of every bit of it. His wealth, his manipulative powers. To live here alone, as the house fell gradually apart, without servants, or any authority or commitments. And without Anna.

Had he been glad when Uteka eventually died? Yes, she had suffered so. And he had never known her. She was like a book he had meant to read, had begun to read several times, only to put it aside, unable to remember those pages he had already laboriously gone through.

With Anna it was easy, but then, she was not a book at all. She was a demon he had himself invented (Vonderjan did not realize this, that even for a moment, he thought in this way), an oasis, after Uteka's sexual desert, and so, like any fantasy, she could be sloughed at once. He had masturbated over her long enough, this too-young girl, with her serpentine body (apple-tree and tempting snake together), and her idealized pleas always for more.

Now he wanted to leave the banquet table. To get up and go away and sleep and grow old, without such distractions.

He thought he could hear her, though. Hear her fast starved feeding breathing, and for once, this did not arouse him. And in any case it might not be Anna, but only the gasping of the sea, hurling herself far away, on the rocks and beaches of the Island.

It—he—paints her lips with its long and slender tongue, which is black. Then it paints the inside of her mouth. The tongue is very narrow, sensitive, incites her gums, making her want to yawn, except that is not what she needs to do—but she stretches her body irresistibly.

The first set of hands settles on her breasts.

The second set of hands on her ribcage.

Something flicks, flicks, between her thighs . . . not the staff of the penis, but something more like a second tongue . . .

Antoinelle's legs open and her head falls back. She makes a sound, but it is a bestial grunting that almost offends her, yet there is no room in her body or mind for that.

"No—" she tries to say.

The *No* means yes, in the case of Antoinelle. It is addressed, not to her partner, but to normal life, anything that may intrude, and warns *Don't interrupt.*

The black tongue wends, waking nerves of taste and smell in the roof of her mouth. She scents lakoum, pepper, ambergris and myrrh.

The lower tongue, which may be some extra weapon of the tail, licks at a point of flame it has discovered, fixing a triangle with the fire-points of her breasts.

He—it—slips into her, forces into her, bulging and huge as thunder.

And the tail grasps her, muscular as any of its limbs, and, thick as the phallus, also penetrates her.

The thing holds Antoinelle as she detonates about it, faints and cascades into darkness.

Not until she begins to revive does it do more.

The terror is, she comes to already primed, more than eager, her body spangled with frantic need, as if the first cataclysm were only—foreplay.

And now the creature moves, riding her and making her ride, and they gallop down the night, and Antoinelle grins and shrieks, clinging to its obsidian form, her hands slipping, gripping. And as the second detonation begins, its face leaves her face, her mouth, and grows itself faceless and *only* mouth. And the mouth half rings her throat, a crescent moon, and the many side teeth pierce her, both the veins of her neck.

A necklace of emeralds was nothing to this.

Antoinelle drops from one precipice to another. She screams, and her screams crash through the house called Blue View, like sheets of blue glass breaking.

It holds her. As her consciousness again goes out, it holds her very tight.

And somewhere in the limbo where she swirls, fire on oil, guttering but not quenched, Antoinelle is raucously laughing with triumph at finding this other one, not her parasite, but her twin. Able to devour her as she devours, able to eat her alive as she has eaten or tried to eat others alive. But where Antoinelle has bled them out, this only drinks. It wastes nothing, not even Antoinelle.

*More—more—*She can never have enough.

Then it tickles her with flame so she thrashes and yelps. Its fangs fastened in her, it bears her on, fastened in turn to it.

She is arched like a bridge, carrying the travelling shadow on her body. Pinned together, in eclipse, these dancers.

More—

It gives her more. And indescribably yet more.

If she were any longer human, she would be split and eviscerated, and her spine snapped along its centre three times.

Her hands have fast hold of it. Which—it or she—is the most tenacious? Where it travels, so will she.

But for all the *more,* there is no more *thought.* If ever there was thought.

When she was fourteen, she saw all this, in her prophetic mirror, saw what she was made for and must have.

Perhaps many thousands of us are only that, victim or predator, interchangeable.

Seen from above: Antoinelle is scarcely visible. Just the edges of her flailing feet, her contorted forehead and glistening strands of hair. And her clutching claws. (Shockingly, she makes the sounds of a pig, grunting, snorting.)

The rest of her is covered by darkness, by something most like a manta ray out of the sea, or some black amoeba.

Then she is growling and grunting so loudly, on and on, that the looking-glass breaks on her toilette table as if unable to stand the sound, while out in the night forest birds shrill and fly away.

More—always more. *Don't stop—*Never stop.

There is no need to stop. It has killed her, she is dead, she is re-alive and death is lost on her, she is all she has ever wished to be—nothing.

"Dearest . . . are you awake?"

He lifts his head from his arm. He has slept.

"What is it?" *Who are you?* Has she ever called him *dear* before?

"Here I am," she says, whoever she is. But she is his Anna.

He does not want her. Never wanted her.

He thinks she is wearing the emerald necklace, something burning about her throat. She is white as bone. And her dark eyes—have paled to Venus eyes, watching him.

"I'm sorry," he says. "Perhaps later."

"I know."

Vonderjan falls asleep again quickly, lying on his back. Then Antoinelle slides up on top of him. She is not heavy, but he is; it impedes his breathing, her little weight.

Finally she puts her face to his, her mouth over his.

She smothers him mostly with her face, closing off his nostrils with the pressure of her cheek, and one narrow hand, and her mouth sidelong to his, and her breasts on his heart.

He does not wake again. At last his body spasms sluggishly, like the last death-throe of orgasm. Nothing else.

After his breathing has ended, still she lies there, Venus-eyed, and the dawn begins to come. Antoinelle casts a black, black shadow. Like all shadows, it is attached to her. Attached very closely.

Is this her shadow, or is she the white shadow of *it*?

9

Having sat for ten minutes, no longer writing, holding her pen upright, Yse sighs, and drops it, like something unpleasant, dank or sticky.

The story's erotographic motif, at first stimulating, had become, as it must, repulsive. Disgusting her—also as it should.

And the murder of Vonderjan, presented deliberately almost as an afterthought (stifled under the slight white pillar of his succubus wife).

Aloud, Yse says almost angrily, "Now surely I've used him up. All up. All over. Per Laszd, I can't do another thing with you or to you. But then, you've used me up too, yes you did, you have, even though you've never been near me. Mutual annihilation. That Yse is over with."

Then Yse rises, leaving the manuscript, and goes to make tea. But her generator, since the party, (when the music machine had been hooked into it by that madman, Carr) is skittish. The stove won't work. She leaves it, and pours instead a warm soda from the now improperly-working fridge.

It is nighttime, or morning, about three-fifty a.m.

Yse switches on her small TV, which works on a solar battery and obliges.

And there, on the first of the fifteen mainland (upper city) channels, is he—is Per Laszd. Not in his persona of dead trampled Gregers Vonderjan, but that of his own dangerous self.

She stands on the floor, dumbfounded, yet not, not really. Of course, who else would come before her at this hour.

He looks well, healthy and tanned. He's even shed some weight.

It seems to be a talk show, something normally Yse would avoid—they bore her. And the revelation of those she sometimes admires as over-ordinary or distasteful, disillusions and frustrates her.

But him she has always watched, on a screen, across a room when able, or in her own head. Him, she knows. He could not disillusion her, or put her off.

And tonight, there is something new. The talk has veered round to the other three guests—to whom she pays no attention—and so to music. And now the TV show's host is asking Per Laszd to use the piano, that grande piano over there.

Per Laszd gets up and walks over to this studio piano, looking, Yse thinks, faintly irritated, because obviously this has been sprung on him and is not what he is about, or at least not publicly, but he will do it from a good showman's common sense.

He plays well, some melody Yse knows, a popular song she can't place. He improvises, his large hands and strong fingers jumping sure and finely-trained about the keyboard. Just the one short piece, concluded with a sarcastic flourish, after which he stands up again. The audience, delighted by any novelty, applauds madly, while the host and other guests are all calling *encore!* (more! More! Again—don't stop—) But Laszd is not manipulable, not truly. Gracious yet immovable, he returns to his seat. And after that a pretty girl with an unimportant voice comes on to sing, and then the show is done.

Yse finds herself enraged. She switches off the set, and slams down the tepid soda. She paces this end of her loft. While by the doors, forty feet away, the piano dredged from the Sound still stands, balanced on its forefeet and its phallic tail, hung in shade and shadow. It has been here more than a month. It's nearly invisible.

So why this now? This TV stunt put on by Fate? Why show her this, now? As if to congratulate her, giving her a horrible mean little failed-runner's-up patronizing non-prize. Per Laszd can play the piano.

Damn Per Laszd.

She is sick of him. Perhaps in every sense. But of course, she still wants him. Always will.

And what now?

She will never sleep. It's too late or early to go out.

She circles back to her writing, looks at it, sits, touches the page. But why bother to write any more?

Vonderjan was like the enchanter Prospero, in Shakespeare's *Tempest,* shut up there on his sorcerous Island, infested with sprites and elementals. Prospero too kept close a strange young woman, who in the magician's case had been his own daughter. But then arrived a shipwrecked prince out of the sea, to take the responsibility off Prospero's hands.

(Per's hands on the piano keys. Playing them. A wonderful amateur, all so facile, no trouble at all. He is married, and has been for twelve years. Yse has always known this.)

Far out on the Sound, a boat moos eerily.

Though she has frequently heard such a thing, Yse starts.

Be not afeard: the isle is full of noises,
Sounds and sweet airs, that give delight, and hurt not.

She can no longer smell the perfume, like night-blooming vines. When did that stop? (Don't stop.)

Melted into air, into thin air . . .

10: Passover

They had roped the hut-house round, outside and in, with their amulets and charms. There were coloured feathers and dried grasses, cogs of wood rough-carved, bones and sprinkles of salt and rum, and of blood, as in the Communion. When they reached the door, she on her bare, navy-blue feet, Jeanjacques felt all the forest press at their backs. And inside the hut, the silver-ringed eyes, staring in affright like the staring stars. But presently her people let her in, and let him in as well, without argument. And he thought of the houses of the Chosen in Egypt, their lintels marked by blood, to show the Angel of Death he must pass by.

He, as she did, sat down on the earth floor. (He noted the earth floor, and the contrasting wooden bed, with its elaborate posts. And the two shrines, one to the Virgin, and one to another female deity.)

Nothing was said beyond a scurry of whispered words in the patois. There were thirty other people crammed in the house, with a crèche of chickens and two goats. Fear smelled thick and hot, but there was something else, some vital possibility of courage and cohesion. They clung together soul to soul, their bodies only barely brushing, and Jeanjacques was glad to be in their midst, and when the fat woman came and gave him a gourd of liquor, he shed tears, and she patted his head, calming him a little, like a dog hiding under its mistress's chair.

In the end he must have slept. He saw someone looking at him, the pale icy eyes blue as murder.

Waking with a start, he found everyone and thing in the hut tense and compressed, listening, as something circled round outside. Then it snorted and blew against the wall of the hut-house, and all the interior stars of eyes flashed with their terror. And Jeanjacques felt his heart clamp on to the side of his body, as if afraid to fall.

Even so, he knew what it was, and when all at once it retreated and galloped away on its shod hoofs, he said quietly, "His horse."

But no one answered him, or took any notice of what he had said, and Jeanjacques discovered himself thinking, *After all, it might take that form, a white horse. Or she might be riding on the white horse.*

He began to ponder the way he must go in the morning, descending towards the bay. He should reach the sea well in advance of nightfall. The ship would come back, today or tomorrow. Soon. And there were the old buildings, on the beach, where he could make a shelter. He could even jump into the sea and swim out. There was a little reef, and rocks.

It had come from the sea, and would avoid going back to the sea, surely, at least for some while.

He knew it was not interested in him, knew that almost certainly it would not approach him with any purpose. But he could not bear to *see* it. That was the thing. And it seemed to him the people of the Island, and in the hut, even the chickens, the goats, and elsewhere the birds and fauna, felt as he did. They did not want to *see* it, even glimpse it. If the fabric of this world were torn open in one place on a black gaping hole of infinite darkness, you hid your eyes, you went far away.

After that, he started to notice bundles of possessions stacked up in corners. He realized not he alone would be going down the Island to the sea.

Dreaming again, he beheld animals swimming in waves away from shore, and birds flying away, as if from a zone of earthquake, or the presage of some volcanic eruption.

Nanetta nudged him.

"Will you take me to St Paul's Island?"

"Yes."

"I have a sister there."

He had been here on a clerk's errand. He thought, ridiculously, *Now I won't be paid.* And he was glad at this wince of anxious annoyance. Its normalcy and reason.

11

Per Laszd played Bach very well, with just the right detached, solemn cheerfulness.

It was what she would have expected him to play. Something like this. Less so the snatch of a popular tune he had offered the talk show audience so flippantly. (But a piano does what you want, makes the sounds you make it give—even true, she thinks, should you make a mistake—for then that is what it gives you. Your mistake.)

As Yse raised her eyes, she saw across the dim sphere of her loft, still wrapped in the last flimsy paper of night, a lamp stood glowing by the piano, both of whose lids were raised. Her stomach jolted and the pain of shock rushed through her body.

"Lucius—?"

He was the only other who held a key to her loft. She trusted Lucius, who any way had never used the key, except once, when she was gone for a week, to enter and water her (dying) plants, and fill her (then operable) refrigerator with croissants, mangoes and white wine.

And Lucius didn't play the piano. He had told her, once. His *amouretta,* as he called it, was the drum.

Besides, the piano player had not reacted when she called, not ceased his performance. Not until he brought the twinkling phrases to their finish.

Then the large hands stepped back off the keys, he pushed away the chair he must have carried there, and stood up.

The raised carapace of the piano's hind lid still obscured him, all but that flame of light which veered across the shining pallor of his hair.

Yse had got to her feet. She felt incredibly young, light as thin air. The thick silk of her hair brushed round her face, her shoulders, and she pulled in her flat stomach and raised her head on its long throat. She was frightened by the excitement in herself, and excited by the fear. She wasn't dreaming. She had always known, when she *dreamed* of him.

And there was no warning voice, because long ago she had left all such redundant noises behind.

Per Laszd walked around the piano. "Hallo, Yse," he said.

She said nothing. Perhaps could not speak. There seemed no point. She had said so much.

But "Here I am," he said.

There he was.

There was no doubt at all. The low lamp flung up against him. He wore the loose dark suit he had put on for the TV program, as if he had come straight here from the studio. He dwarfed everything in the loft.

"Why?" she said, after all.

She too was entitled to be flippant, surely.

"Why? Don't you know? You brought me here." He smiled. "Don't you love me any more?"

He was wooing her.

She glanced around her, made herself see everything as she had left it, the washed plate and glass by the sink, the soda can on the table, her manuscript lying there, and the pen. Beyond an angle of a wall, a corridor to other rooms.

And below the floor, barracuda swimming through the girders of a flooded building.

But the thin air sparkled as if full of champagne.

"Well, Yse," he said again, "here I am."

"But you are not *you*."

"You don't say. Can you be certain? How am I different?"

"You're what I've made, and conjured up."

"I thought it was," he said, in his dry amused voice she had never forgotten, "more personal than that."

"*He* is somewhere miles off. In another country."

"This is another country," he said, "to me."

She liked it, this breathless fencing with him. Liked his persuading her. *Don't stop.*

The piano had not been able to open—or be opened—until he—or she—was ready. (Foreplay.) And out of the piano, came her demon. What was he? *What?*

She didn't care. If it were not him, yet it was, him. So she said, archly, "And your wife?"

"As you see, she had another engagement."

"With you, *there*. Wherever you are."

"Let me tell you," he said, "why I've called here."

There was no break in the transmission of this scene, she saw him walk away from the piano, start across the floor, and she did the same. Then they were near the window-doors. He was standing over her. He was vast, overpowering, beautiful.

More beautiful, now she could see the strands of his hair, the pores of his skin, a hundred tiniest imperfections—and the whole exquisite manufacture of a human thing, so close. And she was rational enough to analyse all this, and his beauty, and his power over her; or pedantic enough. He smelled wonderful to her as well, more than his clean fitness and his masculinity, or any expensive cosmetic he had used (for her?) It was the scent discernable only by a lover, caused by her chemistry, not his. Unless she had made him want her, too.

But of course he wanted her. She could see it in his eyes, their blue view bent only on her.

If he might have seemed old to an Antoinelle of barely sixteen, to Yse this man was simply her peer. And yet too he was like his younger self, clad again in that searing charisma which had later lessened, or changed its course.

He took her hand, picked it up. Toyed with her hand as Vonderjan had done with the hand of the girl Yse had permitted to destroy him.

"I'm here for you," he said.

"But I don't know you."

"Backwards," he said. "You've made it your business. You've bid for me," he said, "and you've got me."

"No," she said, "no, no I haven't."

"Let me show you."

She had known of that almost occult quality. With what he wanted in the sexual way, he could communicate some telepathic echo of his desires. As his mouth covered and clasped hers, this delirium was what she felt, combining with her own.

She had always known his kisses would be like this, the ground flying off from her feet, swept up and held only by him in the midst of a spinning void, where she became part of him and wanted nothing else, where she became what she had always wanted . . . nothing.

To be nothing, borne by this flooding sea, no thought, no anchor, and no chains.

So Antoinelle, as her vampire penetrated, drank, emptied, reformed her.

So Yse, in her vampire's arms.

It's how they make us feel.

"No," she murmurs, sinking deeper and deeper into his body, drowning as the island will, one day (five years, twenty).

None of us escape, do we?

Dawn is often very short and ineffectual here, as if to recompense the dark for those long sunsets we have.

Lucius, bringing his boat in to West Ridge from a night's fishing and drinking out in the Sound, sees a light still burning up there, bright as the quick green dawn. All Yse's blinds are up, showing the glass loft, translucent, like a jewel. Over the terrace the snake tree hangs its hair in the water and ribbons of apple-green light tremble through its coils.

Yse is there, just inside the wall of glass above the terrace, standing with a tall heavy-set man, whose hair is almost white.

He's kissing her, on and on, and then they draw apart, and still she holds on to him, her head tilted back like a serpent's, bonelessly, staring up into his face.

From down in the channel between the lofts and towerettes, Lucius can't make out the features of her lover. But then neither can he make out Yse's facial features, only the tilt of her neck and the lush satin hair hanging down her back.

Lucius sits in the boat, not paddling now, watching. His eyes are still and opaque.

"What you doing, girl?"

He knows perfectly well.

And then they turn back, the two of them, further into the loft where the light still burns, although the light of dawn has gone, leaving only a salty stormy dusk.

They will hardly make themselves separate from each other. They are together again and again, as if growing into one another.

Lucius sees the piano, or that which had been a piano, has vanished from the loft. And after that he sees how the light of the guttering lamp hits suddenly up, like a striking cobra. And in the ray of the lamp, striking, the bulky figure of the man, with his black clothes and blond hair, becomes transparent as the glass sheets of the doors. It is possible to see directly, too, through him, clothes, hair, body, directly through to Yse, as she stands there, still holding on to what is now actually invisible, drawing it on, in, away, just before the lamp goes out and a shadow fills the room like night.

As he is paddling away along the channel, Lucius thinks he hears a remote crash, out of time, like glass smashing in many pieces, but yesterday, or tomorrow.

Things break.

Just about sunset, the police come to find Lucius. They understand he has a key to the loft of a woman called Yse, (which they pronounce Jizz.)

When they get to the loft, Lucius is aware they did not need the key, since the glass doors have both been blown outwards and down into the water-alley below. Huge shards and fragments decorate the terrace, and some are caught in the snake-willow like stars.

A bored detective stands about, drinking coffee someone has made him on Yse's reluctant stove. (The refrigerator has shut off, and is leaking a lake on the floor.)

Lucius appears dismayed but innocuous. He goes about looking for something, which the other searchers, having dismissed him, are too involved to mark.

There is no sign of Yse. The whole loft is vacant. There is no sign either of any disturbance, beyond the damaged doors which, they say to Lucius and each other, were smashed outwards but not by an explosive.

"What are you looking for?" the detective asks Lucius, suddenly grasping what Lucius is at.

"Huh?"

"She have something of yours?"

Lucius sees the detective is waking up. "No. Her book. She was writing."

"Oh, yeah? What kind of thing was that?"

Lucius explains, and the detective loses interest again. He says they have seen nothing like that.

And Lucius doesn't find her manuscript, which he would have anticipated, any way, seeing instantly on her work-table. He does find a note—they say it is a note, a letter of some sort, although addressed to no one. It's in her bed area, on the rug, which has been floated under the bed by escaped refrigerator fluid.

'Why go on writing?' asks the note, or letter, of the no one it has not addressed. 'All your life waiting, and having to invent another life, or other lives, to make up for not having a life. Is that what God's problem is?'

Hearing this read at him, Lucius' dead eyes reveal for a second they are not dead, only covered by a protective film. They all miss this.

The detective flatly reads the note out, like a kid bad at reading, embarrassed and standing up in class. Where his feet are planted is the stain from the party, which, to Lucius' for-a-moment-not-dead eyes, has the shape of a swimming, three-legged fish.

"And she says, 'I want more.'"

'I want the terror and the passion, the power and the glory—not this low-key crap played only with one *hand*. Let me point out to someone, Yse is an anagram of Yes. *I'll drown my book.*'

"I guess," says the detective, "she didn't sell."

They let Lucius go with some kind of veiled threat he knows is only offered to make themselves feel safe.

He takes the water-bus over to the Café Blonde, and as the sunset ends and night becomes, tells one or two what he saw, as he has not told the cops from the tideless upper city.

Lucius has met them all. Angels, demons.

"As the light went through him, he wasn't there. He's like glass."

Carr says, slyly (inappropriately—or with deadly perception?), "No vampire gonna reflect in a glass."

12: Carried Away

When the ship came, they took the people out, rowing them in groups, in the two boats. The man Stronn had also appeared, looking dazed, and the old housekeeper, and others. No questions were asked of them. The ship took the livestock, too.

Jeanjacques was glad they were so amenable, the black haughty master wanting conscientiously to assist his own, and so helping the rest.

All the time they had sheltered in the rickety customs buildings of the old port, a storm banged round the coast. This kept other things away, it must have done. They saw nothing but the feathers of palm boughs blown through the air and crashing trunks that toppled in the high surf, which was grey as smashed glass.

In the metallic after-storm morning, Jeanjacques walked down the beach, the last to leave, waiting for the last boat, confident.

Activity went on at the sea's edge, sailors rolling a barrel, Nanetta standing straight under a yellow sunshade, a fine lady, barefoot but proud. (She had shown him the jewels she had after all brought with her, squeezed in her sash, not the ruby earrings, but a golden hairpin, and the emerald necklace that had belonged to Vonderjan's vrouw.)

He never thought, now, to see anything, Jeanjacques, so clever, so accomplished at survival.

But he saw it.

Where the forest came down on to the beach, and caves opened under the limestone, and then rocks reared up, white rocks and black, with the curiously quiescent waves glimmering in and out around them.

There had been nothing. He would have sworn to that. As if the reality of the coarse storm had scoured all such stuff away.

And then, there she was, sitting on the rock.

She shone in a way that, perhaps one and a quarter centuries after, could have been described as radioactively.

Jeanjacques did not know that word. He decided that she gleamed. Her hard pale skin and mass of pale hair, gleaming.

She looked old. Yet she looked too young. She was not human-looking, nor animal.

Her legs were spread wide in the skirt of her white dress. So loose was the gown at her bosom, that he could see much of her breasts. She was doing nothing at all, only sitting there, alone, and she grinned at him, all her white teeth, so even, and her black eyes like slits in the world.

But she cast a black shadow, and gradually the shadow was embracing her. And he saw her turning over into it like the moon into eclipse. If she had any blood left in her, if she had ever been Antoinelle—these things he ignored. But her grinning and her eyes and the shadow and her turning inside out within the shadow—from these things he ran away.

He ran to the line of breakers, where the barrels were being rolled into a boat. To Nanetta's sunflower sunshade.

And he seemed to burst through a sort of curtain, and his muscles gave way. He fell nearby, and she glanced at him, the black woman, and shrank away.

"It's all right—" he cried. He thought she must not see what he had seen, and that they might leave him here. "I missed my footing," he whined, "that's all."

And when the boat went out, they let him go with it.

The great sails shouldered up into the sky. The master looked Jeanjacques over, before moving his gaze after Nanetta. (Stronn had avoided them. The other whites, and the housekeeper, had hidden themselves somewhere below, like stowaways.)

"How did you find him, that Dutchman?" the master asked idly.

"As you said. Vonderjan was falling."

"What was the other trouble here? They act like it was a plague, but that's not so." (Malignly Jeanjacques noted the master too was excluded from the empathy of the Island people.) "No," the master went on, bombastically, "if you sick, I'd never take you on, none of you."

Jeanjacques felt a little better. "The Island's gone bad," he muttered. He would look, though, only up into the sails. They were another sort of white to the white thing he had seen on the rock. As the master was another sort of black.

"Gone bad? They do. Land does go bad. Like men."

Are they setting sail? Every grain of sand on the beach behind is rising up. Every mote of light, buzzing—

Oh God—*Pater noster*—*libera me*—

The ship strode from the bay. She carved her path into the deep sea, and through his inner ear, Jeanjacques hears the small bells singing. Yet that is little enough, to carry away from such a place.

13

Seven months after, he heard the story, and some of the newspapers had it too. A piano had been washed up off the Sound, on the beach at the Abacus Tower. And inside the lid, when they hacked it open, a woman's body was curled up, tiny, and hard as iron. She was Caucasian, middle-aged, rather heavy when alive, now not heavy at all, since there was no blood, and not a single whole bone, left inside her.

Sharks, they said.

Sharks are clever. They can get inside a closed piano and out again. And they bite.

As for the piano, it was missing—vandals had destroyed it, burned it, taken it off.

Sometimes strangers ask Lucius where Yse went to. He has nothing to tell them. ("She disappears?" they ask him again. And Lucius once more says nothing.)

And in that way, resembling her last book, Yse disappeared, disappears, is disappearing. Which can happen, in any tense you like.

'Like those hallucinations which sometimes come at the edge of sleep, so that you wake, thinking two or three words have been spoken close to your ear, or that a tall figure stands in the corner . . . like this, the image now and then appears before him.

'Then Jeanjacques sees her, the woman, sitting on the rock, her white dress and ivory-coloured hair, hard-gleaming in a post-storm sunlight. Impossible to tell her age. A desiccated young girl, or unlined old woman. And the transparent sea lapping in across the sand . . .

'But he has said, the Island is quite deserted now.'

ABOUT THE AUTHOR

Tanith Lee was born in 1947, in London, England. After non-education at a couple of schools, followed by actual good education at another, she received *wonderful* education at the Prendergast Grammar School until the age of 17. She then worked (inefficiently) at many jobs, including library assistant, shop assistant, waitress and clerk, also taking a year off to attend art school at age 25. In 1974 (curious reversal of her birthdate) DAW Books of America accepted 3 of her fantasy/ SF novels, (published in 1975/ 6), and thereafter 23 of her books, so breaking her chains and allowing her to be the only thing she effectively could: a full-time writer.

Since then she has written 77 novels, 14 collections, and almost 300 short stories, plus 4 radio plays (broadcast by the BBC) and 2 scripts for the TV cult UK SF series *Blake's 7*. Her work, which has been translated into over 17 languages, ranges through fantasy, SF, gothic, YA and Children's Books, contemporary, historical and detective novels, and horror. This year she was awarded the prestigious title of Grand Master of Horror 2009. She has also won major awards for several of her books/ stories, including the August Derleth Award for *Death's Master,* the second book in the Flat Earth series.

She lives near the South East coast of England with her husband, writer-photographer-artist John Kaiine. And two tuxedo cats of many charms, whose main creative occupations involve eating, revamping the carpets, and meowperatics.

ORIGINAL APPEARANCES

"Where All Things Perish," *Weird Tales,* ed. Darrell Schweitzer, 2001.

"Midday People," *Dark Terrors 6,* UK, 2002.

"Cold Fire," *Asimov's,* ed. Sheila Williams, 2007.

"Crying in the Rain," *Other Edens,* UK, 1987.

"We All Fall Down," *Nature Physics,* 2008.

"The Beautiful and Damned by F. Scott Fitzgerald," *Asimov's,* ed. Sheila Williams, 2008.

"The Isle Is Full of Noises," *The Vampire Sextette,* ed. Marvin Kaye, Science Fiction Book Club, 2000.

Breinigsville, PA USA
26 April 2010
236869BV00001B/27/P